LISA MARIE RICE

MIDNIGHT Kiss

Midnight Kiss ©2020 by Lisa Marie Rice

Published by Lisa Marie Rice

Cover Design & Formatting
by Sweet 'N Spicy Designs

All rights reserved. Without limiting the rights under copyright reserved above, no part of this publication may be reproduced, stored in or introduced into a retrieval system, or transmitted, in any form, or by any means (electronic, mechanical, photocopying, recording, or otherwise) without the prior written permission of both the copyright owner and the above publisher of this book.

This is a work of fiction. Names, characters, places, brands, media, and incidents are either the product of the author's imagination or are used fictitiously. The author acknowledges the trademarked status and trademark owners of various products referenced in this work of fiction, which have been used without permission. The publication/use of these trademarks is not authorized, associated with, or sponsored by the trademark owners.

Message posted in HER: *Is anybody there? Help!*

FELICITY: *Hey, who is this? Just caught the message.*

HER: *Thank God! It's Hope, Felicity. I've got men after me, they broke into my apartment. I saw it on my security app and barely escaped. I'm holing up in a friend's house but I don't know where else to go.*

FELICITY: *On secure phone?*

HER: *Brand new. Didn't have a chance to give you the number which is why I didn't show up. I'm in bad trouble. I've got some scary guys after me. They killed a friend of mine. I've been on the run for hours.*

FELICITY: *Oh hell. Send me your location ... got it. Wait ...*

At exactly 10.15 tomorrow, walk out onto the sidewalk of Lawrence Street and wait on the corner of Lawrence and Hyde. A car will pull up. Password: Dungeons and Dragons. Response: World of Warcraft. The car will take you to an airfield where a corporate jet that belongs to my company, ASI, will be ready for takeoff. The jet will take you to Portland and you will be met by one of our operatives, Luke Reynolds. He's utterly trustworthy. A highly decorated former soldier and a former cop. He will take you to a safe location and we'll take it from there. You'll be safe, honey. Guaranteed.

HER: *Oh God, Felicity! Thnx so much! I think the men who raided my apartment killed a friend of mine. They killed my doorman. I'm so scared. Good thing you were at work and saw my bat-signal!*

FELICITY: *Not at work, in bed. Pregnant and spotting. Under strictest orders not to get out of bed. My husband is being really hard-assed about it.*

HER: *Married! Expecting! OMG!*

FELICITY: *Yeah. Get here safely and I'll tell you all about it.*

One

Portland, Oregon

It was raining when they landed at the airfield in Portland. Near the township of Hillsboro. She checked the map on her laptop when she got onto the plane. It always made her feel more secure knowing exactly where she was going.

She'd been shaking when she got into the plane, a sleek corporate jet with only one other passenger, a perfectly pleasant banker-type who nodded then pulled out spreadsheets and started working his way across the continental United States without saying a word. The pilot had taken one look at her, handed her a blanket and, just before going back to the cockpit, a cup of hot tea.

The banker never even looked up.

Good. If she opened her mouth to speak, she'd probably scream.

Hope envied the businessman, envied him his focus, envied the fact that he was able to just sink into his documents. She wanted to work her way across the country too, lose herself in work, which was her specialty. Work was her happy place. But she'd been running on fumes and was beyond exhausted. She couldn't concentrate on work right now. She'd barely escaped with her life.

This was the first time in 24 hours she'd been safe. Inside the jet, it was all muffled sounds and neutral colors and soft seats. Plus, there was absolutely nobody who would kill her here, 35,000 feet in the air.

With any luck.

Whoever was after her wouldn't know that she was landing in Portland, Oregon because she wasn't on anyone's manifest.

So now was the time for her to stop and try to figure out what had happened, to make plans, maybe even to leave the country. Felicity's company could help her with that. But she'd have to have a coherent story ready to tell them. One that made sense instead of the random insanity that was happening to her.

Analyzing data was her job. She was good at it and got paid well for it. The reward this time wasn't a raise or a promotion, but her life. So this was her chance to stop and try to find out what the hell was going on.

Instead, she fell fast asleep. More like falling into a coma.

Since Kyle had called the previous day, she'd been

on superhigh alert. Hadn't eaten, hadn't slept. Probably had adrenaline coursing through her veins instead of blood.

Adrenaline crash. All nerds knew them. Forty-eight and even seventy-two hour work binges, when sleep was for sissies, for the brain-dead, followed by crashing hard for twelve hours. Like that. Only with death and danger thrown into the mix.

She fell asleep the moment she buckled her seat belt and realized that there was no one who wanted to kill her inside this steel tube that was soon going to be unreachably high up in the stratosphere. She slept through the trip, through the descent, through the landing, and only woke up when someone touched her hand.

She was torn out of a nightmare, gave a raw, whispery scream and flung her arms up over her face. Because in the dream someone was shooting her in the face and a good way to avoid that is to throw up your arms, which will of course stop a bullet.

"Hey."

Killers didn't say 'hey'. Did they?

She was scrabbling in her seat, wrenching at something holding her down, before she even opened her eyes.

"Hope." She opened her eyes and saw a man standing right in front of her. He didn't look like a crazed killer and his voice was low and deep and calm. And he knew her name. "My name is Luke. I'm Felicity's friend. I'm here to help you."

The words bounced around in her head, only three words making any sense. Luke. Felicity. Friend.

But she was still bound somehow, with no freedom of movement.

"May I?" the man said. Holding up his hands. Why was he doing that? To assure her he didn't hold weapons? But those hands were *big*. Those were hands that could *hurt*.

But they didn't hurt. Before she could react, he reached down to her lap, she heard a metallic click and was free of the seat belt.

And the cloud in her head lifted.

Hope was smart. Her essential self was basically what went on in her head. It was frightening to be out of it even for the few moments between waking up and realizing where she was. It was a sign of her exhaustion and stress that she'd reacted so badly.

She looked up at the man standing in front of her. Luke. His name was Luke Reynolds and her good friend Felicity had sent him to help her. To protect her. And she'd almost attacked him. If she hadn't been strapped in by the seat belt, maybe she'd have tried to punch him.

Though ... to tell the truth, he looked pretty unpunchable. He was tall, very lean and all muscle. Sinewy and tough-looking. She'd have only hurt her hand if she'd punched him.

"Sorry." Her voice was a croak, still rasping from sleep. She drew in a deep shuddering breath. "So sorry."

"Nothing to be sorry about." His deep voice was even, emotionless. He reached to the side and gave her a floppy hat and sunglasses, though from what was visible through the airplane portholes, it was overcast. "Please put these on. The sunglasses are Reflectacles and distort facial features. The hat has a hidden light under the brim which makes it impossible to film your face. We have stairs with a canopy and a vehicle waiting at the bottom of the stairs. Felicity said you needed to stay undetected."

She nodded. For some reason she was finding it hard to keep up. It took her a moment to realize he was handing her a disguise.

Disguises were good. Particularly high-tech ones. Yeah. She believed in tech the way other people believed in God.

"Thanks," she said, glad that her voice was less croaky.

He nodded.

Hope felt creaky and disoriented, a little like she felt after a 48-hour work binge and she was inserting herself back into meatspace. She looked around. The businessman she'd been on the flight with had disappeared. She'd barely had a glimpse of him before she'd fallen into her coma. A pilot stood at the cockpit door, waiting.

For what?

For you, dummy. He's waiting for you.

Luke was waiting too. He indicated the door with his hand.

Hope looked around. There was a sequence to getting off a plane. Unbuckle, get up, get something — get what? Then she remembered. "I don't have any luggage, not even toiletries."

She had only her laptop backpack with her.

Luke nodded. "Felicity had some stuff put together for you. It's waiting in the car."

He looked at her bare head. "Please put the glasses and hat on."

He'd said this before.

"Oh." Feeling unsettled, she put the floppy wide-brimmed hat and huge sunglasses on. They were heavy. "Sorry."

"Don't be sorry." He reached out to touch her arm. "You're having an adrenaline dump. It's ok. We'll take care of you."

Well, that was a novel concept. Someone taking care of her. She'd been taking care of herself for a very long time.

The steps were covered and the sides were a transparent plastic. Paranoia gripped her. Anyone with binoculars could see her. If they had a powerful enough camera, they could photograph her. She knew exactly how amazingly efficient facial recognition had become. Yes, she had special glasses and a special hat but this was new tech. It sometimes failed. And if someone had a sniper rifle …

Luke took her elbow gently and nudged her forward. "I know what you're thinking," he said. "That there's danger." She glanced up at him. If he was working for Felicity's company, which was a security company, he was probably professionally paranoid. Part of the job description. Paranoia was a new feeling for her and she didn't like it. Fear wasn't fun.

"Yes. That's exactly what I'm thinking," she said.

"But there is no danger. Don't worry about it." They were walking down the steps. With his free hand he touched the transparent sides of the portable stairs. "It's transparent to you, but no one can see through on the other side. You'll see once we're in the car. The hat and the glasses are overkill. Literally no one can see you but me, and I'm on your side."

Well, that was … reassuring.

They walked down the stairs. Luke Reynolds matched her, step by step. He looked like he could leap down the stairs but he matched her slow pace exactly. It felt … safe. She'd lived completely on the alert these past 24 hours, unconsciously ready for flight at the slightest provocation. But with this man by her side, she knew he'd see danger before she ever could, and he looked perfectly capable of reacting.

His big lean body next to hers radiated heat and safety. She wasn't even aware of being cold until he was next to her and she had to stop herself from leaning into him. For the heat. For that feeling of strength he exuded so effortlessly.

The canopy of the stairs actually overhung the vehicle's roof. And someone had stationed the vehicle so that she stepped straight from the safety and anonymity of the covered stairway into the passenger seat without ever touching the ground.

The windows didn't look dark but from the outside she hadn't been able to see inside the vehicle at all.

Luke rounded the hood, slid into the driver's seat and drove off.

"Look behind you," he said and she did.

Oh my god! The transparent sides weren't transparent at all. They were opaque. Absolutely nothing showed through. Not the railing, not the steps, nothing.

"See?" She turned wide eyes toward him and he nodded. "No one in the world knows where you are," he said softly. "So relax."

And she did. For the first time in days. Muscles unclenched and she drew in a deep breath for the first time in what felt like forever.

Luke punched a button and classical music flowed gently into the cabin of the car. Just loud enough to be heard, to weave gentle fingers over her body, but not loud enough to stop conversation.

She turned in her seat to look at him. For the first time she noticed how amazingly good-looking he was. It had taken a while because he didn't put out those 'I'm so handsome it hurts' vibes like most handsome men did. He was entirely matter of fact, entirely unaware of the effect he was producing, and one of the handsomest men she'd ever seen. Even in the movies. Lightly tanned, with sharp, clean features, ice blue eyes, sharp blade of a nose, firm mouth. Actually ... grim mouth. Because he was here for serious business, protecting a woman under threat.

Man, he was *hot* though.

Hope needed to stop thinking what she was thinking. What she was thinking was entirely unlike her. Hope didn't flirt and it usually took her months to work up an attraction. This instant — *thing* he inspired was kind of scary. Her entire body was awake, hormones firing, skin sensitive. He was such an eye magnet she turned her head to look out the passenger side window.

"So. Where are we going?" she asked the window, then looked back at him. Because he *was* such an eye magnet.

However, not knowing where he was taking her was so weird.

God. Her entire job was doing one thing while thinking five or six or seven steps ahead. She wasn't thinking ahead now, just following this man, moment by moment, not knowing where she was going. When was the last time that happened?

Had the danger and fear knocked something loose? Something she didn't know she had? Was she going to be sandbagged by her hormones at the wrongest moment possible?

Luke glanced at her briefly and it was like the sun shone on her for an instant.

"The company hires a suite in a very nice upscale hotel. No one will know you are there because it's booked under another company's name. We'll have room service and you can debrief me knowing you're safe." He looked over at her, head to toe. She was dressed for work. Black stovepipe pants, oversized forest green linen top, oversized black linen jacket. "It's a deluxe hotel, and you'll fit right in, if anyone sees you, which they won't," he said. He blew out a breath. "Sorry I'm not dressed for it. I've been on a stake-out."

She slid her eyes back over to him. His blond hair was too long and he had blond scruff softening a hard jawline. Not the deliberate kind of scruff that took a barber to curate. The real deal, that came from not shaving. He had on faded jeans, a shapeless, long-sleeved, grayish tee that had been washed too many times and a blue flannel shirt over it like a jacket. Everything rumpled.

Whew. It lifted her spirits.

She had her first smile in days. "Don't worry. At my company, formal dress means your shoes match and your pants are zipped. You're almost overdressed."

Two

Luke hadn't expected Felicity's friend to be so goddamned *pretty*. Maybe he should have. Felicity herself was a beautiful woman. The most beautiful woman in the world, according to her husband, Metal. He'd probably shoot the face off anyone who denied that.

But in Luke's head, the odds against having two pretty women computer nerds were high. He'd spent ten years in the Army, most of them as a Ranger. A lot of fellow soldiers in the Army who were analysts or in communications were women, and as sexless as their computers to him. Most were more like bots than people.

Not this woman. She was looking out the window to her right so he could keep sneaking glances at her without coming off as skeevy. She was more than pretty. She was beautiful. Delicate features, huge green eyes surrounded by thick black lashes, perfect ivory skin, short spiky blue-black hair. Slender and fragile-looking, though it was hard to tell because she wore oversized clothes as if trying to hide herself from the world.

Her whole body language was — don't look at me. Well, yeah, if she had killers after her, she definitely didn't want to be seen.

Though with regular-fitting clothes and without possible killers after her, people would look at her. Definitely. Men, in particular.

She was in big trouble, though Felicity had only given him the bare bones of her story. *It's better if Hope tells you herself,* she said. And yeah, that made sense. A secondhand story wouldn't do anyone any good. They'd have plenty of time for her to tell him what was going on. Where they were going, they could stay for a while, figuring things out. Luke didn't start work at ASI for another two weeks and he was absolutely certain that no one knew where Hope Ellis was. ASI was good at that.

Well, unless Satan himself — armed with excellent gear — was after her. Always a possibility. After his recent experiences, Luke wouldn't swear that the devil himself was not alive and kicking in Portland, Oregon.

Nice little city. Gentle, responsible people around. They obeyed the laws, gave to charity and recycled. But there were monsters here, too. He was living proof of that.

They were at the hotel. Luke drove past the façade and around the corner. ASI had a separate entrance with security cameras that could be turned off from the garage up to the top suite. They'd already checked in. No one on earth except ASI knew where they were and Luke would lay his life on the line that no one at ASI would leak the info, or could be bought or coerced into talking.

He believed in ASI when he no longer believed in much of anything, particularly the law.

Hope's eyes were large as she glanced at the façade as they drove by. "This is a fancy hotel," she said.

"Yeah." It was. Way beyond the architecture and design, it was in part a safe house and a lot of money had gone into making it secure.

She turned her head to look at him as he plunged into the garage, turning right into an area off-limits to other guests.

"I have money to repay your company," she said earnestly. "Not to mention the private plane over. As a matter of fact, my parents left me a lot of money and I earn very well. But the thing is —"

Luke held up a hand and she cut herself off. He parked and turned fully in his seat toward her. His heart clenched a little because she was looking so worried. So pale and fragile, curled against the door. As if nobody would help her if she couldn't pay right away. As if she were expecting to be abandoned. She looked so small and vulnerable in her oversized clothes, pale face turned anxiously toward him.

"Don't say another word." He put command in his voice and saw her blink, startled. He wanted to stop this right now. "Money is definitely not an issue here. You are a friend of Felicity's and she's asked us to do her a favor. Felicity has done endless favors for everyone in the company, she's gone out of her way countless times. Everybody is dying to do something for her. As a matter of fact, the guys envy me because I happened to be available when you called her. A lot of our operatives are on missions and several are OUTCONUS. That's —"

"Outside the continental United States," she said. "Yeah. I worked for the NSA for two unpleasant years."

Luke clutched the steering wheel so hard his knuckles turned white so he wouldn't slap himself upside the head. What was he thinking? She sat there, looking so vulnerable, looking like a frightened twelve-year-old, and he'd just assumed that he could talk to her as if she were one.

This was an accomplished professional, one of the best in a hard field, and she'd worked on issues of national security all her professional life. Her security clearance had probably been higher than his when she worked at the NSA.

"Sorry."

She nodded.

"Anyway, doing a favor for Felicity is something all of us want to do. Desperately. So you've got me and you've got a company of pretty competent guys on your side." He gave a half smile. "Even if most of them are squids."

"Navy." She smiled back, the smile shaky but there. He nodded, pleased.

"Okay." He gave a light pat to the steering wheel and unlocked the doors. "Now that we've got that out of the way and now that you've understood that you have a lot of people who want to help and we wouldn't take a penny of your money no matter what, let's get up into the room and have a debrief."

She nodded and opened her door. Luke wanted to get around the car to help her down from the vehicle but before he could, she hopped out gracefully and went around to the back of the car and waited for him to open the trunk.

There were two small wheelie bags in the back. He'd packed for a mission of about four days. If it got extended, he'd either order new clothes online or use the hotel's laundry service. Someone else had packed Hope's bag and he just hoped she had everything she needed, because they were going to stay put until they figured out what was going on.

He didn't want them to go out unless necessary.

He rolled both of the bags toward an elevator against the back wall. There were security cameras, but his cell had an app to turn the cameras off. There'd be no record of their arrival. At the elevator, he rolled his eyes at the 'Out of Order' placard taped to the doors and pushed a button. The doors opened and he punched ten.

They stood, staring at the elevator doors. "Neat trick," she said after a moment. "With the Out of Order sign."

He nodded. Yeah, his company — his future

company — was full of neat tricks.

There were only four suites on this floor. He already had the electronic key out and ushered her into the west corner suite, smiling as the door whooshed slowly closed behind them. It was made of reinforced. The mild paranoia that always gripped him when on a mission slowly abated. They were as safe as he could make them. He knew only the bare bones of her situation but he imagined that she'd spent the past 24 hours in a state of high anxiety and dread.

She could relax now.

He watched her as she walked into the living room area. The room was designed to be relaxing and it did its job. Her shoulders dropped a little, her fists unclenched. She noted the two bedrooms, shot a glance at him, was reassured and let out a soft breath.

"Would you like some tea?" he asked and her face lit up.

"Oh God, yes! Thank you!"

Chicks and tea. You'd think it was crack cocaine and oxytocin rolled into one. He left their bags and walked over to the refreshments table against the wall. A water boiler, a billion types of black and herbal teas, an espresso machine with every flavor of coffee capsule, and in the fridge would be a selection of fruit juices. Luke would help himself to a finger of the excellent whiskey at the wet bar.

There was some kind of ritual to tea but he just boiled the water, stuck a tea bag in a cup and poured the hot water over it, figuring she needed the tea fast, not perfect.

"Sit and I'll bring you your tea. Would you like a cookie or something with it?"

She looked down, consulting her stomach, and shook her head. "Later, maybe," she said softly. "But thanks."

He nodded at the couch and she sat at one end. When she was sipping her tea, he sat in the comfortable armchair perpendicular to it and sipped his own equivalent of tea. A very nice single malt. Ah, that went down well. Trust ASI to have only the finest whiskey on tap. There'd be some local brews in the small fridge too. They'd have been chosen by ASI operatives and they'd be good.

He sat, sipped and waited. She was settling her nerves, gathering her thoughts, and he let her. Getting intel was always tricky when the source was unsettled. He didn't know much about her situation, but he understood that she'd had a brush with violence. Violence would unsettle anyone who wasn't a battle-hardened former soldier and soon-to-be ex-cop. Violence didn't unsettle *him*, it pissed him off.

And it pissed him off doubly as he watched her.

Everything about her spelled delicacy, from the fine collarbones, to the slender graceful hands, with that small knob at the wrists. She would have looked like a child dressed in an adult's clothes if it weren't for the intelligence blazing out of those green eyes. Someone wanted to hurt this smart and pretty young woman and that *really* pissed him off.

She'd been bone white when she sat down but the hot tea was putting a little color in her cheeks. Good. She was beginning to realize it was time to fight back and that she had people on her side. He didn't know much about her background, except for the fact that Felicity had said she was alone in the world. No family and no boyfriend. Which was odd, considering how incredibly pretty she was.

She was so attractive it was a distraction. When Luke was in work mode nothing distracted him, ever. He was intensely focused when on the job. He was here to protect an innocent young woman and that kind of thing was what he was born to do. There was a long line of Reynolds men behind him who had been cops and firefighters and warriors and it was in his DNA to fight to protect.

How could someone so smart and so pretty be so freaking alone?

Never mind. She had him now and behind him was a solid wall of good guy badasses with resources up the wazoo.

Now she not only had some color in her cheeks, but instead of sitting ramrod straight, she was relaxing back into the cushions. When she put the teacup back in its saucer on the coffee table and sat back, he knew it was time.

"So, do you want to talk about it?"

"The trouble I'm in? Yeah." She sketched a smile. "But I think I'm going to have to start from way way back. Is that ok?"

Luke took another sip of the Talisker, watching her carefully. "We have all the time in the world. Start anywhere you want. Actually, the more intel I have the better. So you can start from the Pleistocene as far as I'm concerned."

He wasn't taking notes on this first run through. It would stop her flow. They'd go over it again and again. Later, he'd take meticulous notes and pass them on to Felicity, who'd intercept them anyhow if he didn't send them to her, and then on to the ASI operators. But he was team leader on this and he'd be the one to judge who and how many to call in. Some problems were single-operator problems. Some required a lot of heavy hitters.

Whatever Hope needed, she'd get.

Luke was prepared for anything. She'd worked for the NSA. She was a female computer nerd and he knew they ruled the world. Felicity even had a sign above her workplace computer stating **Who run the world? Girls!**

It was clear to Luke that he and the guys back in the office were essentially muscle. Well-trained and lethal, sure, but muscle. The smarts were with people like Felicity and Hope, who were the ones who really ran things.

He was ready to hear about any kind of far-reaching conspiracy, massive fraud or theft in the upper reaches of government, treason, a possible EMP device coming to America's shores, killer viruses, the zombie apocalypse ... anything.

But he was taken completely by surprise by the next thing she said.

"I never got on with my parents."

Three

At any other time, Hope might have broken out in laughter at the look on Luke's face. She wasn't in a laughing mood but oh, boy. He was doing his very best to keep a perfectly bland expression on his face but it was as if he'd reached for a stick and picked up a rattlesnake instead.

Not what he was expecting.

Still, it all started from there — from her family. From what she thought had been her family.

She'd always felt something was wrong.

In her mid teens, she realized that she was scary good with computers. When she also realized she felt absolutely nothing for her parents, it occurred to her that it could mean she was somewhere on the spectrum. She wasn't — she knew that now. But for a while she made it a point to read social cues and facial expressions to convince herself she could.

Her self-directed course on human behavior led her to hack into the FBI's course on body language and she'd studied it thoroughly, paying particular attention to microexpressions, which meant that she could read Luke Reynold's expression pretty well.

The wheels were almost visibly turning in that incredibly handsome head of his. Was he being shanghaied into being a shrink? Had she mobilized vast resources — that private plane ride across the continental US alone probably cost $50,000 — for a family squabble?

"Not what you think," she said.

"Not thinking anything," he replied, which was a lie.

"This isn't a therapy session," she said.

"Good thing, because I'm no therapist," he said. Instead of taking a small sip of his whiskey, he gulped the rest of it down.

Yeah, Luke Reynolds didn't look like a shrink. He looked exactly like what Felicity said he was. A former soldier and a cop. Totally reality-based guys who didn't speculate and didn't do feelings. Certainly not the touchy-feely kind that came with discussions of family. Every inch of that lean and muscled body was meant for action, not reflection.

Which was great. Because reflection was her field and action was his.

Hope was in big trouble, had no idea why, and needed a Luke.

"Hear me out." Hope leaned forward a little, body language for *hear me out* to go with the words.

He nodded his head soberly.

None of this was going to be easy. She gathered her thoughts and resolved to be as clear and as concise as possible.

Here goes nothing, she thought, and began.

"My parents weren't good parents. They weren't bad parents, either, really. They were just indifferent, wrapped up in themselves, so they farmed out the parenting. We always had money, though I'm not too sure where it came from because I never saw them work. I'm investigating that right now. My parents hired nannies to look after me and they hired really good ones. At the age of ten I was sent to a boarding school that by sheer chance happened to be exactly what I needed. It had an excellent academic program, gifted teachers and a student body of kids like me — with parents who had more money than parental instincts. I had a good time, made good friends, got a superb education. At first, until I was about fourteen or so, I'd go home for Christmas and Easter and summer vacations, but then I stayed over at the school for extra courses in the summer, which is why I graduated at sixteen. I ended up staying with friends for Christmas and Easter after that. My parents ... didn't mind."

He was listening carefully, to his credit. There was a reason she was telling him this and he understood that.

"The only time my parents showed any strong feelings about me was when I said I wanted to study at Stanford. For some reason, that agitated them no end. My father put his foot down and said he wouldn't pay for it. I was pretty sure I could get a scholarship and anyway I was already writing code for pretty good money so I knew I could pay my own way. But one evening both of them begged me to stay in Boston. Cried, even. Begged and cried so much I … gave in. I have absolutely no idea why they were so set against Stanford. But it was the first thing they'd ever asked of me, so …" she shrugged. "I went to MIT. About six months ago, they retired, though for the life of me I don't know what they were retiring from. Neither of them worked a day in their lives, that I could see. They bought a condo in Clearwater, Florida and spent the winter there."

She stopped, sipped more tea. It was lukewarm, but that was okay. It gave her a moment to gather her thoughts. She'd never really laid her family life out like this. Hadn't even thought about it much, really, until very recently. When the past reached out and tried to take a big bite out of her.

She met Luke's eyes. They were a light blue, a beautiful color, but bloodshot. Either the man had been on a bender or he wasn't sleeping. She didn't think Felicity would have entrusted her to an alcoholic. Felicity had mentioned that he'd been having problems.

Welcome to the club.

She drew in a deep breath. "Spoken out loud like this, I'm wondering why I wasn't more curious about them. But — your family is like the ocean for a fish, I guess. Just there. What you swim in. Do you know a lot about your parents' past?"

"Everything," he said. "I was close to my parents and I knew most everything about their lives."

"Knew? Are they gone?"

A spasm of pain crossed his face, uncontrollable. "My mom died when I was eighteen. I lost my dad a couple of months ago."

He still felt that loss, it was clear. It made her even more aware of how strange her family was, how cold and uncaring. "I'm so sorry."

"Thanks." He bowed his head briefly. "Go on."

"Well, like I said, I never questioned my family much. I had nannies, then boarding school and then I discovered computers and the hacker community and my parents were like this background noise that never interfered with anything. They paid for my schooling, weren't mean to me, made sure I didn't want for anything. But that's about it. They never took any kind of interest in me, in what I was doing."

For the first time it occurred to her what she was really saying. She wasn't describing parents. She was describing guardians.

"Then — then they died suddenly. In an accident. They hired a plane to get to Kingston and it went down over the Cayman Islands. I didn't know for a week. It was the bank that notified me."

His eyes narrowed until only the pale glow of his irises showed. "This is a shrink question but — how did you feel about it?"

"I was appalled. I was appalled that I didn't find out sooner, that I didn't feel more than some sadness. Thinking about it, though, I also realized they hadn't tried to make me love them. They — they just went through the motions. There was a memorial service I organized and which only a few people attended. They hadn't made many friends. I blew up a photograph of them I had and put it on an easel. Some friends of mine came. One had studied genetics at MIT and was a buddy of mine. Kyle Ackerman. He spent the memorial service studying their photographs and afterward came up to me and asked me if I'd been adopted."

Luke's eyes narrowed even further. "Isn't that a big assumption to make?"

In answer, she handed over a photo she kept in her backpack. It was a glossy hi-def copy of the photo at the memorial. Luke studied the photo carefully, flicked a glance at her, then continued studying it.

She knew what he was seeing. Two people who looked nothing like her. Not one trait in common. Both Neil and Sandra Ellis were ruddy-faced, with sandy brown hair, brown eyes, high broad cheekbones, round faces. She had pale skin, inky black hair, green eyes, a long narrow face.

"Kyle — my friend — saw my face when he said that, because it was something I'd long suspected. He said to get some of their DNA, for both of them, and to bring the samples to him. He had just founded a gene testing startup, sort of like 23andMe, only faster and very thorough. It's in beta at the moment and he said he'd do the testing for free. He pulled out a swab for my DNA and took it then and there. I inherited the condo in Florida and the house in Boston. The will was very clear. I had the keys of course. There hadn't been time to clear out the house so I found combs with hair still in them, toothbrushes. Kyle told me what to look for. I sent the material to Kyle and he was fast. He came over himself and sat me down. This was four days ago."

She watched Luke watching her. His expression was neutral but there was no doubt she had all his attention.

He had hers, too. He was so distracting. He had a male model's good looks — fine, chiseled features, blond stubble softening a hard jaw, amazing light blue eyes — but it was as if his looks didn't belong to him. Most good looking people went through life with an air of privilege, preening. Nature's aristocrats. But Luke didn't, he didn't even seem to be aware of what he looked like. Maybe because he also looked exhausted, like he'd run a marathon through a forest fire. Backwards.

"And?" he asked.

Hope shook herself. Damn. She must be really exhausted to get caught up in the good looks of a man sent here exclusively to protect her and try to help her get to the bottom of what was happening. Getting lost staring at him wasn't cool.

She sat up straight. This was serious business and she couldn't lose track drooling over a handsome man. Even though he was — whoo — really good-looking. Very hot. What guys called eye candy when talking about women. In her line of work, there weren't many good looking guys. None, actually. She would have sworn she was immune to handsome faces, only turns out she wasn't, not at all. She just hadn't been exposed to many. Not in real life anyway. Most handsome men she'd seen were up on a screen.

"Hope." He carefully kept exasperation out of his voice but it had to be there.

"Hmm?" His eyes were light blue with narrow striations of dark blue.

"Hope. Kyle? DNA?"

Oh God, there she was again, mooning. At least she wasn't drooling. Was she?

She surreptitiously ran a hand over her mouth, which — yes, thank you God — was drool-free.

Kyle. DNA. A dead friend. A lifetime of lies. Danger built right into her DNA. That was enough to bring her down to earth.

"Yeah. Kyle came right over and showed me the DNA results." If she closed her eyes she could see the scene. Kyle, his friendly, droopy face unusually sober and serious, sitting on the edge of her couch in her pretty, tiny apartment, right under her original Star Wars poster. Another story of hidden genetic connections. Luke Skywalker's father had turned out to be a monster. And hers?

"And ... who were they?" Luke said and she realized she'd gone into another fugue state.

She needed to sharpen up, focus. Focus is what

would keep her alive.

"Well, not my parents, for one." Luke straightened a little at that. "I was right. There was no genetic connection at all between me and my parents. Both of them were mostly Slav. Polish and Russian extraction, Kyle said. I am of English extraction with some Irish thrown in. But that's not all." She plucked at an afghan that was hanging over the back of the couch. It was made of cashmere and touching it soothed her. "Not only were they not my parents, they weren't man and wife, either. They were siblings."

Luke blinked, which she was sure was an expression of great astonishment for him. He didn't seem to be someone who wore his feelings on his sleeve. She gave a wry smile.

"Yeah. They were brother and sister." Hope held up a hand. "That isn't quite as skeevy as it sounds. Or maybe it is, I don't know. Not sure of much of anything these days. But I never actually saw them kiss or even hug. They slept in separate bedrooms. And looking back, they didn't behave like man and wife. I don't know if they behaved like brother and sister because frankly, I don't have any experience in that field, but they were more like partners in an endeavor than — than a couple. So clearly, that endeavor was to be Neil and Sandra Ellis and to pretend to be my parents."

Luke's eyebrows drew together in a scowl. So expressive it was as if he'd spoken.

"Yeah." She had felt the same way.

"So if they were — were pretending to be your parents, there was a reason."

"Uh huh. I think they were *paid* to pretend to be my parents. Like a job."

He thought it over. "Well, this is so weird, why not? What led you to that conclusion?"

"Like I said, they always had plenty of money, but I never saw them work. Ever."

He leaned forward a little, the frown still there.

Yes, that was exactly what *she* felt like too. The more you knew about the situation, the more you felt like you'd fallen into a rabbit hole.

"And the adoption angle?"

Hope nodded sharply. "Yeah. That's the only thing that makes sense. I have looked — and trust me when I say I'm pretty good at looking, it's what I do — and I can't find anything. Though I don't have the resources to hack into the systems of every adoption agency in America and — given that I seem to be English and Irish — abroad. I spent a sleepless forty-eight hours searching every adoption agency I could find, including some in England since apparently that's my main heritage, with no luck at all. But in the meantime I asked Kyle to attack the problem from another angle."

"You asked your friend to match your DNA to as large a database as possible."

She nodded. "By this point he was as intrigued as I was." She smiled a little. "I think part of that was that he was an Ashkenazi Jew and his family could trace its roots back five hundred years, uninterruptedly. He said he couldn't fathom not knowing where he came from. So I sent him another DNA sample from me and he said he'd get back to me in a couple of days. I spent those days scouring the web and pacing in my apartment."

"And?"

She looked at that handsome, exhausted face and sighed sadly. "Yesterday, Kyle called me up, really excited and — and worked up at the same time. He said he'd got some astonishing results, results that could change everything. That he was on his way over."

Luke's jaw muscles clenched. "That's what he said? He found that your possible parentage could 'change everything'?"

"His exact words. I saved his call to a cloud server. It ends very badly. Can I open my laptop?"

"Sure." A wave of uneasiness crossed his face. "But —"

"Don't worry. I have a very strong proxy IP. No one can find me." She pulled out her laptop and felt better just touching it. It was a piece of hardware, yes. But it was also her life and it had never let her down. Unlike people. "So, when I turn on the audio file, you'll hear a loud background noise. It'll be his car." She glanced at Luke. They'd driven here from the airport in a car so soundproofed there hadn't been a whisper of noise from the engine. "He doesn't know anything about car mechanics or maintenance and his car probably has the equivalent of three or four serious diseases."

Luke was bent forward, elbows on knees, big hands clasped between them. His face was intent and she knew that he would pay very close attention.

"Okay, here we go." She clicked on the file and the room was filled with a loud hum and then Kyle's breathy, high-pitched voice, vibrating with excitement. "Hey Hope! Got some ... some amazing results from the DNA analysis and matchup. I didn't want to email them to you because ... because, well, you'll see. It's like you're related to Bigfoot, only not so nice. So I'm on my way to your place. At first I shot blanks more or less everywhere, and I thought maybe the DNA wasn't on file. It took me some time to cycle through a bunch of databases and I wasn't getting anything. But you know a specific set of DNA files became classified years ago."

She shot Luke a questioning look and he nodded. There had been a massive scrubbing of DNA files of top officials of Homeland Security, the CIA, the FBI and the Secret Service.

"So, technically, some big shot DNA has been removed from the data banks. But whoever scrubbed the files wasn't very good because they left a ... space, I guess you could call it. Sort of like a missing brick in a wall and footprints leading away from it. I called in our good friend and hacker extraordinaire, Dragondude95, who lives for puzzles like this and he found our missing DNA. He said it was in a super secret file behind firewalls and fire-breathing dragons and the name was actually *redacted,* so he had to climb over some more firewalls. And shit, Hope, you won't believe who you are related to! I mean, *closely* related to! Your grandfather, in fact. This is serious shit and given what's going on at the moment, it could change everything. Absolutely everything. I'm talking history-altering, game-changing shit. Can't wait to see your face when you realize who it is because —"

The loud screeching of torn metal, shattering glass, a scream. Hope looked down at her knees, because she knew she was listening to the sound of a friend's death. Murder. Each time she heard the recording, it felt like the accident went on and on and on. This time, too, the crashing noises went on forever. But finally the noise stopped and there was the sound of groaning, then screaming.

A crunching sound. She'd listened to the recording three times before realizing what it was. The sound of shoes walking over shattered glass. She was expecting it, but she still jumped at the sound of a gunshot. The screaming stopped abruptly. On the recording was a moment of shocking silence, then the crunching sound again, fading. The killer walking away.

Luke's face had tightened, the skin over his cheekbones taut, the brackets around his mouth deep. He'd gotten it immediately.

"He was killed," Hope said numbly. The words were hardly out of her mouth when she realized she'd said a *no shit, Sherlock* thing, but Luke only nodded soberly.

He touched the side of her laptop with a long finger. "ASI has sound engineers on call. They're good at isolating sounds." He shot her a look. "Do you know where this happened?"

Hope nodded, throat tight. She blew out a breath. Waited for her throat to loosen up enough to talk. "Yeah. I hacked into police radio. It was on the corner of Madison and 4th. It's a straight line from his office to my house. He'd obviously gone into work, logged onto the company system and ... and realized what the results meant. Though now we'll probably never know. He knew I'd be home because I told him I was conducting research to see if I'd been clandestinely adopted. He called me en route and — and that happened."

"Okay, you give me the make and model of his car and his phone and we'll see from his GPS what his route was, just to be certain." He frowned. "I'll have to wait to ask Felicity. Her husband, Metal, would have my head if I called right now. He guards her naptime like a dragon guarding its hoard of gold. She wants to see you, but Metal nixed that for the moment."

"I can do it. I'm not a hacker, per se, I'm a data analyst, but this is easy stuff. I can do it. I've been too — too shocked to analyze Kyle's death, but I can do it now."

"And I'll have a sound engineer analyze the footsteps. I think maybe from the gait and the volume of the crunching maybe we can estimate height, weight. Certainly the engineer can analyze and identify the caliber of the weapon."

Caliber of the weapon ... Hope shuddered. Maybe it had been her exhaustion, maybe the fact that all of this was entirely outside her experience, but she hadn't really focused on the essentials. All she really knew was that someone had shot and killed her friend Kyle Ackerman.

Because of her.

The police report said it was a shot to the head. Like an execution. She made a mental note to find the medical examiner's report, however hard it was going to be to read. She'd study it, pass it on to Luke and his teammates. She owed Kyle that much.

He'd died for her, after all.

It all came down to her, to some kind of — what? Some kind of original sin? Something in her origins, in her background, that was dangerous and that had gotten someone killed. And might just kill her.

Hope bowed her head, exhausted, trembling, sad beyond words. To her shame, a tear fell down her face and plopped on her clasped hands.

Oh God. She couldn't let him see her crying. She couldn't —

A large, warm hand covered her clasped hands. She was cold all over except at that point where his hand touched hers. They sat there for a moment, while she got herself under control. She lifted her head to apologize but he spoke first.

"None of this is your fault," he said. "You haven't done anything wrong. And I know it feels terrifying, but you're not alone anymore and we will get to the bottom of this."

He said it like an established fact. The sun will rise in the east tomorrow. We're going to get to the bottom of this.

"It's too late for Kyle," she whispered.

Luke gave a sharp nod. "It is. Kyle was an innocent and someone with something to gain killed him. The world is full of people like that. The kind of people who just swat other people out of the way when it suits them. We have to stop them. That's what ASI is all about. They don't let things like this stand."

Hope looked at him. At the brackets around his mouth, the jaw muscles clenched. He meant every single word. It was like cracking open a door to a world she'd never suspected existed, except in fantasy games. A world where evil was real and present and there were brave men and women who fought it. Hope had no idea if she was brave enough to be a warrior but she was sitting next to someone who was. He'd been a decorated soldier, Felicity said.

Which meant that he'd been shot at and hadn't run away. Had run into danger. Into fire.

"So what did you do next?" he asked.

"I knew where Kyle was from police radio, so I hacked into the traffic cams. It took me a few minutes and by the time I saw the traffic cam view, whoever shot Kyle had gone. I just — I just looked at the scene. At the smoking ruins of his car. At his torso, half out of the upside-down driver's seat window. He'd been trying to crawl out when —"

Her voice cracked and she looked away, willing the tears back. Thinking of Kyle, who'd survived a bad car crash only to be shot while trying to crawl away.

And all because of her. Because of something in her past clawing its way into the now.

Emotion welled up, unstoppable. It took her a moment to be able to speak. Luke's big hand tightened around hers.

She drew in a deep breath, let it go. "Something caught fire. The car didn't explode like in the movies, but it did start to burn. Then suddenly EMTs showed up and then the police. No sound of sirens, of course."

Another terrible memory. Kyle half-in, half-out of the vehicle, being pulled all the way out, the bullet wound in the head horribly visible, a black hole. Blood pooling in a black puddle around his head. The police stretching yellow tape — which showed up light gray in the black and white video — around the car. The EMTs loading poor Kyle onto a gurney, then into the ambulance and driving away.

"And then?" Luke asked, after she fell silent, memories like nails driven into her heart.

"Then I followed them on traffic cams. I wanted

to follow where they were taking him. I thought I'd go where they took him, to pay my respects to him." She glanced at him. His jaw had tightened even more. You could cut glass with it. "What?"

"Bad move."

She sighed. Yeah, it would have been a bad move.

"You're right, it would have been a terrible move, but I wasn't thinking straight. I was following the traffic cams when my cellphone pinged."

"Some alert you'd set up?"

She nodded. "The security system in the building. From the lobby." He'd immediately understood. It had taken her precious seconds to understand the sequence of events. Kyle talking to her on his cell, then the alert. She'd been slow all along the way in a deadly game where catching up after the fact meant death. Where speed meant life.

"Four men walked into the lobby with ski masks on. My building has a doorman, Geraldo. He doesn't man the front desk much but he's pretty good about paying attention from a small room behind the front desk. There are monitors covering the grounds, the lobby and the corridors. He must have pressed an alarm button. I watched him come out from the small room and one of the men just —"

Her voice went hoarse. She closed her eyes and saw the scene inside her eyelids. She'd never forget it, the casual brutal killing, the utter shock and horror of it. She opened her eyes to find Luke watching her, head tilted slightly. Showing no surprise at all at her next words.

"They — they were walking fast, like ... marching, almost synchronized. As they walked by the front desk, Geraldo came out from the back room. One of the men just lifted his arm. He was holding a gun and to my shame I only noticed then that they were all armed. He lifted his arm straight out and shot Geraldo in the head. Without even aiming. Just put his arm up, shot Geraldo, put his arm back down and carried on without breaking his stride. Like stepping on an ant. They filed into the elevator and I could see in the cam them punching in the 5th floor. My floor."

Geraldo had dropped like a stone, the only evidence of him being there a slight pink mist in the air and blood spattering the door behind him.

"They traced the call." Luke's voice was pensive. "Came after you right away. Almost simultaneously."

She nodded.

"Two teams. One for your friend and one for you. That's a lot of manpower. You'd have to assume they had other teams ready."

"Oh God." The breath left her chest in a painfully jagged whoosh. She hadn't put it all together. She'd just reacted to all the events, but hadn't analyzed them. She was an analyst but not this kind. Not the real-world real-time killers-on-the-loose kind. "That's — that's really scary."

He dipped his head, face sober. "It is. But you escaped."

That iron anchor on her chest lifted, just a little. "I did. My apartment is around the corner from where the elevator opens. I threw my laptop in my backpack, put a burner cellphone in the microwave, turned it on and grabbed a couple of other burner phones I always keep around."

He cocked his head. "Cell in the microwave, eh? That was good thinking. Most people would hesitate, particularly if they had an expensive cell. And most people keep a lot of data in their cell's memory."

She shook her head. "It was just a burner. I have a very expensive cell, yes, but I can always buy a new one. I keep all my contacts and info and messages in the cloud, and trust me when I say that the data there is secure. It was just a burner though, so I was essentially trashing a piece of plastic. I could smell melting plastic as I went out the door. The burner was a distraction. I knew they'd spend a few minutes trying to salvage it. Buy me some time."

"That was good thinking on your part."

She sighed. "I think in terms of computer security all the time. But never in terms of personal security. Got a real crash course in that."

He looked straight into her eyes. "You're a good student."

Yes, she was. She'd gotten straight As all her life. But this — this was another school. A hard, cruel, pitiless one, and she didn't think she'd aced the exams. A friend of hers had died, as had the doorman of her building. Maybe if she'd thought it through, maybe if she'd taken a moment to consider consequences, Kyle and Geraldo would still be alive.

But no. She'd been breathless with curiosity, burning up in a fever of restlessness to *know*. To know whether this vague feeling of unease around her parents was on her or was on them. It hadn't even occurred to her that opening that door might be dangerous. That she might be cracking open a door onto a monstrous hell.

"Don't." Luke's voice was deep and low. He'd put his hand over hers again and again she felt that sense of strength and warmth. She caught her breath. No, not warmth — *heat*.

Oh God. She was never distracted by beefcake, never. Not that handsome men were thick on the ground where she worked. Either at her current company, at the NSA, or even at university. Slump-shouldered, either painfully thin because they forgot to eat or dumpy because the only thing they did besides work the keyboard was eat pizza, with dubious grooming habits, the men she'd been around most of her adult life did not inspire lust.

The few times she'd forced herself to go on dates or go clubbing, the men had been better looking and better groomed but — like children. Preening in fancy clothes, dropping restaurant names, checking to see what effect they were having on her.

Awful. That was the effect they had on her. Usually she couldn't wait to get back to her cool, empty apartment and get back online, where interactions were fun and impersonal.

This man didn't do any of that. He didn't preen and he didn't try to impress. This man was a man, in the full sense of the word.

She rarely saw real men. That must be why all her hormones woke up at the very worst possible moment. What was the point of hormones rising up, raring to go when there was nowhere to go? This was strictly a frightened customer/professional protector scenario.

But *damn*! He was just so incredibly attractive. It was unfair that she had to deal with such a good-looking *male* male when she was so tired and scared. Like a male model, only a little scruffy and unshaved. Which actually made him even more attractive.

Oh God. Sandbagged by her own hormones.

He was so serious. He exuded seriousness from every pore. She was in so much trouble and here she had a freaking *soldier* protecting her. A brave one, too. Felicity had texted her the basics on Luke Reynolds, thinking it would reassure her. It had. He'd won medals for valor. Had been in Special Operations, SpecOps, they'd called it at the NSA. Brave and smart and dedicated to helping her.

Why, oh *why* were her hormones betraying her now?

Her hand under his was trembling and she looked down. He snatched his hand away as if he'd presumed too much. When, actually, she wanted to crawl onto his lap and lick his face. Throw her arms around that strong neck and lay her head against that broad chest.

It wasn't fair.

"Tell me the rest of the story." He looked her in the eyes and she almost got lost in them. Manly men weren't supposed to have beautiful eyes but this one did. Just her luck. Light blue, with thin lines of dark blue and dark eyelashes though he was blond. She sighed, looked down, gathered her thoughts which were not of him. Not, not, not.

He nodded as she looked up again. "How'd you get out without anyone seeing you? Anyone with operational experience would have posted men at the front and back entrances. I don't know what kind of manpower they had but they'd have covered all contingencies."

"They probably did. But my apartment is part of a pretty big complex, a gated community of twelve apartment buildings. What isn't visible, and what you can't know unless you have property there, is that they are all connected via underground passageways, so people can get from one building to the next underground if it's raining or snowing. The laundry rooms and garbage bins are there, and everyone has a storage locker. The elevators to go up to the apartments don't go down to the basement, there are separate elevators down to the basement. So unless they did major research and hacked into the architect's studio, they wouldn't know about the underground passageways and the special elevators. I was in the special elevator to the basement before they made it up to the fifth floor. I followed them on the hallway security cameras. I ran down the basement corridor as fast as I could. In ten minutes I came up in a small alleyway twelve buildings away. It leads directly to a bus stop. I waited in the alleyway for a few minutes until a bus came. It covered the video cam across the street. The camera couldn't catch me boarding. I got off right in front of the apartment of a friend of mine who's away for two months on a course. She asked me to water her plants twice a week and I had the keys to her apartment in my backpack. I don't think anyone would ever connect us. I stayed there all night. I hacked into Kyle's work computers. He's pretty good at security and it took me a while. But when I finally got in, his entire system had been trashed. His company will have to start over. Even the data stashed in the cloud was gone."

Luke stared at her, unblinking. "That would take a lot of talent."

She nodded. The fact that someone had killed Kyle's entire IT department had frightened her almost more than the killing of Kyle himself. Any idiot with a gun can kill. It took talent and resources to wipe out Kyle's company's system.

"By evening, I realized I needed help, so I called the HER room."

"Come again?" For a moment she was distracted by his frown. Damn, he was so handsome even frowning was a good look on him. "What's a her room?"

That called up a slight smile. Just thinking of the HER room made her feel better, safer.

"The HER room. It's a Blockchain-encrypted storage folder in the darkweb shared by the four of us. There were originally three of us in the same office at the NSA, we were the ones who set it up. This was before Felicity. Me — Hope — Emma and Riley. H.E.R. We founded it a couple of years ago when we were working together at the NSA. We had the Boss from Hell who managed to be oppressive, incompetent and sexist, all at once, and all at maximum volume. We were setting up a database of all the known means of communication of ISIS, and it required focus and he was always there, looking over our shoulders, complaining and making stupid comments because he didn't understand the parameters of the database. Backstabbing sexist creep. Belittling us while waiting for us to make our breakthrough so he could claim credit." She glanced angrily at him. "Did you ever have a boss like that?"

"Once. In the Army. But everyone hated him and he was eventually rotated back to Washington. Never in law enforcement."

"Then you've been lucky."

He bent his head. "I have. But you haven't."

"No." She tried hard to control her breathing because just *thinking* about Kevin Dolby made her gnash her teeth and her cerebral circuits short out. "We needed a way to communicate because we suspected he had our workroom wired for video and sound."

That surprised Luke. "Really?"

"Well, it *was* the NSA. It's the Palace of Paranoia and it's very likely even the bathrooms were wired and there was an AI somewhere monitoring us, always. So we created an out. A special message board in the darknet where you have to beat fire-breathing dragons and climb a mountain of thorns to get in. Impenetrable. And it can also display text steganographically. The messages can be embedded into whatever is on the screen. I wrote that little algorithm. We could complain about Dolby and no one would know. We also warned each other if some other particularly obnoxious guy was coming our way. And we helped each other out with problems."

The skin had tightened over Luke's cheekbones. The skin over his temples pulled as his jaw muscles clenched. "You got a lot of that? At the NSA? Harassment?"

She sighed, looked down at her hands where her fingers intertwined then pulled apart. "We got a lot of that, yeah. Not just at the NSA. We're used to it, but sometimes it just … it just rankles, you know? We were working so freaking hard and we just kept getting undercut. So it was hard."

His mouth was a thin line. He nodded jerkily.

"Anyway, it was our safe room, the HER room. Felicity was admitted by popular acclaim though she wasn't at the NSA long. We talked, vented. When one of us has a problem she just sends up the bat-signal and help is on the way. So I sent up the bat-signal. It's weird that Emma and Riley didn't answer but Felicity answered right away. I didn't actually know where she was and that she was married and pregnant. Not only pregnant but with orders to stay in bed because she could lose the baby."

"Babies." A faint smile crossed Luke's face. "Twins. Boys."

Her face lit up. "Oh my gosh! How wonderful! I hope her husband treats her right."

Luke nodded. "Oh yeah. He loves her. He takes really good care of her. She is his life. He was the one who arranged for everything. The pickup in Boston, the flight over, me. Any friend of Felicity is a friend of his. And mine."

Hope hardly heard him. Only heard — *he loves her. He takes really good care of her. She is his life.* Hope wasn't jealous of Felicity, not a bit. Felicity hadn't had it easy and she deserved every ounce of happiness life could give her.

But oh ... to have someone love you. Really love you. What must it be like? Hope had friends who were fond of her, but no man had ever loved her in her life. Emma, Riley and Felicity loved her but none of them even lived in the same city.

Well, that was pathetic. Right now she was in danger, a friend had died because of her, her doorman had been killed and now a brave man — a decorated soldier — was right here, right now, ready to lay his life on the line for her.

That's what she should be thinking about, not romantic notions of love.

She was tired. That was it. All that adrenaline coursing through her system, it had made her loopy and sloppy.

"So." She tried to straighten her spine. "That's it. That's basically all I know. Well, except for one more thing." She tried and failed to keep the misery out of her voice. "Whoever my real father is, apparently he wants me dead."

Four

Whoever my real father is, he wants me dead.

Those were the saddest words Luke had ever heard. How could anyone want this woman dead? Let alone ... *her father?*

She looked so fragile and delicate, perched at the edge of the seat of the sofa as if she would fly away at any moment. So pretty and so smart. Felicity hadn't said much about her — there hadn't been time — but she said Hope was wicked smart and coming from a wicked smart woman herself, it really meant something.

Felicity hadn't mentioned she was also wicked pretty. Not that Luke was noticing. Not much, anyway. Pretty as she was, she was also in imminent danger. Big time. Her story was horrifying and it took a lot for him to keep his cop face on. Expressionless and stolid, when inside he was screaming.

He'd expressed the fact that the shadowy forces against her were powerful without letting on that they might be facing fucking Satan himself, on steroids. Anyone who could corral two teams of efficient operators within the space of maybe half an hour ...

that was serious shit. Maybe even government serious. Certainly, the only entities that could field that kind of operational reaction that fast would be US military SpecOps, maybe the CIA Special Activities Division and one or two private security companies, but they'd have to operate on the East Coast.

Or be everywhere, which was even scarier.

This was a woman who had serious enemies. Enemies who had infrastructure, resources and weaponry. She had nothing of that, not even tactical awareness. She had smarts and was nice. That was what Felicity said and he'd seen nothing that would contradict that.

Smart. And nice. Those weren't good qualities to deal with the bad guys of the world. Particularly if one of them was her fucking *father*. Or grandfather. Who wanted her dead.

Luke had dealt with a lot of shit in his life, as a soldier and as a cop. But he'd never had to deal with anything like this. His own dad had been the best. Aloysius Reynolds, pure Irish, a twenty-year cop, had been the best husband and dad ever, in the history of the world. When Luke's mom had cancer, his dad took leave and never left her side. She died with her hand in his. And when Luke had had his troubles, his dad had been by his side one thousand percent. In fact, Luke's troubles had broken his dad's heart.

He missed his dad, fiercely, every single fucking day.

His dad had never once raised a hand to him. He

sure as hell hadn't tried to kill him.

That was a level of viciousness he'd never encountered, not in fifteen years as a soldier and a cop. No wonder she was almost paralyzed with terror.

Luke watched her carefully as she spoke. She was exhausted and terrified but she spoke cogently, even elegantly. Every aspect of her spoke of a stable, intelligent young woman. Who also happened to be amazingly pretty. Not head-turningly beautiful, she was too understated for that. Beautiful women reached out and grabbed your hormones by the balls because nature programmed them for that. Not Hope. She just sat quietly and waited for you to notice the perfect skin, fine features, green eyes surrounded by black lashes, the shiny blue-black hair. She was quiet and made you come to her but once you did ...

Shit.

What kind of man would want this young woman dead? How could a *father* not be supremely proud of a young woman who was so smart and brave? He just couldn't wrap his head around a father wanting a daughter dead. Ordering her death.

Luke had come across great depravity as a soldier and as a cop but this ... this was just too much.

He always did a good job, the best he was capable of. But by God, he was going to defend this young woman with everything in him. Luckily ASI was on board, and ASI had resources. They'd pull out all the stops for Felicity because she was loved, but once they got to know Hope, they'd pull out all the stops for her own sake.

He hated that lost look on Hope's white face. The look of someone who'd suddenly had the gates of hell wrenched open right in front of her, with fanged monsters reaching out to grab her. She needed some sense of normalcy, otherwise she'd spiral into despair. Luke had no idea how resilient she was, but he did know that to track down those who wanted to hurt her, he needed her help.

Only she had the knowledge necessary to crack this, inside that pretty head of hers, but if she was beaten down, she couldn't access it.

Normal ... what was normal?

Well, food.

Leaning forward, he tapped her gently on the knee. She startled, looked him in the eyes. Her own were full of fear and misery.

"Hey. I think we need to take a break. You are completely safe here. I know you've been on the run and you must be running on fumes. This place has a great restaurant. How about we order in some food?"

That earned him a shaky smile and a nod. He didn't want it to — this was a job, or if not a job, a favor to Felicity — but his heart simply turned over in his chest. She was doing her very best in a very shitty situation. Which, basically, was what being a Ranger and a cop was all about.

"Here." He stretched out, grabbed the room service menu and sat next to her. He ran his finger down the choices. "Do you eat meat?" She was probably vegetarian. He just hoped she wasn't vegan because the chef here made full use of eggs, cheese and butter.

But she surprised him. "God, yes, I eat meat. Love it." Her finger landed on the page. "Pepper steak. I love pepper steak. Is it good here?"

He smiled at her. "Oh yeah. I'll have it myself. With fries?" And was delighted when she nodded.

She pursed her mouth, considering. "Maybe we should also order a salad? Just to even things out? Sneak in a few vitamins?"

"Okay. And then since we've been really good about the salad, how about a slice of blueberry cheesecake? To die for."

"Oh God." Her eyes closed and a smile tilted her lips up. "Pepper steak, fries and blueberry cheesecake. I can already feel my arteries hardening. Can't wait."

While her eyes were closed, Luke sneaked a guilty look at her lips, soft and naturally pink and so very kissable.

Whoa. Jesus, where had that come from?

Do. Not. Go. There. He told himself sternly. He had to be really harsh with himself, drill-instructor harsh, slap-yourself-upside-the-head harsh because operators don't get involved with their protectees. Fastest way on earth to lose someone — have your head up your ass, giving an opening to whoever was gunning for your client.

Not gonna happen.

"Okay." He stood, put some distance between them. "While I order, do you want to take a shower? I'm told there's more or less everything you might need in the bag Summer put together for you."

"Summer?"

"A friend of Felicity's. She put the bag together for you, since Felicity herself doesn't have much freedom of movement these days. Summer's a journalist. You might have read some of her stuff? Used to run a political blog, Area8. She just published a book, is writing another one."

Luke shook his head in admiration. Man, he was good with a lot of stuff but he couldn't ever write one book, let alone two.

Hope stood, too, giving a little gasp. "Summer Redding-Delvaux?"

He nodded. "That's the one."

"I used to read her blog all the time! And I have her book, *The Massacre,* on my ipad. Felicity recommended it. Be sure to thank Summer for me."

Luke nodded. "Will do. She told me to tell you that you should find more or less everything in there. For all your, ahm, needs. That's what she said." He could feel just a touch of heat rising along his neck.

"Okay." Hope picked up the wheelie and disappeared into the bedroom Luke indicated, and then into its en suite bathroom. After a moment, he could hear the shower. The showers at the hotel were amazingly luxurious and he hoped the four shower heads, one of which had a choice of lavender-scented, lemon-scented or rose-scented water, would make her feel better.

The food would definitely make her feel better.

The food arrived and he arranged it on a small table he pulled out from the wall. A bottle of a good California red was open and breathing when she came out of the bathroom, a puff of lavender-scented air coming out with her. Oh, man. He was tongue-tied for a moment. The shower had put some color in her face and she looked rested, as if the shower were the equivalent of a nap. Often it was.

She was dressed in an outfit Summer had provided — a turquoise cotton sweater and dark blue pants. She was a little smaller than Summer so the clothes hung on her but the effect was just to make her look more delicate. Fragile. Like a strong wind would blow her away.

She also looked unspeakably beautiful.

"Hey," she said into the silence and it jerked him out of whatever it was that made him stare at her. Luke quickly ran a hand along his chin just to make sure his tongue wasn't hanging out and shot to his feet.

"Hi. Hey. You look great! Fabulous. Ahm ... I mean you look like the shower did you good. Showers are great. Food's arrived." *She can see that, you moron. Quit while you're ahead.*

He held out a chair at the small dinette table and held his tongue.

"Thanks." Hope sat, turned her head to smile up at him. "Aren't you going to sit down?"

Fuck. Since when being in a room with a beautiful woman made him tongue-tied? Since fucking never. He always kept his head — the big one and the little one — strictly under his control. Plus, he would soon be working at a place where a whole bunch of his colleagues were married to beautiful women he would see often. And in his old life as a cop, his boss, commissioner Bud Morrison, was married to a good-looking woman. And an heiress. Not that you'd know it from Claire Morrison's behavior.

So he should be used to female beauty. No reason to feel like he had two left tongues.

He sat, lifted the covers of the dishes and oh, man. The pepper steak and fries gave off smells almost as good as Hope coming out of the shower.

She leaned forward over her plate, closed her eyes, sniffed. "Oh wow. That smells delicious." She was smiling, but her hands were trembling.

It knocked that clumsiness right out of him. "When was the last time you ate?" His voice came out harshly, almost as an accusation.

"Ate?" Her dark brows drew together in confusion, as if she didn't recognize the word at first. Her eyes rolled up and to the right, trying to remember. "Ahhh … I was really anxious waiting for Kyle's analysis results and my stomach just closed up. And since — since the accident. No." She drew in a deep breath. "Since Kyle's murder, and the murder of

Geraldo, I've had two protein bars and a sandwich. There was food on the plane apparently but I just fell asleep."

"I want you to eat every single bite," he said seriously.

"Yes, mom." Hope rolled her eyes, but she was smiling.

Picking up the bottle of wine, he half filled her glass then his. Only a finger for him. They were safe, but still. "It's a good red from Napa Valley. Have you ever been?"

She sipped and sighed. "Oh man, yes, that's good. Nope," she answered his question. "Before today, actually, I've somehow never been further west than Chicago. I told you that when I got accepted at Stanford, my folks just went wild." She put down the glass, eyes distant. Then shook herself. "God knows why. They insisted on me studying in Boston so hard I just gave in. That was when I thought maybe ... maybe they wanted to see more of me. So weird, when we barely saw each other all the years I was at boarding school and MIT. But turns out they didn't really want to see more of me. They just had a thing about travelling out west, I guess. Why are you still wearing your shirt? It's warm in here."

Luke knew how to switch gears. He had on a heavy flannel shirt that doubled as a jacket, and it *was* warm in here.

"I'm armed." He watched her face carefully and saw the barely concealed wince. "I will stay armed.

And I'll sleep with my weapon close by. I didn't want to freak you out, so I kept the shirt on."

She was silent a moment, searching his eyes. "Considering the fact that you're armed for me, to protect me, I think I will allow you to take that hot flannel shirt off. And by the way — thanks. Felicity texted me you're volunteering to help me? You're not a part of her company? I didn't quite get it."

"It's a long story." Long and sad and infuriating. "I am — was — a cop, ex-military, and my contract with the police force ends at the end of the month, but I'm on leave. And ASI has recruited me and I'm slated to start in two weeks, but am not officially on the payroll yet. So I guess, like an actor that's between parts, I'm an operator between jobs."

She cocked her head. "There's a story there you're not telling me."

There was. He didn't tell it to many. It was painful. "Hmm. It's sad and bad."

She looked him in the eyes. "I know all about sad and bad," she said softly. "Tell me."

He wrestled with himself briefly and lost. He was going to tell the story. For the first time, he suddenly realized. Everyone he knew had lived through it with him. He'd never told it to an outsider.

Maybe now was the time. Maybe now he had some distance. And to a sympathetic audience, as well. She was looking at him with sadness in those intelligent eyes, but interest as well. A good combo.

He was going to do this.

"Okay. I was in the military for almost ten years. The Army. Most of that time I was in the Rangers, which is —"

"SpecOps," she said gently. "Yes. I could at one time recite the Ranger Creed by heart. At the NSA Emma, Riley and I worked with General Orenson to develop a …" She stumbled, bit her lips. Whatever they had developed, it had probably been highly classified. "Develop something for them."

He smiled. "The General was something else, wasn't he?"

She smiled back. "He was. Tough but fair. Also a lightweight when it came to alcohol. We did a really good job and completed it the day before he was retiring. He invited the three of us out to dinner and Riley drank him under the table. It wasn't hard to do."

Luke laughed out loud. The General had been a good guy, very strait-laced. The thought of a female nerd drinking him under the table was good gossip. Next time he met with his Ranger teammates he was going to pull that story out. It would get him a couple of beers, at least.

Hope leaned forward on her elbows. "So —" she prodded. "You were a Ranger?"

"Yeah." Luke nodded. "I liked being a Ranger. But my dad started having a few health issues. And then he had a heart attack."

She nodded. "And you were close to your father."

Ah … Christ. She wasn't even aware of the longing in her voice.

"I was. He recovered but I knew I needed to be around him. So I resigned my commission and applied to join Portland PD. My dad had been a cop all his life. I knew the ropes already and hell, I grew up with half the force. My dad was really good friends with the Commissioner, Bud Morrison."

She was watching him carefully. "You liked being a cop, too," she said gently.

He bowed his head. "I did. A lot. I like being useful. After a few years on patrol I passed the exam and got my badge. Assigned to Homicide."

"Homicide," she said softly. "I'll bet you were good at that too."

He gave a half shrug. "I solved my fair share of cases. Had good backup at Portland PD, which is well run. And then I ran into a case that nearly broke me. A young college student, brutally raped and murdered, her body left under a bush in Washington Park."

Hope's mouth fell open. "I remember reading about that case! The Sigma Phi Five! That poor girl! What she suffered! And at the trial, it turned out the policeman —" Her eyes widened with horror. "You! You were the policeman!"

Luke couldn't stop the spurt of anger. Still. He thought he'd gotten rid of most of it, but nope. "I was."

"They — they crucified you on the witness stand. I remember that."

He nodded. "We solved the case, thanks to quick DNA analysis. There were five of them, but we only found the DNA of four of them on the body of the young girl. The fifth was a bystander. He was guilty. He was there and he didn't stop them. But he didn't rape her. The other four had really powerful fathers. One a sitting Senator, two tech billionaires and a famous actor. The father of the fifth kid, the one who didn't actually do anything but was just there, was just a high school teacher. The kid took the fall for all of them."

"The four got off scot-free," Hope said. "I remember that. And I remember that they were guilty in everyone's eyes."

"Except for the jury, because they hired the best legal muscle in America and they cast doubt in every direction, like some evil sorcerer's dust. And some fell on me."

She nodded. "I remember. It was in all the newspapers for a while. I don't normally pay attention to true crime, but this was unavoidable."

Luke's back teeth ground. He should be over this. He was starting a new life, a new job, but it still burned. They'd gone over his military career with a fine-tooth comb and though there wasn't anything to find, they'd manage to dig up a fellow Ranger from under a rock who'd testified that Luke had disobeyed orders once and had stolen arms from the armory. It wasn't in any way true, but they made it sound true. Jacko's father, Dante Jimenez, who was a former

DEA investigator, found out that the Ranger suddenly had a hundred grand in his bank account.

The lawyers had dug up nonexistent dirt on the office that analyzed the DNA, on the coroner and on the chain of evidence.

But most particularly they came after him with everything that $700-dollars-an-hour lawyers could throw at him.

Luke had had to hire lawyers of his own and had exhausted his savings and, worse, his father's savings. They'd been about to dig into the small trust fund his grandmother had left him when the trial ended. The four rapists and murderers got off scot free. The fifth kid was convicted of manslaughter, sentenced to ten years and would be out in four.

The pressure on Luke had been horrible. His father had died two weeks later of a coronary. He'd died, essentially, of a broken heart.

His boss, Bud Morrison, the Commissioner, had been ready to wage war on the four men and Luke realized that Bud was willing to lay his job on the line.

Luke had been broken, he didn't want Bud to be broken. Because if there was one lesson he'd taken away from the whole sorry mess, it was that money talked. Loudly. The men, together, had several billion dollars in assets and they felt they could do what they wanted and fuck everyone else. Bud wasn't bending, so Luke quit.

Bud hadn't been happy and had been vocal about

it, until Luke told him he was accepting a job at ASI. Bud stood down because it was a good place to be.

Luke knew he'd carry some of the dirt of the trial around for the rest of his life. But the men he knew and respected knew the truth and that was enough for him.

"I'm so sorry," she said, and laid her hand over his. It was a simple gesture, but comforting. "It must have been hell."

"Yeah, it was. I lost my father, who basically died of a broken heart. I lost my job, which I loved. But I'm moving on to ASI, which is a really good place to work. And those four kids are psychopaths. Sooner or later they're going to hurt someone else and then the law will fall on them like a ton of bricks."

"Good."

"Enough about me." Luke meant it. He was sick of thinking of the past. Right now, he wanted to focus on her story, which was dangerous, and was dangerous *right now*. "I think we should finish our meal."

She waited a moment, searching his eyes, then nodded. "Sure."

She dug in, enjoying the food. The shower and the hot food were doing their work. Color bloomed on her skin. The white brackets around her mouth disappeared.

She didn't feel the need to fill the airwaves with her voice, which Luke found restful.

She'd taken one bite of the blueberry cheesecake and was rolling her eyes in delight when Luke's cell rang. He checked. Felicity. "Gotta take this. Felicity, hey."

Hope's eyes shot to him. She put down the fork and he put Felicity on speakerphone but not video. He placed the phone against the bottle of mineral water so they could talk hands-free.

"Hey, Felicity," Hope said quietly, leaning forward to speak into the cell's microphone. "How are you feeling?"

"Hey back," Felicity said. Her voice sounded tired. "There are still three of us in one body. Not easy. Just checking in. How are things going there?"

"I'm feeding her," Luke answered.

"Good. I imagine that between the death of a friend and intruders in her home, she hasn't been able to eat properly in a while."

Hope leaned forward a little, affection blossoming on her face. Luke knew how she felt. Felicity always thought of others before she thought of herself. "Thanks for everything, Felicity. I owe you for this. I honestly didn't know where to turn."

"No problem, honey. You'll find my company full of good guys who are remarkably good at dealing with trouble."

"Just what I need," Hope said, with a glance at Luke.

Luke gave a half smile. That was an excellent description of ASI. Good guys who were good at dealing with trouble.

Felicity sighed. "I'll be helping you guys some

more as soon as I fend off a DoS attack. Wily thugs are attempting to crash through our cloud servers. Luke, you know what a big piece of business our cloud computing service is."

He did. It represented 10% and climbing of ASI's corporate income. Felicity had designed it all.

"You've got an ongoing attack?" Hope frowned. "Who do you think it is?"

"The Romanians, I think," Felicity answered. She sighed heavily, audible over the speaker. "The Timisoara gang. They're good. It's a massive attack."

Hope sat on the edge of her seat, took the phone from Luke. "Talk to me," she said softly.

Luke deliberately hadn't switched to video out of respect for Felicity. He stacked the plates and put them outside the door for the room service staff to pick up while he listened to Hope and Felicity talk geek.

Christ. Deep math. He'd been good at math in school but not like this. This was scientist-level shit. Well, if Hope could help, that would be great. He knew the company was under attack at least three or four times a month. They did a lot of government work, kept a lot of secrets. Felicity had put a magic spell around their computers but the spell was breaking down.

He tuned back in.

"So the parameters change on a randomized basis, second by second. Basically it would take a quantum computer to crack it. I've got the whole thing on my laptop. I'll send it to you as soon as we're done."

"Oh man." Felicity breathed a sigh of relief. "If it works, we'll be eternally grateful. Just name your price —"

Hope threw up her hands, though Felicity couldn't see her, an expression of horror on her face. "No! God no! I can't begin to thank you and your company for what you're doing for me! Consider it a down payment on what I owe you. In fact —" she glanced at Luke. "I don't know what the plan is for tomorrow, but if I have some down time could you throw some problems that you should be working on my way? I get itchy when I'm idle and I would love to help you out."

Silence. "I don't know …" Felicity said finally.

"You know my security clearance when we were at the NSA." Hope put a wheedling note in her voice. "It was the highest possible. But at any rate, if you want, send me routine stuff, send me scut work, anything. Something. Have me do the cyber-equivalent of alphabetizing your spice rack, polishing your silver. Mopping the floors. *Pleeeeeze?*"

Luke didn't smile because it wasn't a smiling situation, but it was hard not to. Hope had hitched herself onto the arm of the couch, one leg swinging back and forth. She looked like a twelfth grader begging to go to the movies. She was irresistible.

Felicity didn't resist.

"OK. I hate hate hate this, but I really can't take care of our work load right now." Luke heard Metal's deep rumbling voice in the background. "Temporarily," Felicity said firmly. "It's just temporary. So yeah, if you can take care of some work for me, I'd be grateful."

Hope pumped her fist. "Yes! Just send it over, I'll take care of whatever you throw my way, and be grateful for it."

"Don't be too grateful, Hope." Felicity was fading fast. Her voice was thready. Luke stood, knowing Metal would put an end to it in a moment. "One of the tasks is to analyze worldwide usage data for a new social media app that wants to replace Facebook. We're expected to study the security aspect. It's terabytes of data."

"I eat terabytes of data for breakfast." Hope had watched Luke rise and rose herself. "Listen, let's get off the phone. I'm sending you my security software and you send me the Facebook wannabe data." Her voice turned sober. "Take care of yourself."

"As my husband would say, roger that." The connection closed.

Still standing, Hope turned to Luke. She opened her mouth to say something but it turned into a gigantic yawn, instead.

"Okay, princess, time for bed," Luke said. She blinked owlishly, nodded and picked up her laptop.

Like for Felicity, her laptop seemed to hold some kind of magical property for her, not to mention being a security blanket. Luke had serious respect for Felicity. She always did amazing work, did it fast, perfectly and with a smile. Everyone liked her a lot and depended on her more than they were comfortable admitting.

Maybe for a while they'd found themselves another Felicity. Dark-haired, green-eyed, smaller, but just as smart and just as nice.

And incredibly beautiful.

Luke shut that thought down immediately because his body responded in a rush of blood to his groin. A hard-on for a young woman who was locked up with him and whose life was in danger — maybe from her own father — wasn't cool. He needed to keep it in his pants. Not that he'd had any problems reining it in at work before. But there was something about this fairy-like woman that got under his skin.

"Going to bed," she mumbled and Luke stepped right in her way. There were things he had to tell her and she had to pay attention.

He stood in front of her long enough to get all of her attention. He needed to reassure her.

"So, Hope. This is the way it is. You can sleep in as long as you want," he said. "Breakfast will be any time you want. I just need you to know that you are as safe as safe can be here. The hotel's security team is alerted and will let me know if anyone comes up to this floor or if there are any issues at all. The door is reinforced and alarmed and I am armed. Nothing — and trust me when I say nothing — will happen to you."

He said it without smiling, sober as a judge,

meaning every word.

She sketched a shaky smile. "Unless the zombie apocalypse happens."

"Then, too. I know to aim for the head and I'm an excellent shot." He didn't smile back. "Still, no zombies tonight, guaranteed. Sleep well."

She nodded and walked into her bedroom and he let out a breath he didn't realize he was holding.

This wasn't going to be easy and not because she had killers after her. That was the easy part.

Five

Hope finished unpacking the bag Summer had prepared for her and, as promised, Summer had been thorough. Hope had enough clothes for at least a week and she could always order online, Luke had said. Anything she needed would be ordered off a company card and delivered to the company and then brought to them. Summer, like her, had apparently perfected the art of dressing Nerd Chic. Comfortable clothes made of excellent fabric, well cut, but sporty. Clothes you could look good in even when working twelve-hour days.

Summer had included new underwear that was a little large, a new toothbrush and toothpaste, minimal makeup and tampons and — whoa. A box of condoms at the bottom. A *box*.

It contained more condoms than the times she'd had sex in her life.

Standing there like an idiot, with the box in her hand, she blushed furiously. Hope rarely blushed and if she did, it wasn't about sex, it was when she made a very rare professional mistake. Sex didn't play a big part in her life. Ordinarily, she'd have smiled and put the box of condoms away, but she stood there like a dork, package in hand, while intense heat prickled through her entire body.

Because, well, condoms meant sex and she had the sexiest man she'd ever seen in the next room. Luke Reynolds was, as they said, sex on a stick.

Hope worked in a man's world, but the man's world she was in wasn't full of men. Not *men* men, anyway. It was full of humans with a Y chromosome who were really interested in a) data, b) software, c) money. If they were interested in women, that came way, way down in the list and after office hours. And since most everyone worked fourteen-hour days, sex didn't play a big part in their lives, either.

In her classes at MIT, at the NSA and now at the hedge fund that she had probably resigned from, since she'd gone AWOL, there wasn't an ounce of testosterone. The rec room goodies were more interesting than the men.

But Luke Reynolds ... huh. While being utterly serious, even grim, he simply oozed sex. He was built — though maybe too lean — but that wasn't it. Or at least that wasn't all of it. He just was a man in the truest sense of the term. After that initial flurry of terror when he'd woken her up in the plane, she'd felt nothing but safe with him. It was like he'd thrown a magic male protective net over her. And all the time they'd been together, he'd been armed. The men after her were armed, but so was he. He'd been a special forces officer and then a cop, a detective. No doubt he *was* a really good shot, just as he said. But above all, he seemed serious and focused on her.

She was a job, sure. He hadn't made any moves of any type, neither physically nor verbally. He'd been a perfect gentleman every single second. But he couldn't help being so dazzlingly handsome.

In Hope's most desperate moment, Felicity had thrown her a lifeline. A man who could and would protect her. Hope was really really grateful. But why did he have to be a hormone magnet? Why? Was this fair?

No, it wasn't. But life wasn't fair, she knew that. Had known it for a long time. All of her life, in fact.

So she'd tuck the condoms back into the bottom of the wheelie and forget about them. Nothing to do with her.

So many layers of anxiety, she thought as she got into the super comfortable bed with the billion thread-count sheets. They smelled of a lavender-scented fabric softener and felt like satin.

There was a whole column of things to be worried about. The shadowy men after her, who'd been willing to kill. The identity of her parentage. Someone in her family who'd been willing to kill. Probably was still willing to kill her. Possibly her father. The absolute lack of a path to follow to figure out what was going on. How could she sleep?

She couldn't.

All she could do was try to close her eyes and let

her anxious buzzing brain work on the issues. So she closed her eyes, just to rest them for a moment, then she opened them again.

But when she opened her eyes, there was light around the thick curtains drawn over the big windows and on the ceiling was projected *9.30*. She'd programmed her cell to project the time onto the ceiling even when the monitor went dark, so she'd always know what time it was.

She stared at the ceiling, puzzled. It had been 10.15 when she'd crawled into bed. Had she somehow fallen into a wormhole and travelled back in time?

No. It took her dull brain a full minute to realize that it was 9.30 *the next morning.* She'd slept almost twelve hours. When was the last time she'd slept twelve hours straight? Never, that was when.

She moved her head to the left, to the right. The room was beautiful, well-appointed, with even a small armchair and sofa set. The bathroom was luxurious, too. She was on the run, but with style.

If she died, presumably ASI would make sure she was buried in a superior mahogany coffin with brass handles.

God knows no one else would care.

Whoa.

She had to stop this, right now. Gloomy and depressing thoughts would only make her gloomy and depressed, and not help her in any way. What would help her was being clear-headed. And speaking of help, she'd made a promise to Felicity and had every intention of keeping that promise.

She threw back the rose-patterned comforter and slid out of bed. A quick shower, then she dressed in stretchy black jeans and a green cotton sweater and walked barefoot into the living room area.

Luke immediately stood up. Startled, Hope wondered why on earth he was standing up. Was he planning on going somewhere? But he didn't move, just watched her walk toward him out of those gorgeous light blue eyes.

And then she realized he'd stood up like a gentleman would when a lady entered the room. The men she knew didn't have old-fashioned manners. No manners at all, actually. Most of them had no idea how to behave in society.

So having such a capable and tough man stand when she entered a room made her feel ... like a lady.

Luke smiled at her and she smiled back.

"Sorry I slept in so late," she said and the smile disappeared.

"God, don't apologize," he said frowning. "No problem. At all. You needed it, you've been operating on fumes the past couple of days from what I can see. I only ordered breakfast a quarter of an hour ago and it should be arriving right about —" The doorbell rang. "Now."

Luke pulled out the small side table and set two small chairs beside it. In a moment, Luke had made a little breakfast table, then walked to the door. There wasn't a peephole, but a little screen to the side of the door. Luke waved at her to get out of the line of sight and she did, retreating to her bedroom, waiting while she heard the sounds of the waiter rolling a cart in, the low murmur of male voices and then the door closing.

Another moment, then Luke called softly for her to come out. She walked back into the living room area. She could have found her way by smell alone. There was a feast on the table and Luke had had the waiter leave the cart because there wasn't room on the table for everything.

Two pots — one for coffee, one for tea, she imagined. Another pot of milk. Pancakes, syrup, a rack of whole wheat toast, a big plate of link sausages, scones, pots of yogurt, a big bowl of steaming oatmeal with blueberries sprinkled on top, a plate of croissants, an omelet, a huge platter of sliced fruit, pats of butter and an array of tiny jam jars.

It was almost more than she ate in a week.

Luke was still standing and she understood that he wouldn't sit down until she did. So she sat and unfurled a huge napkin. Linen, thank you very much.

This was so different from her usual breakfast, gobbling down a pot of yogurt over the sink.

"I didn't know what you liked so I ordered a little of everything." Luke was watching her carefully, as if unsure whether he'd done the right thing or the wrong thing. Hope tried to remember the last time someone cared what she ate.

"Thanks so much," she said softly, and his face cleared. "But — could someone become suspicious that you're ordering so much food?" She glanced at the cart. "And two plates and two cups and saucers?"

"Coffee? Tea?" Luke was holding up both pots. She indicated the coffee and he started pouring. "This two bedroom suite is registered in the name of two men, booked by a big fertilizer concern in Idaho. Credit card is in the company name. Two businessmen in a nice hotel, their company saving money by booking a two bedroom suite instead of two separate bedrooms."

She nodded, pouring hot syrup over pancakes that smelled like heaven. It all smelled like a sweet and savory heaven. The pancakes were perfect, crisp on the outside, fluffy on the inside. From what she could tell, the syrup was real. Came from a tree and not a factory. Everything tasted fresh and not factory-made.

"I've been holding Felicity off," he said casually, putting two slices of toast and some sausage on her plate. Hope couldn't remember the last time someone actually served her food and who wasn't a waiter. "She's called three times."

Hope looked up. Luke didn't look worried or tense, so it wasn't an emergency. If it had been, he'd have woken her up. "Do you know what it was about?"

"Yep." He kept his face expressionless.

"Am I — am I in trouble?"

"Nope." The sides of his mouth curled up, almost a smile in that oh-so-handsome but oh-so-grim face. "The opposite in fact. Felicity found herself unable to hack your security system. She was pleased but also irritated. Not much is unhackable by Felicity. She's impressed and —" His cell rang. He glanced at it. "Speaking of the devil."

He grinned and held the phone out to her.

Hope put Felicity on speaker and video and smiled at her on the screen. Felicity had some color in her face and was sitting up. She sounded upbeat and less tired than the evening before. "Hey! I thought I was good! This is an absolutely new paradigm."

Hope smiled and sipped her coffee. "Yeah. Basically asymmetric-key encryption that shifts every second."

"Like you said, you'd need a quantum computer to break it and even then ..."

Hope was so pleased. Felicity got it, but then of course she'd get it. "We'll be okay until the Singularity."

"And by then it won't matter. Because Skynet will have taken over."

Hope smiled. It was their favorite meme. The Singularity was coming and Skynet would follow but for right now, it was OK. "Right."

"Listen, Hope. I know you said you didn't want to sell the system to us ..."

"God no!" Hope was delighted to give it to ASI. She'd been wondering how to use her system that was so secure it was almost scary. Who to sell it to? Not the US government. There were parts of the US government that definitely needed sunshine, not an unbreakable wall. Not her company. Her ex-company by now. Her hedge fund didn't deserve it. They were all greedy fucks who'd walk all over their grandmothers' faces with cleats for an extra 1% margin of profit. Nope. ASI sounded like a good place for her system to land. They'd helped Felicity. After a little research last night before falling asleep, she'd learned that they'd helped a number of other people, including Summer Redding-Delvaux, her hero.

Felicity smiled at her. It was like she was in the room with them and it warmed Hope's heart. "Listen honey. We work sometimes with Black Inc. They really helped us out recently on something I can't talk about. But it was serious stuff and they came through. Would you be willing to sell your system to them? It's exactly what they need."

"No."

Felicity blinked. Luke turned his head sharply toward her.

"No?" Felicity said.

Hope shook her head. "I won't sell it to them but I *will* give it to them. If they are your friends and helped you in a bad situation —"

"The worst situation." Felicity's mouth tightened.

"All the more reason to give it to them."

"Well ... that's generous."

It wasn't. Hope had more money than she could use in ten lifetimes. Felicity was helping her every way she could in a difficult period for her. For some reason her other two friends, who would usually be there for her, were AWOL. Emma and Riley. As soon as they saw her bat-signal, they'd get in touch but for now it was Felicity and her team, who turned out to be absolutely ace. And if Black Inc was their friend, Black Inc was her friend, too.

"Just hope it's useful."

Felicity gave a small, evil smile. "It would sure be useful to the CIA. They have been leaking like a sieve lately. But they won't get it."

Hope gave a small evil smile right back at her. "Nope. But you guys and I guess Black Inc will be safe. For a while. The best that can be hoped for."

"I agree." Felicity sighed. "Listen. I'm nearing the end of my leash, or at least the amount of work Metal is allowing me."

There was a bass sound in the background that sounded like a growl. Hope looked, startled, at Luke. He gave a shrug.

"So before I am forced to go dark," Felicity continued. Her voice was weaker than before. "I tried to crack the nut of your parents' origins."

"Not my parents." Hope was clear on that.

"No. The people impersonating your parents. I traced something back to Sacramento."

For a moment, Hope was lost. "Sacramento

what?"

"California. Sacramento, California. There's a string there but I didn't have time to pull it. I'm sending my files ... now."

Then Felicity's face disappeared and Hope stared for a moment at the dark screen. California. California. She had no connection whatsoever with California.

"What's the deal with the security system?" Luke asked and Hope had to wrench her mind back to her firewall, when just about every molecule of her mental hard drive was fixated on California.

"Oh, that. Well, essentially, I set up a system where you establish your own DoS attack — a Denial of Service — to safeguard your system. Imagine there's a highway between outsiders and your files. It's a two-lane highway and cars go by slowly enough for you to have a shot at crossing it at a run. You have to time it carefully and there's a little danger, but it's doable."

He was listening carefully, head cocked to one side, probably wondering where she was going with this. "Okay."

Hope nodded. "Now imagine you still want to get over to the other side. But now it's a twenty-lane superhighway, full of trucks going 100 mph, and it's bumper to bumper traffic. And as soon as you think you've seen an opening to cross *one* lane, another truck whizzes by unexpectedly. There are twenty lanes to cross. My algorithms shift every ten seconds.

You'd need a quantum computer to deal with the firewall and those don't exist yet. Not in any meaningful way."

Luke thought a moment. "And by the time they do, we'll be living under the jackboot of Skynet, as you said, and it won't make any difference."

She beamed a smile at him. "Exactly." It was nice to see he got it.

"On behalf of ASI and on behalf of Black Inc, I thank you. Computer security saves lives. You about done there?" He nodded at her plate and she realized she'd been eating and had stopped. She consulted her belly and it was full so she nodded.

"Good." Luke rose. "Housekeeping will take care of this. Can you pack again? Put everything back in the wheelie Felicity sent you?"

Hope was still thinking of her firewall. "What?"

Luke took her elbow gently and guided her back to her room. "Pack. Please."

"We're going somewhere?" She'd just arrived in Portland and they were leaving?

"Yeah. Sacramento."

Six

Willard Hotel
Washington DC

"Senator, it's time." Court Redfield's personal assistant, Leland Barton, heroically kept from glancing at his expensive Phillipe Patek watch, but it was clearly an effort. His young face was carved with worry lines, giving a flashing glimpse of what Leland would look like in thirty years' time. Thank God Leland wouldn't be around *him* in thirty years' time.

Leland was a moron and Court entrusted him only with the most mundane of tasks and never paid attention to what he said. Hiring Leland as his 'personal assistant' was a token to the old boys' network, and assured the help of Mercer Barton, who owned a slew of radio and TV stations in the Midwest, in exactly those states he needed to win this goddamned thing, the Presidency.

Court cleared his voice and pointed his finger at Leland. Court was worried sick, but his voice betrayed nothing. He'd been the Deputy Director of the CIA for seven years and if nothing else, it taught him how to hide emotions and put command in his voice. "Has my son Bard arrived?"

Leland pretended to consult his cell, pursing his lips. But Court knew the answer. "No, sir." Leland lifted his round face, big moist eyes sorrowful. Amateur liars never blinked when lying but then blinked eight times more often after the lie. And now Leland was creating a small wind eddy with his blinking. "He, ahm, sent a message that he'd be delayed." An orangutan could tell he was lying.

Bard had done no such fucking thing.

This time, Court had been adamant. He'd ordered Bard to be here. Bard needed to be by his side when meeting the big donors of his party. Bard's absence was bad news. The worst. Particularly with the announcement he was about to make. He was making a run for the Presidency, for the office he'd been born to. Court was destined to be the leader of the country. His son was a decorated war hero and should be by his father's side, on this day of all days. *Fuck.*

Why wasn't he here? Of course, they weren't close, had never been close. But goddammit, Bard's entire life was duty. He was a warrior, a fucking SEAL. *Always do the hard thing* was their unofficial motto. And though Bard long ago cut himself off from the family and the Redfield money, he did his duty. He was on mission when Maddy died, but he came home for the funeral. He hadn't cut himself off from his mother, Maddy, though Maddy, too, had become estranged from Court. Had asked for a divorce before breast cancer took her away.

Court had since married twice, but Bard hadn't come home for either of the marriages.

Court could count on the fingers of one hand the number of times he and Bard had actually had a discussion over the past thirty years. And most of the times had ended with Bard slamming the door behind him.

Court didn't need to be loved, but he did need to be obeyed and damn it, Bard should be here now as he prepared for the move that had been decades coming.

If he wasn't here, did that mean ... Did Bard know what had happened all those years ago? *Could* he know?

Court shut that thought down immediately. Of course Bard didn't know. Court had seen to that. The entire connection had been severed, completely contained, for almost three decades. And the person who'd made the connection again, via freaking DNA, was dead. But the girl ... the girl who was improbably alive ...

She'd be dead too. Soon. For the second time. If Court had had any idea that the girl had survived, he'd have dealt with it long ago.

How the hell had she survived? Who'd taken care of her?

Maybe he should have checked, sent a man to the

morgue to see the bodies. But those had been different times and he hadn't had many people on call. He had them now, by God. He had a fucking army, and they were highly competent, the best of the best. Former SpecOps soldiers, recruited when he was heading the Special Activities Division of the CIA and totally loyal to *him* now. Considering he paid them a fucking fortune, they'd better be loyal.

He'd once calculated that his little army had cost the US government a hundred million dollars to train.

And now they were his.

His son, the best of SpecOps, a legend, should be one of them. Should be by his side, right fucking now.

Instead he had two bodyguards in front and three behind him. Two already in the dining room, waiting. If anyone so much as yelled at him, they'd be quietly taken away. His Pretorian Guard looked after him well.

And still, it should be his fucking son looking after his father. Where was he?

Inwardly, Court seethed as he walked along the plush gold-patterned carpeting of the long elegant corridor toward the dining room. He could hear the excited jabbering halfway down the hallway. Rich men, excitable like children. How they'd squeal when he gave them a new toy.

Where the *hell* was the girl? The DNA scientist had kept the girl's name off the test, only a code was given.

Court's own DNA had been taken off the national database, but he'd left instructions to leave a tripwire to notify him in the unlikely event someone tried to trace his DNA. A stroke of luck and paranoia.

He'd nearly had a heart attack when his most trusted tech in the CIA — and who now worked secretly for him — told him that his DNA was being checked. At first he hadn't worried. The top levels of national security agencies — all seventeen of them — had had their DNA scrubbed from any files accessible from the outside. But there'd been a hole in the scrubbing procedure and his file apparently had been accessible. Hard to get to, yes. But it was doable and someone had done it. Luckily his tech had put in that tripwire and they were warned. They'd tracked the scientist down — a Dr. Kyle Ackerman, genius geneticist, now CEO of a company specializing in DNA analysis.

The scientist was easy to get rid of — nerds rarely pay attention. Ackerman hadn't noticed the car trailing him until it was too late.

His own tech had had some difficulties in cracking Ackerman's code and finding out who had ordered the DNA test, but he'd managed it and told Court. It was a name that meant nothing to him. Hope Ellis. But the photograph of her meant a lot. His heart had skipped a beat when he'd seen a copy of her NSA badge. She looked so much like Bard and

Court's own father it was crazy. She was of their blood, there was no contesting that.

Ackerman had been talking to her when he'd been eliminated.

The girl nerd — not even in his head could he think of her as his granddaughter — turned out to be surprisingly hard to take out. She'd disappeared. Nothing in her file said she had experience as an operator. She'd worked in national security — for the NSA — but only in an analytical capacity. She'd never been trained. And yet she'd disappeared.

Which meant she'd had help. This was a problem that was fast growing viral and needed to be stopped. Right. Fucking. Now.

He thought he'd gotten rid of her and her bitch of a mother twenty-five years ago.

He needed to get rid of her now.

But first he had to find her.

And keep Bard in the dark. That was what scared him more than anything. Not that an illegitimate child could show up during his campaign. Nowadays, that could be massaged. Turned into a tiny little flurry in one news cycle and nothing more.

No. What had Court sweating as he walked down the corridor was the idea of Bard finding out that Court had … done what he'd done. Bard had said he loved the girl, which was ridiculous. Court had done what had to be done. But Bard would never understand. Bard already hated him. Bard was a trained killer and Court would not swear that Bard wouldn't kill him.

This had to be stopped, the girl had to be eliminated before any of this became public.

He stopped before a door and let his man open it. From now on, all his doors would be opened for him.

As he walked in, the excited jabbering rose to a crescendo. A fund raiser. Only not for a Senate seat. For the big job. Several billion dollars on the hoof were in the room, which smelled of freshly-pressed clothes and expensive cologne and expensive wine.

Everyone here for him.

His press secretary bent his head to the mike.

"And now, ladies and gentlemen, the moment you've all been waiting for. Let's give it up for the next President of these United States, Senator Court Redfield!"

And the room roared with cheers.

Portland

Hope dug in her heels.

Luke was surprised. He'd seen it all and he'd done it all and he was rarely surprised when it came to people, but this stopped him in his tracks.

Hope Ellis was small and pretty and cerebral. And

soft, he thought. Well, what else would someone who worked with computers be?

But nope, she wasn't soft at all. There was a core of steel there.

She absolutely refused to leave until she'd solved Felicity's problem. Felicity hadn't thrown her the equivalent of polishing the silver. She'd thrown her something thorny, apparently. And Hope was dug in like a tick.

Luke explained, slowly and carefully, that there was a thread to tug in Sacramento. One of ASI's corporate jets was even now on the tarmac, waiting for them. They'd borrowed a safe house in Sacramento from Black Inc, another company that was quivering with eagerness to help her as repayment for the magical mystery firewall that had their tech people salivating. There was a whole machine revving up, just waiting to go and … she dug in her heels.

"But —" he began, in his reasonable tone.

"No." Hope's voice wasn't adamant or stubborn. There was no emotional overtone at all. That 'no' was said as if he'd offered her a whiskey and she'd said no. No biggie.

Except it was.

She pulled out the chair from the side table that was acting as a workspace and she sat and pulled her laptop toward her. She'd been working since breakfast, had taken a coffee and muffin break and was now settling back in.

Luke was … well he was at a loss. If this were an

operation where her life was in immediate danger, he'd have no compunction in tossing her over his shoulder and getting her out of there. But her life was in no immediate danger. If anything, she was super safe right where she was.

"Hope, it really would be best to get going." Said quite reasonably. With absolutely no irritation in his voice, which was an act of heroism right there.

She touched a key and her screen came to vivid life, colors so bright they almost hurt the eye. Her screensaver was ...

"Rivendell," he said. The Peter Jackson version.

That earned him a quick upside look. "Right." She gave him a slow elevator look, boots to hair. "You're too built to be a nerd. What is this?"

He took a step toward her. "When I was eleven and discovered Lord of the Rings, I was short and underweight. I looked about seven and I was bullied. I discovered books, dived into them and didn't come up again until I started growing. So in a real way, Tolkien saved my bacon. And my dad. He saved my bacon too."

She stopped, put her hands in her lap. "Tell me about your dad. I love good dad stories."

He just bet she did. Her own father wasn't her father after all and had ignored her, from what he understood. And maybe her biological father was trying to kill her. So he could imagine that good dad stories were appealing.

Well, he was happy to oblige. He'd had one of the

best.

Luke perched on the edge of the table and felt her interest as a palpable thing. God she was just so irresistible — that pretty face turned up, those intelligent eyes focused like green lasers on him.

"My dad was the best," he began.

Her pretty face fell. "Was. You told me."

He nodded, sighed, feeling that punch to the heart he always felt. "Yeah. Unfortunately." He wouldn't repeat that his dad had essentially died of a broken heart right after the trial. It wasn't the time for sadness. "Anyway. Seventh grade. Middle school. I was the runt of the class. Short and scrawny. Classic nerd. Straight As. D&D, Lord of the Rings, Harry Potter. Bullied mercilessly by a gang of tough older kids who were much bigger than me. The main bully was Lou Garrett. Mean son of a bitch. I used to come home with black eyes, once with a cut that required ten stitches. But my dad … he didn't do the TV dad thing. Go to the bully's house, talk with the asshole's father, talk to the school principal. Nope. That would have just painted a bullseye on my back. He took me to the gym of his good buddy and former Marine, Nelson Harmer. Known as The Hammer."

She winced. "Ouch."

"Nah." Luke shook his head. "He was a good guy and always took me to my limits but never beyond. I trained hard, three afternoons a week, for seven years. During those seven years I shot up a foot and a half and put on fifty pounds. The Hammer made sure it was all muscle. After the first year at the dojo no one bullied me again. And that is the story of how I can be a former Ranger and still know Rivendell."

That brought a smile to her face. "What happened to the bully?"

The thought always made him happy. "He's asking customers if they want fries with that."

"Oh, man." Hope sighed. "I do love me a happy ending."

Luke leaned forward. He'd taken the tense expression off her face, which was good. Now for the rest of it. He made his voice very gentle. "Hope, we really need to go to Sacramento. Metal has turned off Felicity's phone and he just texted that she is sleeping and he won't have her disturbed. But she found something that seems to lead to Sacramento. You have her files and you can figure out what she found on the way down. But I think we need to be there."

Hope turned in her chair until she faced him completely. She touched his knee and instinctively, he put his hand over hers. It felt small and soft, but he understood now that *she* wasn't soft.

"I get it, Luke. Absolutely. But whatever might be there in Sacramento has been there for the past twenty-nine years and can wait a day longer. Right here, right now, Felicity needs me." He opened his mouth and she held up a hand. "I know her job isn't at risk. I know she is a very valued member of your company, as she should be. But I also know her and know how sad and frustrated she is that she isn't keeping up with the workload. If I can help take even a pound of that weight off her shoulders, then that's what I'm going to do because it's my absolute priority. Are we clear on that?"

"Absolutely clear."

He looked deeply into her eyes. Fiercely intelligent and focused. Amazingly beautiful forest green interspersed with streaks of bright yellow. For a second, he spaced out on her eyes, falling into them so intensely the world disappeared.

She wasn't defiant and she wasn't challenging him. He understood that. It wasn't rebellion — but it *was* stubbornness. Hope was absolutely committed to helping Felicity and wasn't about to be swayed.

And, fuck. Luke understood that, understood it to the bone. Loyalty to teammates was bred into him. He'd learned loyalty at his father's knee. Loyalty was absolute and not conditional.

You weren't loyal to your friends when it was convenient and it suited you. You were loyal, always. Even when it was hard. Especially when it was hard.

He sighed. "Okay."

She lifted her fingers from his knee and looked at him, surprised. "Okay?"

Luke nodded. "Yeah."

"You're a soldier. Were a soldier. And a cop. Those are professions where you're used to being obeyed."

He gave a wry smile. "Yep."

"But you're not freaking out at not being obeyed."

"Nope. I'm not going to convince you with words. And that's all I'm willing to use. It's essentially your show."

"That's a nice example of cooperation. In a spirit of compromise, I'm going to work as hard as I can and as fast as I can."

Luke deliberately didn't smile at her earnest words. "Okay. Fast is good."

She nodded, turned around and ... disappeared. He'd never seen anything like it. Soldiers — and especially SpecOp soldiers — knew how to focus. Fuck, their lives depended on it. During briefings, studying maps, getting ready for action, a soldier was nothing but focus. But this — this took it to a whole other level. Hope sort of leaned forward and essentially entered her laptop. Her fingers flew over the keyboard like a pianist playing rock music. The Elton John of keyboarding.

She also disappeared Luke right off the face of the earth. When he understood that she wasn't even aware of his presence, he took himself off to be useful somewhere else. He settled in another area and cleaned his weapons, rearranged his go-bag, took care of some admin on his own laptop, which Hope would probably consider a pitiful thing. It was the latest of a popular brand, but didn't look anything like Hope's laptop, which was so advanced it seemed like an alien artifact, beamed down from space.

He was thinking with interest about lunch when there was a soft sound of satisfaction. He turned and watched Hope punch a key.

"There!" She cricked her neck to the left and then to the right and stood up.

Luke held the menu in his hand and watched as she folded down her laptop. "Done?"

"Yeah. I sent it off to Felicity. Can I talk to her now?"

He punched the number on his cell and got Metal's plain mug.

"Yeah?" Metal looked like he'd just fought the battle of Pellenor Fields, all by himself, and lost. "What?"

"Hey man." He tried not to wince. But he had to ask. "How's it going?"

"How do you think it's going?" The words were aggressive, but his tone wasn't. He was beat. Luke felt really sorry for him. "She's still spotting and she wants to go back to work." He shot an acid look to the side, clearly aimed at Felicity. Who was also awake.

"Can I talk to her?" Hope asked.

Luke held out his cell.

Hope was smiling as she took it. "I want you to listen, not talk," she said, trying to sound authoritative. Her voice was too soft to be commanding, but there was steel there. "I sent you my conclusions re the file. You can go through them if you want, but I think you'll agree with them. I'd feel good, I'd feel really good, if you just fed them straight to your bosses and took a nap instead. In that file you sent me, there were a few outstanding issues with regard to your command server, just a little flotsam and jetsam, and I took the liberty of cleaning it all up. I think you're all caught up, now. So Luke and I are going to ..." she shot him a look and he nodded his head. "We're going to go chase that lead in Sacramento, but you can always shoot me an email if something needs doing. I'll drop everything."

"Thanks, Hope." Felicity sounded tired. "Emma got in touch from San Francisco. She was worried about you but I told her you're in good hands. She said to send her stuff to do because she's bored. And for you to get in touch via HER room, if you need help. So between the two of you, I'm completely covered and you've got backup. I'm going to switch off now and sleep for a while."

"For a couple of years," Metal's voice said to the side. "I'll wake you up when the boys go off to college." Metal disconnected.

Hope handed Luke's cell back to him.

"Do we know any more about Sacramento?" he asked. Up to now Felicity had called it a thread.

"I'll check when we're in the air." She squinted at him. "The plane has wi-fi. Right?" It was said in the same tone someone else would use to ask if the airplane had wings.

"Yep." Her face smoothed out. "It also has a bathroom with a shower, food and beverages." The plane also had enough weaponry to start a small war, full combat gear, including armor for five people, gas masks, bioweapons detectors, a Geiger counter and parachutes, and enough survival gear to survive the apocalypse for a week.

No flies on his guys, no sir.

"Cool. Let's go." She'd already stowed her laptop. She hitched her backpack onto her shoulder and made for the door.

"Just a minute, Lara Croft." Luke tugged at her elbow. "Aren't you forgetting something?"

She touched her backpack again and frowned. "What?"

"Luggage. We don't know how long we're going to be in Sacramento. Don't you want your things, even if they are basically Summer's things?"

"Sure." She smiled. "You carry the bags. Felicity says that the guys at ASI are the muscle."

That was true. They were. Without a word, Luke went to get their bags.

Seven

Presidential suite
Willard Hotel

It had been an excellent dinner, netting pledges for over ten million dollars for his campaign, and above all netting support from the movers and shakers. But he was tired.

Court Redfield loosened his tie and sat down on the overstuffed armchair in the suite's living room. He opened his mouth but before he could speak, a cut glass crystal tumbler half full of a single malt whiskey was put in his hand.

He looked up at the man who'd put it there and nodded.

The man nodded back.

Good man. The best. Captain Lorne Resnick, formerly of the USMC, then of the CIA's SAD, where Court had met him. While DD of the CIA, Court had met many highly capable men who went … unrecognized. Underpaid. Underused.

Court recognized their potential. There was a lot to be said for highly trained and competent men willing to do anything as long as you paid them enough. He kept a small army of them on retainer. Their main task up until now had been to make problems go away.

Court had made many friends in Congress. He knew a lot of stories. He was the kind of man other men confided in. Trusted. The kind of man you told your darkest secrets to, your wildest dreams, your deepest desires, your greatest fears. Late at night, in his darkened den, after a couple of whiskies, men opened up to him. It was essentially the same story, over and over again. They had problems, they wanted things. Court's men could make things happen, make problems disappear. They could bend your enemies to your will.

It was never a crass quid pro quo. Money never changed hands. Nothing like a written contract. Just an … understanding. Between gentlemen. No questions asked, no payment requested.

Except, the next time Senator Court Redfield needed votes for an industry tax break or deregulation, he had it in the bag. And the money poured in, off the books, offshore. He had a fucking fortune in untraceable accounts in Panama, Gibraltar and St. Thomas. His lifestyle didn't change. You can only drive one car at a time. He had property but not anything flashy, nothing to catch anyone's eye. A nice house in Virginia, his old home in Sacramento and a condo in Florida. He drove a staid late-model sedan. His clothes were off the rack. His mistresses were quiet and discreet. He didn't need the things money bought you, he wanted the power money gave you. So he built his power base. And his army.

He had forty men at his command, all ex-military, almost all former SpecOps, the ultimate beneficiary of the hundred million dollars Uncle Sam had spent training them. Then the military fucked up by not paying them, or not paying them enough. Men who had earned the equivalent of several PhDs, spoke several languages, were almost Olympic-level athletes, who risked their lives daily — they earned basically what a bank teller earned. And if they were seriously injured, they went into the maw of the VA and never came out.

Court was smart. He paid his men a base salary of half a million dollars a year, completely off the books, completely tax free, and he saw to it that they got the finest medical care in the world.

They were loyal and worth their weight in gold.

He stared into his tumbler. He had no qualms about giving kill orders. And his men had no qualms in carrying them out. He just had to make sure no one made the connections.

"Resnick," he said.

Resnick's head came up. "Sir."

"There's a problem."

Resnick nodded. "That's what we're here for, sir."

"It's ... delicate."

Resnick nodded again.

Court's team dealt with hard issues all the time. They were smart, efficient and discreet. For a moment, Court had a flash of anger so strong he felt it crackle in his bones. When this problem first emerged almost three decades ago and Bard was being bull-headed as usual, Court had called in a team of men he wasn't familiar with. They'd reported that the job was done. Court had never heard anything to the contrary since then, until two days ago. If those men had done their goddamned job right the first time ...

His fists clenched, his breathing grew harsh. Resnick watched him, head cocked and Court calmed. Goddammit, only Bard could make him lose his temper, even for a moment.

He should have double-checked, made absolutely sure.

No use thinking that way. The team leader on that job was dead. Resnick had been in high school.

This was in the past goddammit! It should have fucking stayed in the past!

Court sighed. "I have ... an issue. As I said, it's particularly delicate now that I've declared my candidacy."

Something flashed in Resnick's eyes and Court knew what it was. Resnick headed his personal, private army. It was one thing to head the army of a powerful man, a man who'd been number two in the CIA, a man who was currently a sitting Senator and

Chairman of the Armed Forces Committee.

It would be an entirely different thing to be the head of the private army of the president of the United States, with the entire might of the US government behind you. Resnick was about to become the most powerful military man in the world, without being subject to military rules. No wonder his eyes were gleaming.

"Here." Court handed Resnick a flash drive. Resnick bent his blond head over it, turning it over in his hands. The flash drive was made of a special titanium alloy. The contents of the flash drive would dissolve in a flash of heat half an hour after first being opened, but the titanium exterior would remain intact, a perfectly normal but non-functioning flash drive. "Everything you need is here. It will self-destruct half an hour after opening."

Court had debated redacting names. What he'd just handed Resnick was like a ton of C-4 with the detonator ready to blow. Any hint of what was on the flash drive to the outside world and he'd be a dead man. Not just in the political sense, either. Bard could never know. No one could ever know but particularly Bard could never know.

Court hadn't redacted in the end. All the intel was in the clear. He trusted Resnick, who'd proved himself trustworthy over and over again. Inside that flash drive was essentially a confession of murder 25 years ago. Resnick needed to have that info to do what had to be done.

"That intel is highly confidential," Court said, keeping his voice emotionless. But something must have bled through because Resnick's head came up sharply.

"Understood, sir. You can count on me."

Yes, he could. Resnick was a money man. People were driven by sex, money or power. Sometimes by all three. People driven by sex were pathetic and burned out early. What was left was money and power, two highly respectable motivators. Resnick had been born poor and Court understood very well that the money Resnick was accumulating was precious to him in a way he himself could barely understand. He'd come from money and had always earned very well. To him, money was the ladder to power. A tool, nothing more. But to Resnick, it was life itself.

Resnick was amassing what to him was a fortune. He could never earn anywhere else what Court paid him. Court knew Resnick would rather rip out his lungs than forego the money he was being paid.

He'd be discreet. Oh yes.

Shit happens, but Court was counting on shit not happening with Resnick. It was also helpful that Resnick hated Bard. He wasn't going to talk to Bard, tell him the truth. Which was lucky because if there was one person in the world Court feared, it was his son, Bard Redfield.

But Bard at the moment was probably OUTCONUS, having ignored his father's invitations to take part in his campaign. So be it.

"Who do we have in California?" Court asked.

Resnick frowned. "Not many operatives, sir. Four. Hawkins, Peters, Colucci and Li. How many operatives do you need?"

Damn it! The Ellis creature was one girl, an expert in computers and data analysis. No military training. But she must have powerful protectors if she'd been able to evade his operatives in Boston. And was able to vanish off the face of the earth.

But if she started digging deep, there was one place she was bound to go.

Court weighed efficacy and discretion. His men operated well as a team but this was delicate stuff. Not everybody would be as comfortable as Resnick with killing your own blood. So for the moment, he wanted Resnick alone. If he needed help, he could call it in.

"As many as you can, but put them on stand-by. Pull off everyone you can from non-urgent tasks and have them wait by a plane. I want you to head this team up, but if you can finish the mission on your own, that would be preferable. Intel is there in the flash drive. I want you in Sacramento tomorrow. You'll know where to go and what to do."

Resnick closed his big hand around the flash drive. For a moment, Court hesitated. That flash drive was like a bullet propelled from a gun, stopped an inch from his chest. There were secrets in there that had been kept for 25 years. Secrets that would derail his presidential run if what he planned to do came out. Secrets that would send him to jail.

Secrets his son could never know. God knows their relationship was fraught enough.

Goddammit! Court's eye caught a portrait photograph in a silver frame on the bookshelf next to his desk. Bard, in full dress uniform, with an impressive array of his medals on his broad chest. The last official photo of him, and only because the Navy insisted. He was so young and so handsome and looked like what he was — a goddamn hero. Someone any father would be proud of. A real asset.

Even more of an asset would have been Bard leaving the military after an appropriate period, marrying an appropriate woman and having appropriate kids. Court could have had another portrait on his shelf, with Bard, a smiling wife and kids. Maybe a fucking dog. On a slope of green lawn, celebrating July 4th.

Instead — nothing. Bard had stayed in the military and stayed almost invisible, on covert missions abroad. The very few snapshot photos in existence of his son were on ops. An almost feral being, a tough, frightening man with a graying beard, weather-beaten skin, in filthy combat clothes. Not photogenic, not polished. He looked like what he was — a killer.

After that woman, Bard never had a long-term relationship, never married. Not even close. It was like he married the fucking Navy.

So Court was forced to campaign with a ghost son, unobtainable, invisible, legally banned from talking about what he actually did in the Navy.

Also — a son who hated his father.

Getting rid of that girl and her spawn was supposed to bring them closer together, but it hadn't.

Bard just got angrier and angrier. More and more remote. Tougher and tougher.

To the point that Court was actually physically frightened at the thought of Bard realizing what he'd done all those years ago. Bard wouldn't kill his own father, would he? Would he?

Court didn't have an answer to that.

What was supposed to have cemented their relationship by getting an intrusive, trashy little money-grubber out of the way had turned into a mile-high wall that no matter what he did, Court couldn't climb over.

Court was rich. Massively rich, though the wealth was mostly hidden. Still, he'd made it clear that Bard could be rich, too. Way way beyond anything a military career could bring. But Bard couldn't be bought by the prospect of a loan or gifts from his father. He banked almost his entire salary. He lived a spartan life, bunking in the Bachelor Officers Quarters when he was Stateside, living in camps when he was deployed. He had no property to his name and completely ignored Court's hints at leaving him property. There wasn't anything Court could give him that Bard wanted.

He hadn't even wanted a big military career. Bard should have been an admiral by now, and would have been if he'd made even a slight attempt to rise up. He hadn't. He just stayed in the field well beyond what was expected of him.

Bard was also completely indifferent to his father's campaign. Didn't give a shit. Once Court lost his temper and alluded to the fact that one day soon he could be Bard's Commander in Chief.

Bard had simply glared at him. "You'll never be *my* Commander in Chief. Forget it. If you win the presidency, I'll resign my commission and go to work for Black Inc." Taking Bard completely out of the chain of command.

Black Inc was a powerful security company run by former SEAL Jacob Black. He and Bard had been friends forever. Court had tried recruiting Black's company for an off-the-books job when he was DD at the CIA, but Black refused. And threatened to report him to the Congressional Oversight Committee.

Resnick and his crew hadn't refused, which had been a stimulus for creating his own small army. His army never refused him anything.

"Is that all, sir?" Resnick's voice was emotionless. If he'd noticed Court getting lost in his own head — which happened often when he thought of his son — he gave no sign.

"Yes. Get to Sacramento and call your men in if you need to. But only if you need them."

Resnick stood. "Yessir."

"Oh, and Resnick?"

"Sir?"

"Whoever you find that has a bearing on your mission, they are to be terminated. Especially the ... main actor. This has to become a dead end. Are we clear?"

"Absolutely, sir."

He turned and walked out the door.

Court's head suddenly fell forward as if too heavy for his neck. The past had reached out, a raging torrent he thought was underground, but which had punched its way through to the surface. It would carry him away if he wasn't careful. He blew out a shaky breath, staring at the ground for a long, long time.

There was no margin for mistakes now.

Eight

Portland

They did what they'd done the previous day only in reverse.

Hope was in her super-secret spy getup — big floppy hat with the secret lights under the brim, funky high-tech sunglasses, a wad of toilet paper inside her sneaker to change the gait — and instructions to *keep your head down*. That last had been said a billion times by Luke, as if she were unable to process a four-word instruction.

One last thing, Luke had said. Keep your hands palms-down. Satellite photos were astonishingly high resolution these days and a really good shot of a finger would give you a fingerprint as sharp as dipping it in ink and rolling it over the police blotter.

It was hard to keep your head down, particularly when your floppy hat brim dipped down beneath your eyeline, basically giving you a view of your sneakered feet and not much else.

Plus, she was dragging the wheelie and carrying her backpack. It was clear to her that Luke, who had muscles to spare, wasn't short-changing her in the gentleman department. He had an amazingly heavy duffel bag over his left shoulder and his wheelie which he pulled with his left hand. His right hand was kept free at all times. He let her open doors and press elevator buttons.

She understood why. He wanted to keep one hand free to be able to pull the gun that was in his waistband.

The thing was, between schlepping all that stuff, the drooping hat, too big sunglasses, annoying wad in her sneaker that made her limp, she felt like she was walking on an alien planet. Hope played a lot of video games where she was on an alien planet, trying to survive. Instinctively, she wanted to check her environment to make sure no tentacled monsters with three rows of shark teeth sprang out of the woodwork.

Though presumably, keeping a ninja watch out was Luke's department.

They made it down to the sub-basement parking area without incident and once she was buckled in, she could take off the awful hat and terrible sunglasses with a sigh of relief.

"Not made for a life of deceit?" Luke asked, with a sidelong glance.

"Nope. Not even that good at social engineering. Riley's good with that, I'm not. Besides —" she turned her head away, but he could probably hear the intensity in her voice, "I hate lies and deception. Just hate them."

Her entire life had apparently been a lie and at some level, even as a little girl, she'd understood that. And hated it.

Luke was a fast but careful driver as he drove them down unfamiliar streets. She didn't know anything about Portland, still didn't know anything about Portland, since she'd essentially been hiding out in a hotel room. The city center seemed to be relatively small and soon they were in the green suburbs. Not going to the international airport but the airfield.

It was overcast, a few drops falling from the sky, threatening a downpour but not delivering yet on the promise. The Pacific Northwest had a rep as a rainy part of the country. Not as cold as Boston, but wetter. Yesterday there'd been late season snow flurries in Boston. She'd checked the weather. Not that she was homesick, far from it. Now that she was here, out West, she realized she wasn't missing Boston at all. It had never really felt like home. She realized that because she felt exactly the same in Portland as she did in Boston. Pretty city, but there was no connection. That was how she'd felt when she lived in Baltimore, too, the years she worked for the NSA.

She was ... unrooted. Unconnected, unmoored. *All the time.* Like there was a missing piece in her head where most people held the concept of home. The hole had been there all her life. Luckily, she worked among geeks who had tenuous — if any — ties to their hometown. Tenuous ties to reality, actually. Most of them had spent their formative years in the basement on a computer, hacking. All braces and hormones. Connected to the world but not to their physical location.

They all lived in a virtual place called Nerddom.

Luke sped up and she was pressed against the back of the big, soft seat.

The large suburban homes became smaller, the lawns less well kept, the roads filled with potholes and then suddenly they were there, at the outer reaches of the airfield. She didn't even know what it was called. Ordinarily, she'd have looked it up. Her laptop shot her cell, in encryption, its location at all times so that if she ever lost it, God forbid, she'd know where it was. And whoever stole it wouldn't be able to find the geolocator to turn it off and would never crack the password anyway.

If she wanted to, she could find out what the airfield was called. But what would be the point?

She was going where Luke was taking her.

This was new. She wasn't used to not calling the shots. But this whole situation was so baffling, so out of her wheelhouse, beyond her skill set, that she just yielded control to someone who very much looked like he knew what he was doing.

The skies finally opened up and rain fell in thick, rippling gray sheets. The vehicle's windshield wipers had trouble keeping up, rain drumming on the roof, bouncing off the road. The sky was low and steel gray.

Hope hated driving in bad weather but Luke didn't even seem to notice it.

Luke drove them onto the airfield, right up to a small business jet. She didn't know if it was the same one. Its number was painted on the tail but she hadn't had enough bandwidth to notice the number of the plane that took her from Boston to Portland.

Luke parked with the passenger side right up against the moveable steps. She didn't even get a drop of rain on her as she exited the vehicle and climbed the stairs. No one could see her, not even with binoculars. And if someone were checking using IR, all they'd see was a red blob that could possibly be a woman, possibly a small man. But certainly nothing that could identify her.

Luke drove past the steps and exited the driver's side, grabbed both their wheelies and his duffle bag, head down in the rain, and ducked into the steps, coming up right behind her.

She had a whiff of jet fuel then crossed the threshold into the climate-controlled cabin that smelled of expensive leather and, incongruously, lemon. She sat and Luke sat down right next to her.

He'd morphed instantly, from super vigilant warrior to travelling companion, in the time it took to climb up the steps into the jet. From the moment they stepped out of the hotel room, she could sense the tension in him. Not anxiety. He was preternaturally calm. But he also seemed attuned to everything going on around him. His walk even changed — a deliberate heel-to-toe step that looked like he could spring into a run at a second's notice.

A gunslinger's walk, actually. Wildly sexy. Blue eyes cautious, scanning the environment, a gun a microsecond away, ready to draw — yep. An Old West gunslinger. He even had that old-timey sheriff vibe and damned if that wasn't wildly sexy, too.

He oozed pheromones and testosterone without even thinking about it. Hope felt he was ready and willing, and to a certain extent even eager, to engage with the enemy. Gunfight at the OK Corral, coming right up. Though in this case the enemy wasn't the Clanton gang but shadowy entities that shot from the darkness. No matter, Luke was willing to face them.

That taut suspicious look was gone from his face as he sat down beside her with a slight sigh. His face relaxed into easier lines that were just as attractive as before, when he'd been ready for a gunfight at any moment.

He leaned his head back for a moment and closed his eyes.

A suspicion crossed her mind. "Did you sleep last night?" she asked, her voice more harsh than she intended.

"Some," he said without opening his eyes.

He was lying but she didn't call him on it. Had he stayed awake on overwatch, to keep her safe?

With his eyes closed, she could study his face without it seeming skeevy. He had a fascinating face. It was so classically handsome, enough for him to be a male model. Beautifully shaped head, ice blue eyes — when they were open — arrow-straight nose, high cheekbones, sculpted jaw softened by light-colored stubble.

But it was more than a pretty face. It was a face that showed character and determination without a shred of vanity. He had lines in his face that looked brand new.

While they'd been making their way from the hotel to the airplane, Luke had seemed to occupy more space than usual, projecting himself outward. Now he was relaxed.

There was no danger in a seat on a private jet that was now revving up to taxi. Arguably there was no possible danger within hundreds of miles. Someone used to physical danger would be able to let down that shield of vigilance.

Hope didn't know how to do that. Unlike Luke, she wasn't used to physical danger at all. Danger for her came over fiber-optic cable and through the screen of a monitor, and from black hats who at times were halfway around the world. Ever since she'd heard Kyle being killed, seen the men entering her building and on their way to her apartment, the adrenaline had been coursing through her veins and she didn't know how to turn it off.

Work. Work would do it. Work always helped.

No matter what she was feeling, no matter how lonely she got, work helped. Work would help her now.

She'd seen on the tail end of Felicity's work request another issue, one more in her field of data analysis than security. It took her half an hour but she resolved it and smiled. One less thing for Felicity to do. She shot the whole thing off to Felicity in the HER room — *Hope you're resting. Here's the analysis plus the data sets.*

Thanks. The answer came immediately.

Hope sighed. *Shouldn't you be resting? Shouldn't your husband just confiscate your keyboard?*

He did. I'm on my cell under the covers.

Hope smiled. *Rest now or I'm telling.*

Argh! Not you, too!

Go.

Going.

The connection was broken.

Hope looked at Luke. He seemed to be sunk deeply into sleep, nothing moving except a slight rise and fall of his broad chest.

Everything about his body was just so unfamiliar, a new kind of male. This wasn't how most of the men she knew were put together. Maybe there was something to the theory that symmetry was beauty. All the men she knew had something ungainly about them. Kyle — poor unfortunate Kyle — had had extremely short legs, slightly bowed, as if he'd spent his entire life on horseback. Both men on either side of her cubicle at the hedge fund had been awkwardly put together. Larry's left eye had a permanent squint and Ben walked with one shoulder down, as if weighed down by an invisible but heavy bag.

Not Luke. He seemed to have been put together by another, finer hand. Long lean muscles, broad shoulders, big elegant hands. Everything perfect and perfectly symmetrical. Though he could stand to put on some weight. That story he'd told her was horrifying. Enough to make anyone lose weight.

She was glad she'd heard the story firsthand and not from Felicity. Hope appreciated Felicity's discretion. She didn't like gossip. If someone wanted you to know about their problems, they'd tell you. As Luke had done.

She herself was fiercely private, unused to sharing her troubles. Right now all her troubles were right out there for Felicity and her company, including Luke, who apparently wasn't quite with the company yet, to see. And presumably for everyone working at Black Inc to see.

It was horrible.

Nothing to be done about it, though. She couldn't go back and erase what had happened. As always in life, the only way was forward.

She closed her eyes for a moment trying to center herself. And by that she meant trying to be less aware of Luke, who was sitting completely still beside her. He could have been in a coma. So why was her attention focused on him, as if he were this huge black hole? He seemed to exert his own gravity, big body so still next to hers, so close she could feel his body heat.

It was so unfair that her senses were filled with him. She could almost feel the molecules of his big body mingling with hers. She could smell him. Some kind of soap and leather. Even closing her eyes, she could tell he was there, right next to her, because he created a sort of disturbance in the Force.

She'd had crushes before, tepid things in comparison, like a mild case of the flu, mostly for men who were far away. A few actors, the vice president of her company who was French and who she saw twice a year during enlarged board meetings, a great science fiction writer who'd once signed a book of hers.

Certainly never to a man who was *right here*. Right next to her, so close. She brushed his hand every time she moved.

This was so distracting, for a woman who never got distracted, ever. Her focus was legendary, at least wherever she'd worked. In the university computer lab, at the NSA, at her hedge fund. A nerd's nerd.

Not right now. The nerd's nerd was at this very moment filled to the brim with raging hormones, for a man who was beside her strictly for professional reasons and who would probably be annoyed if he knew just how attracted she was.

Focus on the job at hand, she told herself sternly. Something she rarely had to say to herself. If anything, her problem was breaking the focus. She'd find herself climbing out of eighteen-hour work stints, groggy and disoriented, not knowing whether it was day or night outside.

The. Job. It had always been enough, had always filled her life.

She finished another small task that had been on Felicity's to-do list, then concentrated on what Felicity had been able to find out.

A lot, actually. Felicity was not only very good, she was tricky. Able to see under and around, probably because her parents had been Russian spies under Witness Protection. Felicity, too, had grown up in a situation where nothing was what it seemed. So Felicity had a sixth sense for deceit.

The Sacramento connection was tenuous, but definitely there. A reference her parents had given when opening a bank account in Boston. Their first. No previous bank accounts in the city of Boston or in the state of Massachusetts could be found. Digging, Felicity had seen that there was absolutely no record of them in Boston before 1996, though their birth certificates said they had been born there.

On the first application for a bank account, her father had given a reference in Sacramento, California. It puzzled her because they had no connection with Sacramento, or California. But there it was. Their reference was a Bernard Teller, manager of Happy Trails, a trailer park on the edge of the city.

But what was unusual was that two days after giving that reference, it was deleted and another reference given, a man with a Boston address. The new reference was a man Felicity could find no trace of.

Bless her thorough heart, Felicity had found this in a cache of digitized documents covering the '90s.

But the link to Sacramento was there and so they were pursuing it.

Hope was reading this for the first time. She sat there for a long moment, her mind completely disengaged. Feeling her heart beat, slow and steady, feeling her breath moving in and out of her lungs, her fingers numb, her brain a blank.

" — ten minutes."

She turned her head slowly, as if her neck muscles had suddenly turned to wood. Inch by inch toward the sound, feeling as if something were going to crack.

"Hope?" Luke's ash brown eyebrows were drawn together. " — okay?"

She was processing one word out of ten.

Luke raised a big hand and cupped her shoulder. Later, when she was able to think, she'd remember that his touch had been like someone touching a wounded comrade, to see if they were still alive.

His hand shook her shoulder slightly. "Hope?"

Happy Trails. Bernard Teller. *Bernie?*

Thoughts raced, jumbled in her head. So very frightening because she was used to reasoning through things calmly. The world was knowable if you approached it rationally. Things in her head were always clear, never a jumble.

What was in her head wasn't reasoning, it wasn't

verbal or mathematical, it was visual. Broken images floating in front of her eyes, disappearing so quickly she barely had a chance to see them. A park, swings, a jungle gym. A swimming pool. The sounds of men's voices, a friendly rumble in the background. A blonde woman, there and gone immediately.

Her heart gave a painful thump, then another and another, faster, rattling against her rib cage. She brought a hand to her chest, where it hurt. Was she having a heart attack?

"Hope?"

She stared at Luke, wide-eyed. Her chest seized up, her throat closed, her muscles froze. She couldn't breathe! Trying to pull in a deep breath, but only wheezing painfully.

"Hey." Luke leaned forward. "Hey."

His face was close to hers, so close she only saw him, those ice blue eyes looking deeply into hers. So deeply that she wondered whether he understood what was happening to her, since she didn't.

She tried to breathe but no air would come.

And then Luke put up the arm rest, leaned closer and took her gently in his arms. She froze, uncertain what to do. He simply held her so close she could feel his broad chest moving and hear his strong, calm heartbeat. A minute went by, two. Neither of them spoke.

Then something in her chest unlocked and she drew in a deep gasping shuddering breath. Luke dropped his head to rest his cheek on the top of her head and her arms went around him, as naturally as if she'd been doing it since forever. She leaned against him and time stopped. She didn't think about the trouble she was in, the mysteries she couldn't penetrate, the puzzling images in her head, the dangerous men pursuing her, what might await them in Sacramento.

She thought of absolutely nothing at all, she only felt. She felt Luke's warm, hard, lean muscles, the steady beat of his heart. The hard muscles of his back against her arms. That feeling of utter and complete safety. She was safe because she was in a plane, of course, but she was safe because she was in this man's arms.

Her breathing slowed, her heartbeat slowed, she no longer had flashes of frightening images that meant nothing to her yet made her heart beat harder.

Luke adjusted his hold so that she was lying against him. A chill had come over her as if there'd been a sudden blast of Arctic air, but now warmth seeped in, even across her back, because his arms seemed to cover her. A cold tension had held her in its iron grip. Then the grip loosened. Warmth and calm penetrated through her clothes and through her skin. She never wanted to move, just stay like this forever.

Time passed. She had no idea how long. Didn't make any difference because she didn't want to move from where she was. It was like being ... on a beach vacation, floating in the water only it was the beat of a strong heart she was riding instead of the ebb and flow of the waves.

Under her cheek, Luke shifted, pulled her gently back by the shoulders.

Oh no! He was pulling her away! It was so great leaning against him. But — he was right. Much as she'd like to, she couldn't simply spend the rest of her life leaning against his chest. Magnificent as that chest was. There was, like, a time limit on that kind of thing, otherwise she'd do it forever.

He was holding her away from him. Yeah. This was much too nice to last. She didn't want to open her eyes, because she knew what she'd see. A nice man, really handsome, trying to hide his exasperation at having to be nursemaid to a grown woman. Trying to ease her back gently, to be polite, but wanting to put distance between them.

Sheepish but firm.

She sighed and opened her eyes and saw — heat. And fire and flame and red-hot desire. Face taut, eyes closed to slits as he leaned down to her and kissed her.

And kissed her.

And dear sweet Jesus *kissed* her.

Hope had been kissed before but not like this. This was deep and hot and she felt it down to her toes. He kissed her mouth but it felt like he was kissing her all over. Even — even between her thighs. A bit of a shocker, that her vagina contracted sharply when he licked inside her mouth. The back of her head was held in his big hand, as if trying to keep her from running away. When running away was the absolute last thing on her mind. If anything, she wanted to be closer. She reached and wound her arms around his neck and opened her mouth more deeply. Her nose was right against his cheek and she couldn't breathe through her nose but that was ok. She'd breathe through him.

Luke lifted his mouth, just for a second, not enough for her to panic at him leaving her, then his mouth settled down at a slightly different angle, a better angle to taste her.

There was some kind of weird noise in the background that penetrated the fog. She heard it over the heavy beating of her heart that pounded in her ears.

There was a massive jolt that separated them and she looked up. His face was flushed a deep red over his cheekbones. His mouth was wet and slightly swollen. From her mouth! Had that ever happened before?

Why were they separated?

"What happened?" she asked, appalled at her voice. It sounded sexy, almost sultry. Deep and throaty. She almost looked around to see whose voice it could be.

Luke cleared his throat and tucked a lock of her hair behind her ear. "We've landed," he said.

Nine

Sacramento, California

The SUV was waiting at the bottom of the steps. It was a Black Inc vehicle and they were going to a Black Inc safe house. It was all good.

What wasn't so good was his breach of protocol. What the fuck? Kissing Hope was not a good idea. He knew that, he knew the rules. The rules were imprinted on his DNA, rules so strong they didn't even have to be stated. You do not kiss your protectee.

Normally that wasn't a problem. Luke had been on a protection detail four times and his protectees had been male, mainly over sixty and overweight and kissing them hadn't been a temptation.

But damn it, Hope was temptation itself. He hadn't known he was going to kiss her until he was kissing her and it was too late to stop it. And, well, once he started kissing her, stopping was impossible. Insane, even. Who would want to stop kissing that soft mouth, stop holding that luscious, small body?

All the danger signals in his body were switched off and the plane could have been hijacked, the pilot could have jumped out of the plane with a parachute or put a gun to his head and he wouldn't have even noticed. As it was, he was able to let go of her only because they actually landed and it would have been uncool if the ASI pilot came out and had to report back to the head office that Luke was kissing Hope like there was no tomorrow and had a boner to boot.

Getting it down by the time the plane taxied to a stop hadn't been easy either.

He had to do better. So right now, getting going on the mystery threatening Hope's life was more important than kissing her again or — and he had to admit the thought had crossed what passed for his mind — bedding her.

So — first things first.

Luke made sure that Hope was safely inside, settled into the passenger seat and then rounded the vehicle, placing their wheelies in the back seat. His duffel was heavy. He had a Glock 19, an MP5 carbine, several flashbangs and bulletproof vests, for him and her. Hers was going to be huge on her if it was ever necessary for her to put it on. But huge and uncomfortable and cutting into her thighs was better than dead. Night vision goggles with IR capability. He had a Smith & Wesson HRT knife in his boot and a nice big razor sharp Ka-Bar in his bag. And ten boxes of ammo for both weapons. He was loaded for bear.

Knowing Jacob Black and his company, the vehicle would be kitted out with everything but a nuclear bomb. Once he was a part of ASI, he'd be thoroughly briefed on ASI vehicles and Black Inc vehicles but he knew them inside out already. His cell told him that this SUV even had a stealth drone that could be fitted with small explosives and could fly at 20,000 feet for 24 hours.

When he pulled his driver's side door closed, it was heavy and closed with the quiet whump of a heavily armored vehicle.

It was good to know he was equipped because he didn't know who the fuck he was facing. He checked Hope out without moving his head. She'd had a meltdown on the flight down but then so had he. He had never ever been anything less than professional on the job and here he'd kissed her like he'd never been near a woman before. Like she was water and he was parched in the desert.

What had that been about? He wasn't sex-starved. Yeah, it'd been a while, but then he'd been busy fighting off bottom-feeding lawyers, trying to save his reputation and mourning his father. He knew where to find a woman if the itch burned. Bars and clubs did the trick most of the time. He wasn't in the market for a brainy and beautiful programmer who looked like a building had fallen on her. She wasn't his type. She had complication written all over her beautiful face. Luke's life was complicated enough.

But he couldn't have been pulled away from her with a crane.

She was staring out the window to her right so he could study her for a moment. He got it from Felicity that Hope was a genius. She'd shot through college and then grad school like an arrow and had had her pick of prestigious jobs. A woman on a trajectory of success, with one high-level job after another.

And yet — right now she looked like a lost child, slumped in the seat that was engineered for a big man. This successful, beautiful, brainy woman looked fragile, defeated.

Well ... yeah. It was entirely possible that her biological father was trying to kill her. A shot that could come out of the dark at any time. From her *father*.

Luke didn't know too many people, outside the military, who wouldn't be crushed by that kind of stress.

He was ready to take off, but hesitated a moment. "You okay?" he asked quietly.

She didn't even try to ask what he meant.

She nodded.

Luke wasn't fooled. She wasn't OK. She couldn't be.

Of all the things Luke had seen and done and had done to him, this was the one thing that would have broken him. Betrayal, by someone who was supposed to care for you.

He'd been through the shitter. He'd had lawyers charging seven hundred bucks an hour go after him with everything they had. But he'd also had the full support of his big boss, Bud Morrison, the police

Commissioner, the full support of his fellow cops and the full support of everyone at ASI. He'd *felt* that support, like a warm wall at his back.

And he'd had his father, steadfast to the end with unconditional love and support. His father's heart had been broken but he'd never wavered a moment. His heart had given out before his love had.

Hope's *father* might be trying to kill her. Luke had been a soldier and a cop and he'd seen the worst of humanity but this — it was almost impossible to wrap his head around it.

He glanced at her again. So very smart, so very pretty. With good friends who stood behind her. One friend had sacrificed his life for her.

Who would want a daughter like that *dead?*

Well, not on his watch. And not ever.

He started up the vehicle and pulled out. Felicity and Hope were trying to pick up a scent. Maybe Hope had found out something. He would investigate. How he was going to do that, he had no idea. But he'd been a cop and a good one and the terrain always provided something. You just had to be smart enough to find it.

So far the only lead they had was Happy Trails trailer park. It wasn't much and it was a trail that was twenty five years old, but it was all they had at the moment.

The GPS screen on the dashboard showed that the Happy Trails trailer park was on the other side of the city. The GPS recommended route went through the center of town instead of skirting the city.

Hmm. There would be more videocams in a city center than on the outskirts. But passing through the center would save them a lot of time.

Luke trusted that Black Inc's vehicles had privacy protections. The plates would be registered to a shell company and he'd seen for himself that though the smoked glass was not illegally dark, it was impossible to see inside because of the application of a special film. ASI vehicles had that film on the glass of their vehicles as well. It allowed an excellent view from the inside out but no one could see inside.

Hope had pulled out her laptop and was following their route. Only on her screen, it was a top down view, in real time. He could make out their vehicle. The quality of the image was excellent. Crystal clear and detailed.

"You have a drone?" he asked, astonished.

"No." She didn't lift her head. "Not mine."

"Not —" and then he shut up. If it wasn't hers then … it belonged to someone else. And she was hacking into it.

Not in a million years would Luke have been able to a) find a drone in under a minute and then b) hack into it. Clearly, he was in the presence of a Master. Or Mistress. Mistress of the Dark Arts. He smiled a little, because she definitely was a cyberwitch, even if she didn't look it. She looked about twelve, hunched over her laptop.

They approached the historic city center. He

knew some of the buildings dated back to the Gold Rush that had established the city on the Sacramento River. He drove under the speed limit through streets with historic buildings full of touristy shops and trendy restaurants.

Hope looked up from the screen for a moment and did a double take. She straightened in her seat, looking around.

Luke watched her out of the corner of his eye. "What?"

"What?" The face she turned to him looked slightly shocked.

His voice was sharp. "Did you see something? Is something wrong?"

She shook her head. Not saying no, just seeming to try to clear her head. "How can I know if something is wrong? I've never been here before." Her head turned back to looking outside the window.

Luke shut up. Whatever was going through her head was complicated and he was a simple guy. He was here to ferry her around and protect her and he'd do that. There was some deep mystery here and he wasn't the guy to solve it, not on his own. He'd just make damned sure that when the mystery was solved, Hope Ellis would be still standing.

Washington DC

Court Redfield looked at his cell, expecting news from Resnick. But there was no news. Hope Ellis had disappeared off the face of the earth and was still missing. This was bad and came at such an exceptionally bad time. He'd declared his candidacy to a roomful of powerful donors and there was no going back. In a week's time, Court was going to officially declare his candidacy and start his campaign for the presidency, on a platform of moral probity, and his life would be under intense scrutiny.

Already he'd spent a lot of time shielding his money from prying eyes. There was a class of rabid, ferret-like online journalists now who made a point of digging up dirt. His money was hidden but he had to make sure there were no threads anyone could pull.

That was bad enough, to have this going on while his entire team was focused on riding the wave after declaring his candidacy to the money men. They were all expecting him to be focused like a laser beam on the coming campaign, and he couldn't do that while embroiled in this mess. All of this was compromising a campaign he'd been planning for thirty years.

But that wasn't the worst of it. There was still something he feared more than an aborted political campaign. His son, Bard.

All these years, Court had had no idea that Hope Ellis existed. She died 25 years ago, goddammit. He'd made sure of that, or so he thought. Her mother had died and she should have died as well. That pretty girl in Sacramento was supposed to be a bump in the road, someone inconsequential. A way for his red-blooded son to get his rocks off.

When Bard showed an unhealthy attachment to the trailer-park trash, Court had taken steps. He'd had to, right? That woman was going to ruin Bard's life. He'd told her Bard died. Five years later, to his horror, after an article on Bard appeared in the news, she'd written letter after letter, insistently, showing photographs of a daughter. Court had had the letters intercepted. He knew he had to take strong steps. A quiet command to the right man, a quiet exchange of money, and the problem was solved. Even better, the problem was *gone*. Bard had no clue. And life continued.

He'd risen so steadily to the top, step by step — the governorship, Deputy Director of the CIA, the Senate seat. And now he had a good shot at the very top of the ladder, the Presidency. People were tired of the chaos of the past few years and wanted a steady, experienced hand at the helm. Court could promise that. He was a good administrator, a good manager, would keep the ship of state on an even keel after the past turbulent years.

The fact that he wanted the power and intended to earn money off it meant nothing. He was good for the country and the people who counted sensed that.

Really, all he needed was his son by his side occasionally.

Bard. Bard was such a remarkable soldier. A Navy SEAL, for fuck's sake. Spent most of his life abroad, defending his country. That was excellent, on so many levels. And Bard was easy to love from afar, while he was gone on long deployments.

Not so easy when they were in the same room.

Still, Bard was such a superb campaign prop. Court's campaign director was obsessed with him. Bard in his dress whites was an amazing sight and photographs of him being awarded medals were going to play a big role in the campaign.

Everything according to plan.

He sat in his office, rubbing his chest, feeling disaster coming like a freight train. With the potential of ruining his plans and his life. Forced to give the order to kill, well, kill his granddaughter.

It was … a pity. For a moment, Court mourned what might have been. Bard never married and probably never would. The Redfield family tree stopped with him. For just a moment there, Court allowed himself a little sentimentality.

A grandchild. A granddaughter. He held the report on her in his hands and had to admire her. She didn't seem to be a fashion plate, didn't appear to do much with her looks, but she looked like a Redfield. She had the Redfield green eyes and blue-black hair and fine features. She was super smart too. Graduated from MIT at 21…

Smart and good looking. She'd have made a great

addition, an excellent prop. He could picture himself on the campaign trail with a brainy and beautiful granddaughter, an expert in IT, by his side, helping him. He actually needed good help with social media. She'd be so perfect.

Pity.

For an instant, Court thought of acknowledging her. Out-of-wedlock births were no longer a stigma, really, even in his own social class. Hell, half the births these days were out of wedlock. No one really cared. This Ellis girl was so smart and so pretty and had even worked for the NSA. A patriot. It would work. He could make it work. Could even generate a lot of favorable press. Photos of the candidate hugging his newfound granddaughter ... it would tug at a lot of heartstrings.

But ... Bard was no dummy. He'd start asking questions and eventually he'd find out what Court had done. Bard would never forgive him, ever.

Court sighed as he studied Hope Ellis's photograph.

As soon as Resnick found her, she'd be gone, and no one the wiser.

Pity.

Ten

Sacramento

"Here," Hope said abruptly, sitting up straight. "Turn right."

Luke slowed and turned right, into what looked like a field of weeds. On his GPS, the turnoff was in twenty yards but he trusted Hope, braked, and turned right.

Straight into, yup, a field of weeds.

The SUV was armored and sound-proofed but on any other vehicle, the sound of weeds and tree branches brushing against the undercarriage and against the doors would have been loud. They dipped into a ditch briefly and then — Hope was right. He steered the vehicle straight onto an access road that was overgrown with vegetation but that once had been asphalted.

Hope had closed the laptop and was leaning forward, not looking at her cell and not looking at the GPS monitor on the dashboard, just looking straight ahead.

The road under the vehicle became smoother. They were where they were supposed to be.

They passed a section dense with willows and oak that dimmed the sun overhead, then the road curved and there it was.

HAPPY TRAILS TRAILER PARK. The painted words were on a curved section of wood high overhead held up at either end by sturdy poles, surrounded by unkempt grassland and broken sections of fencing. The only intact thing in view was the sign itself.

Happy Trails was anything but happy. At first, Luke thought that it was a deserted trailer park but looking closer, there were a few signs of life. Not many. Mostly it was cars up on wheel blocks, sofas on dry lawns with springs showing, overflowing dumpsters, burned grass on the tiny lots.

A rat ran across the road, furtive as a thief.

He opened the driver's side window and took in the smells. Dust and burnt rubber, the scent of linden trees with a faint overlay of sewage.

Someone shouted and got a shout in return. A dog barked in the distance. A car started up, wheezing and rattling. Definitely not an ASI or Black Inc vehicle. But nothing living moved where it could be seen. Just dirt and stone and desolation.

"Stop the car," Hope said and to his alarm, she didn't even wait. She unbuckled the seat belt, opened the door and hopped out just as he braked to a stop.

Good thing the brakes were in perfect order.

"Hey!" Luke said as she walked fast down the center of the lane. He tried to keep alarm out of his voice as he scrambled to catch up with her. Goddammit! He was her bodyguard so she had to keep her body close to him so he could fucking guard it!

Luke tugged at her elbow to slow her down. It didn't work. He was stronger than she was. Taller, bigger. In shape. A highly trained warrior. But he couldn't get her to slow down without hurting her so he merely lengthened his stride and kept up.

Hope looked like a bomb had gone off inside her head. Her eyes were lit up, like green headlights, huge and mesmerizing. The dusty lane led to a small intersection, where other dusty paths led off. There was a small circle where the paths met and she skidded to a stop, her sneakers lifting a little cloud of dust.

She looked up at Luke, a frown between her delicate eyebrows. "I know this place, Luke. How do I know it? Am I crazy?"

"Maybe déjà vu? You've been here before? Or somewhere similar?"

"No. That I know of, I've never been in a trailer park in my life. I've never been in a place as run down as this before, either. And I've never been to California."

He shrugged, wondering if the stress of her life being threatened was warping her mind. Stress did major damage to people. One soldier in an FOB had been carried off screaming that the Taliban were aliens.

Though, all things considered, he hadn't been that far wrong.

Hope was looking distressed but there was nothing but sober sanity in her eyes.

"Maybe you have been here," he said gently. "But don't remember it."

She shook her head. "Before yesterday, I'd never been west of the Rockies. Hell, never been west of the Mississippi. My parents —" she blinked, cocked her head, as if hearing herself for the first time. "My parents," she continued slowly, "never wanted me to go west. And they never went west, either."

Luke clamped his hand around her elbow. Not painfully, but forcefully. She was going to stay by his side. "Why don't you walk around a little, see if more memories come?"

"Yeah." But Hope didn't move. She just studied the terrain in front of her carefully. Luke stood by her side, quietly. Waiting. She was seeing what he was seeing. A tract that cried poverty and degradation. None of the broken-down trailers looked lived in, though a trailer three lots down the central path had laundry fluttering from a piece of wire strung between a roof strut and a nearby tree. All the other trailer houses looked deserted, unlivable.

A cat wandered down another path toward them. A tabby, looking cared for. It had a collar and glossy fur. The only thing that looked cared for in the whole damned place.

Hope was studying a hedge by the side of the dirt track. The hedge was overgrown, a wild tangle, so thick nothing could be seen on the other side. Suddenly, Hope plunged straight into the hedge. "Swimming pool!" she shouted.

Damn. Luke plunged in right after her. No telling what was on the other side. There could be something sharp, rusty nails. He was up to date on all his shots, including tetanus, but was she?

Damn.

He pushed his way through, following Hope's trail of broken branches. In a moment he was out on another barren stretch of hardpan. *Swimming pool!* That was what she'd said and goddamn if there wasn't a swimming pool right in front of him. Or what had once been a pool and was now a cracked cement hole in the ground full of rotting leaves and dead branches and some dead rats. There was even a cracked diving board at the other end.

Something really eerie was happening here. Hope circled the pool, almost in a trance, looking down at a little sludge in what had been the deep end of the pool. Luke kept pace with her. If this were a horror movie, Hope would be seeing the deep blue of a filled swimming pool and would dive in.

But it wasn't a movie and Hope wasn't making any movements that could turn dangerous. She was simply circling the pool.

Luke could see that it had been a nice pool, once. It was large and surrounded by what had once been an attractive mosaic of blue and white tiles and now looked like a jagged mouth missing most of its teeth.

"Here," Hope said, shifting some yellowed supermarket ads and leaves out of the way with her sneakered foot. "Here was a big crack."

And — there was. A fissure in the cement underlying the mosaic tiles.

At this point, Luke was simply following her lead, following her wherever she wanted to go.

She wandered away from the pool, down another abandoned lane, just a rut in the ground. On either side of the rut were old, rusted trailers. Not the fancy kind, the ancient kind. Abandoned, mostly. There were signs that some had people living in them, but they weren't living lives. Halfway along the rutted path a mangy brindled dog in a rusted cage barked viciously. Luke wondered whether the dog was ever taken out and was tempted to break the padlock with his foot to release the poor creature. But its lips were peeled up showing sharp teeth and its eyes followed their every move, head down, growling.

Releasing it would be kind but probably not wise. And though Luke had a lot of experience with dogs — K-9s and their handlers had saved a lot of lives in the Sandbox — he didn't know if Hope was familiar with dogs. He didn't have any padding to put around his arm in case the dog was feral.

Hope wasn't paying the dog any attention.

Luke didn't know exactly what she was paying attention to. She seemed to be on a secret mission he hadn't been briefed on. She ignored the trailers and the people who might have been in them, touching the top railing made of sun-blasted wood of a fence that formed a sort of perimeter around a small collection of six trailer houses.

Luke winced as she ran her hand along the railing, wanting to tell her to watch out for splinters. But there was no getting through to her.

He pulled out his cell, doing research on Happy Trails while glancing up every couple of seconds to keep an eye on her. He did a quick threat assessment each time he did, but so far there weren't any threats unless there was a sniper up on the branches of an old oak. But there were no branches that would have borne the weight of a sniper and a sniper rifle. The biggest threat was the mangy dog, barking and growling like crazy, but it was in a cage.

He bent down again to his cell screen. He wasn't a computer genius like Hope or Felicity, who were the techie equivalent of Navy SEALs and Army Rangers, but he was ok with tech. And at any rate he was consulting public records. No breaking and entering necessary.

Happy Trails was incorporated in 1980. For many years it was a thriving trailer park, making a tidy profit. After 1991 it started going downhill and was in the red for a couple of years after that. At the last tax report, it had made a profit of $10,546. Barely enough to keep going. There had been a fire in 1997 when Hope would have been six years old. But when she was six years old, she'd been living in Boston. With the Ellises.

Who might be the Sandersons.

Coming to Happy Trails trailer park was a long shot, but it had panned out because Hope's reactions showed that she'd been here before, as a little girl. The path from Happy Trails to Boston was murky and unclear but there definitely was one.

He was scrolling through death notices in 1996 when Hope stopped. She stood there, shoulders stooped, looking exhausted. That was understandable. He suspected she'd taken more than a trip around a semi-abandoned trailer park. She'd taken a trip back through time.

She looked pale, shaky and he took her arm, telling himself it was *not* an excuse to touch her. Not, not, not.

It was costing her a lot and he wanted to get her somewhere where she could regroup. Let her do what she did best — do research online. And while she did that, he could feed her, make her some tea, let her recover from what were traumatic memories. They'd been right to come here but whatever was here to be found, they'd found it. It had given them the certainty that they were on the right path, but it had eaten her up alive. She looked dead on her feet.

Whatever concrete clues there might have been here were long gone.

He turned them around to get back to the SUV parked at the entrance. To get there they crossed a big path he hadn't noticed before. Hope stiffened and pulled away from him, immediately swerving into the new path. Ohhhh-kay. Luke gave a sigh and followed her. Whatever she was doing, she was compelled to do it and he didn't want to stifle her.

Hope walked straight as an arrow down this path, moving in and out of the sunlight, as high trees overhead provided the occasional shady canopy. It had the effect of making her look as if she were walking through spotlights. It made her look like a star on the stage. Luke was beginning to realize she *was* a star, in every sense there was. He was seeing her down, at her worst. Hunted, in danger. Realizing that her entire life was a lie.

But that didn't diminish her. Her sense of purpose, her deep intelligence just shone, like the sun beaming down on her. It was amazing. She glowed in the sunlight.

Unless ... Luke sighed. Unless that was how he saw her. Like a superstar. She sure had superpowers. Beautiful and wicked smart and sexy. That was it. He was attracted to her in a way he'd never been attracted before, which was scary because she was a job and you don't mess with jobs. It was also exciting because she was, yes, a job but she wouldn't be a job forever. And afterwards ...

Gah. While he was slobbering over her cute backside and planning for when he could ask her out, she'd rushed ahead down the path. He lengthened his stride and caught up with her.

Man, it was all *wrong*. Wrong time, wrong place and she was tangled up in something very bad. But the crazy thing was, Luke was feeling really good. He knew all the bad parts about this situation but he also knew he was feeling ... upbeat. The world had been gray and lifeless, mere bony sticks of existence, for a while. Since the trial. He did what was essential because he was a Reynolds and they never faltered. He got up, went to work, ate, worked out, watched some TV, read the newspapers, had the occasional beer with a friend. None of it meant anything, not really. Most of the time he'd felt outside himself, watching himself go through the motions. No colors, no tastes, nothing.

Now he drew in a deep breath, smelling all the scents of the forest. The scent of new leaves, the dust raised by their feet, the wildflowers growing along the sides of the path. His body felt loose and strong, alive in every cell. He welcomed this challenge because at the end of it, Hope would be free and maybe ... hmmm. She'd definitely kissed him back. She was caught up in this too. They were uncovering what had happened to her in the past but once they did, they had the future stretching out ahead of them.

A future they might share.

It felt good to think of the future with hopefulness and not dread. With a woman who enticed him like no other.

The path finally led to a ramshackle wooden cabin fairly deep into the woods. It had shingle sidings that were warped and gray and, in modern-day California, a blaze just waiting to happen. An ancient geezer sat on the rickety porch, like a caricature out of a movie. Not Deliverance, more like Jackass. He had a long gray pony tail, a loose shirt that had been washed a billion times and pants that were too big on him. He looked like someone who'd lost a lot of weight recently.

The old man was watching them steadily, not getting up but not ignoring them either. Luke stopped about ten feet out. He made sure that Hope was on his left hand side. His right hand was down, loose. He could reach his weapon in less than a second. He'd timed it.

"Hey," he said to the old man.

"Hey back." The man wasn't as great a wreck as Luke had thought at first. The entire trailer park was decayed and abandoned and he'd just assumed that the old man would be, too. But though his clothes fit badly, they were clean, and the man's dark eyes were alive and intelligent. "Help you?"

Luke reached out to cup Hope's shoulder. He managed not to frown when he realized she was shaking.

"Yeah, hope you can help," he said easily, smiling. Luke had been undercover, at times, for months. He knew how to assume a persona. Right now he was Easygoing Guy, Mr. Average. Affable, harmless. "I'm writing a family history and trying to chase down all the various branches, before I get down to the writing itself. There's a branch of the family that lived here in Sacramento. Bunch of cousins called Sanderson. My fiancée and I tracked them down to here. It was the last mention of them in a batch of letters I found. They must have moved on — oh — around 1995-1996 maybe, and we don't know where. Is this ringing any bells?"

"Maybe." The man stood up, very thin but agile. He took a step forward and brought his hand up to his chest and rubbed his thumb across the tips of his fingers, in the universal symbol of *gimme*.

Well. Maybe he had intel or maybe not. Only one way to find out. Luke let go of Hope, reached into his right front pocket and pulled out a C-note. His loose money was in his right hand pocket and ordinarily he wouldn't have used his right hand for this. But the man was clearly unarmed. If there was a rifle somewhere, it was in the house, not out on the porch.

Luke leaned forward, holding the hundred dollar bill folded in half lengthwise, held between his first two fingers. The geezer walked slowly down the steps toward him and snatched the note, putting it in his shirt pocket.

"Sandersons, eh?" He looked at Luke then at Hope, and frowned. "Yeah, we had some Sandersons here in the 80s and 90s. Parents were stoners but didn't deal. Kids were straight. Not overly bright but not druggies either. Got into a few scrapes with the law when they were young. Got out of high school okay, the parents took off for Mexico. The kids were going to a community college when they disappeared."

He looked at Hope again, frowning. Hope stepped closer to Luke, an unconscious movement. Luke had to nail himself down not to put his arm around her. "The parents or the kids?"

"Kids. Told you the parents lit out for Mexico. Cheap weed. The kids just disappeared. Well, they weren't kids, they were in their early twenties. But they were gone —" he snapped his fingers. "Like that. Never saw anyone ever again. It was right after the crash."

Hope stepped forward, tense, fists clenched. "What crash?"

Luke held out another C-note between two fingers.

The man stared at her intently. His eyes widened, then his face closed up. He looked at them another moment, gaze lingering on Hope, avoiding the money Luke held out, then turned, walked back up to the porch, entered the shack and slammed the door shut. Dust puffed up from the shingles around the frame.

"Hey!" Luke shouted. He glanced at Hope then vaulted up the steps. He banged on the door with the side of his fist, making more dust puff out. Shards of wood and stucco fell from the overhang. They hadn't said anything to make the geezer clam up. What had happened? He'd been happy to accept the first C-note, why didn't he want the second? Just for a little information.

He pounded on the door for a full minute but there was silence. He was tempted, but the cop in him wouldn't allow him to simply kick the door in. He'd done it before but only with probable cause. He didn't have that here. And the man was definitely uncooperative now anyway. Luke wasn't willing to beat intel out of him.

So Luke simply stood, staring at the unpainted door, completely frustrated.

"Luke?" He turned at Hope's soft voice. His heart clenched when he saw her standing there looking so fragile and lost. "I don't think he's opening that door and I don't think he's going to talk to you."

No, the geezer wasn't going to open that door and wasn't going to talk to him again. And short of kicking in the door and beating the geezer up, which wasn't going to happen, there was nothing Luke could do.

"And you're tired," he said gently.

She nodded her head. "Yeah. Exhausted."

The sun was behind the trees, casting dappled shade. For a moment, branches parted in the gentle breeze and the setting sun beamed a light on Hope's face and all Luke could do was stare. She was exhausted and dispirited but also so incredibly beautiful. The sun lit her face like a spotlight, showing the pale perfect skin, fine bones, that spectacular forest green color of her eyes, the color of the trees around them. Then the beam of sunlight was cut off and what was left was a lovely young woman so tired there were smudges under her eyes.

There was more here to be learned after all, but Luke thought that she wouldn't be the one to learn it. Whatever was here was traumatizing to her. He could come back tomorrow by himself but he didn't want to leave her alone. A four-man team from Black Inc was working in Modesto, helping a bank beef up its security. Maybe they could detach a unit who could come and interrogate the old man. Maybe apply more pressure than Luke was willing to do in the presence of Hope.

Right now, she was close to breaking and he wanted her away from here. There was a connection, a definite connection. That was enough for the moment. They'd made progress.

"What kind of food do you like?" he asked, hoping to jolt her out of her despair and exhaustion.

"What?" Hope turned her pretty puzzled face up to his.

"When we get to the safe house, I'm going to order us a nice meal. I've got the menus of all the local restaurants on my ipad, courtesy of the Black Inc guys. I think there are more or less all the cuisines. And I think we need to have a proper meal. So what would you like? There's even a vegan menu in there somewhere."

Luke repressed a shudder. She liked meat, he knew that. But vegan menus were always high on the list for women. She could order the vegan menu if she wanted, he was ordering steak from an Italian place his buddy Ed said had spectacular food. "So what do you want to eat?"

"Carbs," she answered. "Lots of carbs. Meat. And dessert." She sketched a smile. "Now that you mention it, I'm starving."

"Okay," he said easily, gently turning her around so they could make their way back to the SUV. She stumbled and he put his arm around her waist. It wasn't a hardship. "Carbs and meat it is. What kind of security guy would I be if I saved you from the bad guys but let you starve to death?"

Eleven

Washington, DC

"Well, that went well," Court Redfield's campaign manager said, tablet in hand. Scott Petrie had been hired on the recommendation of one of Court's golfing buddies and it had been an inspired hire. Petrie was efficient and ruthless and Court's polls had risen a percentage point each week Petrie had worked for him.

Court had just finished an interview on CNN and he had no idea how Petrie had done it, but all the questions had been softballs, pitched gently. The interview had been a love fest and he was certain the polls would rise more quickly now.

They were on a roll, he could feel it. If you paid attention, you could feel it like a good surfer can feel the building up of a big wave, even through the board.

If only he didn't have this goddamned mess to deal with. If only he could concentrate on the campaign and not have to worry about Hope Ellis, who was supposed to be dead but wasn't. Goddammit.

And worry about his son, who could never know the truth.

Petrie followed him into the dressing room, silently ticking off items. "Here," he said, "we're already trending on Instagram and Twitter." He tilted his tablet so Court could see ... what? Basically hashtags, phrases and numbers. He was tired and it looked like hieroglyphics to him. He wasn't good with this stuff. He couldn't read it easily like Petrie and his generation could. But he couldn't let on that it was nonsense to him, either. One of his main rivals had been pilloried in the press, print and especially online, when he accidentally mentioned listening to your Walkman. Rex Henry, now known everywhere as T-Rex the Dinosaur. It was Petrie who'd started the meme, the instant he heard the interview.

Petrie was the master of trolling.

Now Court made a point of being photographed either with a tablet or his cell in his hand.

"Great," he said, pushing the tablet away. He sat down and instantly the makeup people surrounded him like gnats. In a flash, he had a makeup cape on and a woman with a very nice rack he deliberately didn't look at was smearing some cream on his face, then removing it with cotton balls. He hated the fuss but at least he didn't have to talk to the makeup people.

Petrie hovered, shifting out of the way of the

makeup people dancing around. Petrie wanted to talk but goddammit, that's why Court hired the man in the first place. To take care of this shit for him.

And he needed to find out what Resnick was doing.

The makeup crew was fast. The cape was whisked away and Court stood up and turned to Petrie and spoke loudly. "Write up a report and email it to me. I need to get home, my wife's not feeling well and she's my priority."

Petrie's eyes dropped to the tablet. He nodded and moved away. Statements like that in public had been Petrie's idea. Court's wife was fine — *her* priority was a divorce in case he wasn't nominated. She'd ride to the White House if she could and if he didn't make it, she had her divorce lawyer on retainer. She was his third. He couldn't afford a fourth, not with the wave of morality he intended to ride all the way to the top.

In the meantime, Court never neglected an opportunity to let slip how tight he and the She-Devil from Alabama were.

It didn't help that Bard hated her. He'd hated number two as well. And he blamed Court for his mother's death.

It was Bard who was his main worry. Bard, son and heir of the Redfield dynasty, who wanted nothing to do with it and especially nothing to do with him. Bard, who'd joined the Navy to get away from him.

Voters could deal with three marriages. They'd done it before. Hell, everyone Court knew had been divorced at least once. It was almost a rite of passage. Voters didn't really care.

But what voters really *didn't* like was the idea of parents and children being estranged. That was one of the last taboos. If your kid didn't trust you, how could a voter?

Things between Bard and himself had been tense since that damned bitch in California.

Bard could have had his pick of girls if he was wanting to settle down. Girls that came from decent families, girls whose families were connected, whose parents would appreciate the thought of marrying into the family of a man on the rise, like Court was. State representative, Governor, Deputy Director of the CIA, Senator and now candidate for the Big One.

Who wouldn't want that? Be married to that?

Bard had been *courted*. Pretty girls, rich girls, had thrown themselves at his feet when he was young. Bard had been discreet, but Court knew he'd bedded a lot of them. Not one stuck. And then he had become fixated on that trailer trash girl, Lucy Whatthefuck. Once she was gone, Bard never had a serious relationship again. The most serious relationship he'd had was with the US Navy, and he'd been ferociously devoted.

So devoted that he'd disappeared for years at a time. Even as a Senator, even as the goddamned deputy head of the goddamned CIA, Court had been able to follow Bard's military career only in broad strokes. As a SpecOps officer, Bard had been almost nonstop on top secret missions not even Court's clearance could give him access to.

Or, for all he knew, Bard had spent the past twenty years at Little Creek, Virginia, two hundred miles from Washington and just hadn't told his father. Court couldn't afford to use official channels to track his son. What father didn't know where his son was? When in truth, most of the time he'd had no idea where Bard was and what he was doing.

All he knew was that his son had erected his SEAL career as a wall between him and his father.

Sometimes Court wondered whether Bard deliberately sabotaged his career to stay away from him. By any measure, by any standards, Bard should have been an admiral by now. He had the combat experience, he had the connections, he even had the goddamned *look* of an admiral. Tall and broad-shouldered. Straight backed and handsome, though weathered. Court had tried to discreetly pull strings behind the curtain and had been assured that of course Bard would advance, but he never did. He'd been a Captain for a decade. He should have become a Rear Admiral by now.

The only possible explanation was that Bard preferred being in the field to being at the top levels in the Pentagon.

God, how the optics of Court standing next to his son, a decorated war hero, wearing a rear admiral's dress whites, would help. It surprised him how much he wanted that because it would just be so goddamned effective. He *yearned* for it.

But no. The two of them had wavelength problems and could barely spend an hour in each other's company without fighting. Bard was easy to love and admire from afar, when he was abroad, on deployment. Not so easy when he was in the same room as his father and contested every fucking word that came out of his father's mouth.

He'd been a rebellious teenager but you factored that in. The serious hatred had begun with the trailer trash. Court had been horrified when he first realized that his son was *serious* about that girl in Sacramento all those years ago. Bard should have just fucked her and moved on. Granted, in the photos she was a really pretty girl. And bright, apparently. But impossible. Since his son was too besotted to see that, Court had had to take steps. Thought he'd done a good job, too. But then five years later, the bitch tried to contact Bard again. And she'd had a child! A girl. At the time, Court thought she was lying. That she'd had a child with some drifter and tried to pass it off as Bard's.

It had actually been a miracle that he'd managed to intercept her letters to Bard. Letter after letter. With photos of the kid. Who, damn it, looked just like Bard.

He'd dispatched two men to Sacramento with a story of a young woman who'd stolen secrets from the CIA. In truth, the men didn't care what the story was. They considered themselves expensive weapons. Point, aim, fire. Two days later Court read police reports about a fatal car crash involving a young Sacramento woman and her five-year-old daughter.

It was after that he decided to set up his small army. A private army, answerable only to him. Best decision he'd ever made.

His army had proved useful over and over again, and Court hadn't given the woman in Sacramento and her daughter a second thought for 25 years.

His heart nearly stopped when he saw the photo of the woman who had engaged the geneticist, the one who'd found his archival DNA.

The female version of Bard. If the two were ever seen in public together there would be no doubt that they were related, that they were father and daughter.

For just a second, Court was ... not sorry, really. He always did what had to be done and never suffered regret. But ... sort of sad that they couldn't claim her. Genius IQ, Harvard, MIT, computer expert, skilled in things Court didn't even recognize. Not a mark against her name, not even a parking ticket.

What a pity. Life played such ridiculously cruel games, sometimes. The mother had been impossible for Bard and by extension for him, but the daughter ... The daughter would definitely have been an asset.

Court sighed.

It was not to be. Not only was it not to be. If

Bard found out that a child of his had been hidden from him, it would not be pretty. Bard wasn't stupid. If he dug into the past, he'd realize what Court had done. And then ...

Court shivered.

Bard was a man who had trained and trained hard to kill. He was a superb shot, he was skilled in hand to hand combat, he was a leader who led willing men at times to their death.

His son was a stone-cold killer.

Court couldn't swear that Bard wouldn't kill him for what he'd done. If Court were capable of feeling regret, he'd regret having killed the child. Maybe he should have given orders to drive the mother off the road when she was alone in her vehicle. That way they could have had the child. Bard would have quit the military, or at least stopped being a field officer. There were plenty of jobs at the Pentagon for a man with his talents, with time to raise a beautiful and smart daughter.

Court sighed. It was a pretty dream but it would never have worked. Bard was professionally paranoid and the first thing he'd have done was investigate the mother and her death.

No, Court had done the only thing he could do. By some wild card of fate, the child hadn't died, had lived, and was now looking for her biological family. If she was smart — and by all accounts she was — she'd find her way back to Sacramento, to that trailer park.

Resnick would intercept her.

Sorry, honey, Court thought, with a touch of sadness. You're likely to be the only grandchild I'll ever have — but you have to go.

He made a note to call Resnick for a sitrep.

Sacramento

The safe house was unusually nice. It surprised Hope. In thriller movies, the safe house was a cheerless anonymous apartment in a cheerless anonymous neighborhood. Flaking walls and an empty fridge. Maybe some cockroaches. Or else a dilapidated and ramshackle farmhouse at the end of a dirt-track road far from anywhere.

Instead, the safe house Luke drove her to was in an attractive, bustling part of Sacramento with restaurants and art galleries and offbeat shops along the streets. Part of a gated community with a guard and landscaping, and inside it was comfortable and well decorated.

Well, hats off to Black Inc.

The entire drive she'd been completely lost in thought. Actually, it couldn't even be called thought — more like drowning in images. What she'd seen resonated strongly, like someone had switched on a tuning fork inside her. It felt like the vibrations would shake her apart. She sat and tried to hide her trembling but it didn't work. Luke switched on the seat heating on her side as well as the cabin heating. It wasn't cold, but she was.

Hope could usually think her way out of problems but there was no thinking her way out of this. There was no rational thread to pursue, nothing really to grab hold of beyond vague impressions, memories so fleeting they couldn't even be called memories, just flashes. A swimming pool and a bright red inflatable tube. A blue bike with trainer wheels. A small dog with long hair.

A beautiful woman. When the woman's face flashed in front of her, too fast to fix it in her memory, her heart started beating so hard she thought she was having a heart attack.

Nothing made any sense.

It was dark by the time they got to the safe house, one of a series of small townhouses, surrounded by large lawns, along a series of winding roads. Luke parked nose out in the driveway. Before getting out, he pulled up an app on his cellphone and started tapping.

"What's that?" she asked.

"The map of the complex and the security cams," he replied distractedly. "Plus the ability to turn them off selectively. There they are. I turned them all off along our route. I'll turn them back on when we're in the house."

"May I see?"

He raised his eyebrows but handed her his phone. "Sure."

Hope took a quick tour of the app. It was simple, but effective. She added a feature — making visible the cams Luke had turned off in the form of a pathway. "Here." She tapped onto the screen. "Looks like you forgot the cams along the driveway just before the security gate. Maybe we should turn those off too? I also memorized the whole thing so you don't have to turn the cams off manually. With one tap, you can turn the same ones on and then off again as long as we follow the same route."

She handed it back to Luke but he wasn't taking his cell. He was looking at her really strangely. "Luke?" He didn't say anything, just stared at her, light blue eyes focused on her like twin headlights.

What the hell?

Luke made a strangled noise in his throat. "Were you familiar with that app?"

What a weird question. "No. Of course not."

"I didn't think so because it was developed especially for Black Inc and they shared it with us. I can't believe what you just did. It took all of us a morning's worth of training to familiarize ourselves with that app. You figured it out in about two seconds."

She shrugged. "Well, it wasn't complicated."

He shook his head and gave a half smile. "It is. It *is* complicated. But you aced it immediately and also figured out where I'd made a mistake. Plus added a function. I think from now on, I should just carry the weapons and the bags. Muscle work. And you do all the thinking."

That coaxed a smile out of her. Her first in a long while. She opened her mouth to reply but her stomach growled.

"That's the third job I have here. Feeding you. Come on, let's go."

Inside, the house was like a luxury hotel suite. Like the hotel they'd stayed in back in Portland, it had two bedrooms. Plus two bathrooms, a living room, dining room and a surprisingly well-equipped kitchen. Not that she'd be using it. She was hopeless in the kitchen.

She watched him as he closed the curtains, put their bags away, switched on the lights. Like watching the enchanted kingdom come back to life when Sleeping Beauty woke up, after the kiss.

Aurora wasn't the only one to wake up after a kiss. In all the terror and horror of the past few days, leaving her chilled and shaken, one thing stood out. That kiss. An infusion of heat and life, a punch to the solar plexus that didn't hurt, that instead infused her with sensations she couldn't name but left her feeling light and free and alive. Just for the space of that kiss, but still.

Everything else was darkness and emptiness.

She looked around. "This apartment is incredible. I thought safe houses were gloomy, with scuffed second-hand furniture and dead flies everywhere."

"Yeah, not here. Black Inc does things with style. But operatives are in Sacramento all the time, so I guess they use this safe house often. The company's HQ is in California. In San Diego. So they often have business here at the state capitol and the big boss wants his men and women to be comfortable and safe. God knows they are often in the field in hellholes."

"What's he like?" Hope sat and patted the seat next to her.

Luke sat, holding his cell. Though he was lean, he still made a dent in the couch. He was heavier than he looked. He finished tapping and looked up. "Who?"

"Jacob Black. He's sort of a legend."

"Yeah, he is. I've only met him a few times. No nonsense. Good leader. Straight shooter."

"Probably the only straight-shooting billionaire in the world."

"He's a billionaire because he's really good at what he does. Not because he wants to be a billionaire. In the field, he lives exactly like his operators."

She sighed. "If you talk to him, thank him for me."

"Yeah. We've all got a stake in helping you. We all feel —" He stopped, studied her. As if he were checking for wounds.

"What?"

Luke nodded, as if coming to an agreement with himself. "We think that whoever is after you is someone either very high up in government or very high up in the security business. There are maybe ten guys — all men — in private security who could command the resources we've seen. And we know them all. Not all are good men, but coming after a woman like that —" Luke shook his head. "Takes a certain kind of person. And in government it would have to be people at the top, too. You've stirred up a hornet's nest, honey, and none of us are happy about that."

She blushed stop-light red at the 'honey' and looked away. "I'm really sorry to be creating so many problems. Maybe I shouldn't have alerted Felicity, I should have —"

A look of horror crossed Luke's face. "God no!"

He picked up her hand, brought it to his mouth. His lips were warm, as was the skin of his face. Warmth spread from her hand down through her body. He pressed a soft kiss in the palm of her hand. Pulling away, she closed her fist, as if to keep the kiss there.

"Somehow you got onto the radar of some bad people, either in or outside of government. Bad is bad. We've all tripped over them. My buddy Matt is — was — a SEAL. A squid. But I forgive him for that. Anyway, his path crossed a CIA operative's path, and he was one of the worst men on the planet. He tried to ruin Matt's life as a prelude to poisoning a major city and almost managed it. But with some help Matt prevailed and we'll prevail here. No one is going to let anything happen to you. Not me, not anyone. You've got a team on your side now, and it's a good one."

She was watching his face carefully, listening to the things he was saying, listening to the things he wasn't saying. He was speaking from the heart, as someone whose life had been ruined. As someone who knew first hand what that felt like.

"Nice thought," she said. It was. Very nice. A team, on her side. The first and only time that had happened had been at the NSA, for about a year. Emma, Riley and she had formed an unshakeable team. And Felicity had joined them for about three months.

They'd put up with round-the-clock work, unspeakably dweeb semi-autistic men, a red-hot crisis a week. None of that mattered and they'd rolled with the punches like pros. Then, the horror of their handsy and bullying boss was too much and they scattered. All four quitting within a week of each other. They kept in touch via HER, the special room in the darkweb they'd set up, but the physical presence of her own team, day-to-day, was no more.

It had been great while it lasted.

"You don't sound convinced." Luke was frowning. Oh man, how could he look so good *all the time*? Frowning, smiling, thinking, driving. It didn't matter what was going on with him, he just looked good. All the time. So amazingly good-looking without being in any way a pretty boy. Fine, stern features, icy blue eyes, clean lines, strong lean body. He could have been a Roman Emperor, one of the better ones before they started electing their horses to the Senate. Or maybe a Roman general, that was more like it.

Yeah, on a rearing steed, sword in hand.

"—you think?" God, he'd said something and she'd zoned out.

"What?"

"You're tired," he said gently. "And you need to eat." He looked up at the sound of a buzzer and smiled. "Good timing. Hope you like what I ordered."

Entry to the apartment was via two locked doors, like a spaceship airlock. Luke had Hope stand to one side and not open the inner door unless she heard him rap out 'Shave and a haircut'. He closed the door behind him and opened the outer door that gave out onto the covered porch. The murmur of voices, the special knock and she opened the door.

Luke carried in what looked like enough food for a football team. Hope followed him to the dining room where they set out two place mats, dishes, cutlery and glasses and he set out the food.

"I got plenty of vegetables. I know you had steak last night, but don't know how often you eat it."

"As often as I can. Love meat," she said, watching as he unpacked the food. "I like everything that's here."

He looked up at her and gave her a rare smile. It was good that he smiled so seldom because his smile was almost blinding and a reminder — as if she needed it — of just how handsome he was. Wow.

"Not picky, eh?"

"What?"

"Well, most women your, uh, size, are uh, your size because they are incredibly picky about what they eat or they eat very little or both."

She scowled, hands on hips. "By, *uh, my size*, are you saying I'm scrawny?"

His face was covered in blond scruff but she could swear that he blushed. Though that couldn't be, could it? Warriors didn't blush.

"God no!" he blurted. "You're perfect! You're gorgeous. I didn't mean at all —"

Hope laughed. "Just messing with you. I'm 'my size' as you put it, because I often forget to eat. I love food, and will eat most anything. But if I'm lost in work, by the time I'm really hungry, it's late and I know by experience that the places that provide food after midnight suck. And it comes cold and greasy. And I always forget to shop. I have some staples like milk and cereal that my fridge automatically orders every week, but my pantry is pathetic."

He looked at her curiously. "You don't cook?"

"At *all*," she said cheerfully. "Never learned. My ... mother didn't cook. I don't think I ever saw her in the kitchen. We had a cook who wouldn't let anyone in the kitchen. Then I spent most of my growing-up years in boarding school, and in college and in most of the places I worked at after that, they had canteens. And of course —" she gestured at the table — "there's always takeout. Do you cook?"

"Absolutely." Luke was still removing the containers from the large insulated bag. "When my mom died, Dad had to learn to cook for me. There sure wasn't money for a cook and anyway he became a pretty decent cook, but with a limited range. It was fine for what it was. But I like lots of different cuisines so I learned how to cook Italian and Mexican and Thai, mainly. At a very basic level, but still. I felt like Italian tonight so that's what we're having. One of the Black Inc guys I trained with particularly recommended an Italian restaurant they use when in the safe house. Traditional, but really good." He leaned over the table of containers and breathed in. "Mushroom risotto, fried polenta, sautéed wild greens, chicken cacciatore, tagliata steak, tomato salad with basil olive oil, panna cotta. Good stuff."

She leaned over, out of politeness, hoping the smells of food wouldn't nauseate her. It happened sometimes, when she was overtired, no matter how hungry she was. Food just made her stomach close up into a tight cold ball.

And she *was* overtired. Exhausted, really. Her emotions had been stretched thin to the point of shattering. She was too tired even to take stock of the day. Of the mind-bending nature of the visit to the trailer park. How she had this knowledge of the park. Somehow, crazy as that sounded, she'd been there before. The information was simply there, in her head, and she had no idea how it was there.

It felt like being tossed around in a stormy ocean.

Her stomach was already tightening when she leaned over the table top and — the smells were absolutely amazing. You'd have to be dead not to respond to them. Her stomach just opened right up and stretched out virtual fingers, curling up. *Gimmee. Now now now!*

"Wow," she breathed. "That smells awesome."

Luke looked up from carting out the food boxes, lifted a corner of his mouth and winked. "Right?"

Oh God. Luke shouldn't do that! Shouldn't give that wildly attractive half smile and a wink, drawing attention to those sky blue eyes. Nope. She was rooted to where she stood, her terrible day and the luscious food all forgotten. All she could do was stare at him, all thoughts gone from her head. No thoughts, just hormones, all suddenly alive and kicking, swirling around in her bloodstream.

She'd been chilled just a moment before, thinking she should have taken a hot shower to warm up. She didn't need to warm up now. No. She was overheating if anything, heat flushing over her skin from head to toe.

It paralysed her, as if someone had put her under a spell. She couldn't move, she couldn't talk. All she could do was stare at Luke. If she'd had room in her head for it, she'd be embarrassed, but she didn't. There was only him, filling her field of vision, his body a magnet for her touch. She had to curl her fingers into the palms of her hands to stop herself from reaching out, because though she couldn't think straight, she remembered very well what he felt like. Like warm steel. He felt like no other human being she had ever touched. He smelled good, too, of soap with a faint overlay of leather.

He watched her watching him and she couldn't move, could barely breathe. The air around them felt charged, like something was about to short circuit.

Like her.

Her hands started trembling uncontrollably. Something had taken her body over and she felt completely rudderless. A broken branch tossed about by a raging river.

He reached her in two strides, placed his hand over hers, large and sinewy and almost twice the size of her hand. She stared down at their hands, so different they could have almost belonged to two species. Her hand was small and soft and about the only thing she did with her hands was work the keyboard. His, however, was powerful and tanned, with a few small white scars, and was clearly used for a number of things.

He was a good shot, he said. He could cook. He was an excellent driver. He was probably really good at ...

Images blossomed in her head as if she were watching clips from movies. Luke, his hand cupping her shoulder, moving down to cover her breast. Crazily, it was as if she could feel his hand on her skin.

Her breast felt heavy, exactly as if he were touching her.

In the movie reel now showing in her head, she was naked on a bed. Sprawled wantonly, legs spread wide, arms out. To her knowledge, she'd never done that except once, at summer camp, when the temperature was 102°. She'd been twelve and hadn't been thinking of sex but of cooling off. Sex was under the covers, preferably in the dark. Not like this, her entire body an invitation.

To sex. That's what this was. Her imagination had sandbagged her and run ahead of her, imagining sex with Luke. Because it was going to happen. No doubt about that.

"You okay?" His deep voice penetrated the fog of imaginary sex that had suddenly filled her mind, that would soon turn into the real deal.

Was she okay? The slight trembling had stopped. She thought about her situation. She was on the run. No idea who her parents were. But she somehow had memories of a broken-down trailer park in Sacramento, California when she'd never been to California.

Those were the cons.

On the pro side, she had the handsomest man alive on her side, protecting her and helping her. He was backed up by a highly competent security team in Portland, with the help of the most powerful security company in the world.

There was a luscious spread of fabulous food

right under her nose.

She was absolutely certain that equally fabulous sex would be in her future soon.

"Fine," she answered, smiling up at him. "Let's eat."

The food was, as promised, absolutely delicious. As delicious as the woman sitting across the small table from him. He was drowning in pleasure as he put bite after luscious bite in his mouth while smiling at Hope. Who was smiling back at him.

Luke wanted sex. Normally, sex would take precedence over food any day and for a moment he wondered at himself, that he was sitting here stuffing his face when what he wanted to do really badly was pick her up, rush into her room — or his, he wasn't fussy — strip her and jump her bones.

She was willing. She hadn't said the words and he'd get the words out of her before taking her to bed, but her eyes let him know sex was going to happen.

So why wasn't it happening?

"This is so good," she said, digging into the risotto. "I really needed this." Color was coming back in her face and her green eyes glowed.

That's why sex wasn't happening. Not right this

minute, at least. Hope needed this. Needed a moment of normality, maybe even a moment of comradeship. Luke wanted to bed her, yes. More than any woman he could remember. But he also liked her, a lot. He'd seen her beaten down and he didn't want to see that ever again. She was so smart and so vital. He liked seeing her the way she was right now, enjoying a fabulous meal. Happy and relaxed.

"Here," he said, picking up a rondel of fried polenta. "Open up."

She opened her mouth obediently, closing her eyes in delight while she chewed. He had a pang when his treacherous mind envisioned that lovely soft pink mouth closing over his — no. He wasn't twelve. He could wait. Just seeing the happiness on her face, when her life had been anything but happy, was repayment for ignoring the boner under the table. "Good?"

She caught her breath and moaned. He smothered his own moan because he was picturing that very expression on her face, under him.

"Oh, man. I've eaten more good meals with you in the past couple of days than I have in the past year."

Luke speared a slice of tagliata steak, delighted at her words. Oh yeah, he wanted to be the source of a lot of happiness for her. Right up there with food was sex and he wanted to put that look of bliss on her face, only not with food. He stared down at his plate, not meeting her eyes. Because though she declared herself a nerd, she was good at reading people and he didn't want her to know what he was thinking right this instant.

Because what he was thinking was a little dangerous. He wasn't happily aroused, a guy looking forward to a good time in bed. He was on a hair trigger. Ready to blow.

And wouldn't that be embarrassing? He hadn't done that since high school.

So the only way he knew to deal with this was to have as few stimuli as possible. Eating. He could do eating. But he couldn't talk and he couldn't touch her. Talking to her would only mess with his head. He found her fascinating and every word she spoke made her even more desirable. And touching her — no way. He wouldn't be able to stop.

So he stuffed his mouth as quickly as manners would permit so he couldn't talk and he couldn't touch her.

She ate more slowly but much less, so she finished before he did. When he saw that she was done, his fork clattered on his plate. There was still some food on it but he ignored it.

He wasn't alone in this. Nope. She was studiously avoiding looking at him, but still she was stealing little glances when she thought he wasn't looking. Luckily, Luke had excellent peripheral vision.

Her hands had started trembling. She put her own fork down, not clattering like his own, but neatly.

They stared at each other, both knowing what

was coming next. But Luke had to have it out there, in words.

"So," he said and stopped. Nothing else came out. Whoa. He didn't have too many words in him.

"So," she answered.

Silence.

"Do you want —" Luke cleared his throat. There had to be better words for this than *do you want to have sex with me?* But at the moment he couldn't think of any. It was like a strong wind whistled in his head, scouring everything but desire from him.

Luckily, he didn't need words.

"Yes," she whispered.

Twelve

He carried her to the bedroom. Hers. Probably because it was the closest.

She'd never been carried as an adult. Actually, she couldn't remember ever being carried as a child, either. Man, it was … it was *great*. Like flying. She wanted to get somewhere but didn't have to exert any effort, all because Luke was carrying her. And not huffing and puffing, either. Perfectly naturally, like you'd carry a book somewhere.

The entire right side of her body was against him, warm and hard. For balance, she twined her arms around his neck, her forearms resting on his strong shoulder muscles, her face against his.

Whoa, forget self-driving cars. This was the way to travel.

When they crossed the threshold together it felt like … like some other kind of threshold had been crossed. From the dining room, where they'd been eating, to this shadowy world of the bedroom where other things were going to happen.

Hope felt a deep tremor of anticipation while at the same time feeling an utter calm. She'd never felt anything in her life was predestined. Everything she had in her life had been gained by hard, assiduous work. Step by step, everything planned out.

Not this. This felt easy and natural. Meant to be. Going with the flow.

Luke didn't look like he felt this was easy. His face was tight, almost suffering. When they got to the bedroom, he gently eased her down to her feet, but kept one arm around her. He was so much taller than she was and held her so tightly against him, she could feel the difference in their bodies keenly. Taller than her, stronger than her, but she didn't feel intimidated at all. If anything, she felt like she held some kind of power over him.

He was looking down at her, face drawn, waiting.

"Kiss me," she whispered.

His eyes narrowed. "Oh, yeah," he whispered back. And kissed her. And kissed her. Mouth eating at hers, as if the boundaries between them could disappear. With the arm wrapped around her waist, Luke lifted her a little so that their mouths could align better. Oh, yeah. Her arms wound more tightly around his neck, their torsos breast to chest. She could feel a deep, regular thumping that she knew was his heartbeat. It wasn't hers because her heart was beating a thousand times a minute.

He licked inside her mouth and she felt an electric thrill run through her, from the top of her head to the soles of her feet. He licked again and her vagina clenched, hard. At this rate, she'd die of overstimulation before they even made it to the bed.

Luke lifted his head, those light blue eyes glowing in the darkened room. The shadows turned him into an almost otherworldly figure, all sharp cheekbones and glowing eyes and teeth. He loosened his hold and she dropped down to her feet, rubbing against his massive erection while slipping down his body. Luke hissed in a breath.

"Sorry," she whispered.

He flashed a grin, that beautiful face going from grim to amused in a second. "No problem," he said softly. "Why are we whispering?"

They were whispering because this felt so … so momentous. Something huge was happening, something that would split her life into two. Before Luke and After Luke. But she didn't have the words to say that, so she just shook her head.

Luke's gaze was fixed on her face. "Hope. I want you like I want my next breath."

"But?" Surely there was a but here?

"But." Luke huffed out a breath. He was holding her by the shoulders, strong hands gripping her tightly. "Okay. This is hard."

Startled, Hope looked down. Yep, very hard.

Unexpectedly, Luke laughed. "Yeah, that too. The thing is — God. I mean Felicity said you were very pretty and she was wrong. You're beautiful, and — I'm messing this up."

Hope was watching him carefully, trying to make sense of what he was saying. Ready to agree with him, whatever it was. If he was backing down, she'd smile, shoo him out, get into bed and stare at the ceiling all night, devastated. But she'd never let him know that.

"It's okay." She tried to smile, but it came out wobbly.

"No," he sighed. "It's not. Like I said, Felicity told me you were really pretty but it never occurred to me because I'm focused on the job, always."

She blinked. "Okay."

"Gah." Luke shook his head. "What I'm trying to say is that I packed for trouble, not pleasure. I don't think it occurred to me that you'd be irresistible."

Whatever it was, it was her fault? Hope frowned and opened her mouth to reply but he beat her to it.

"I don't have condoms, honey. I'm so sorry. It's — it's been a while for me and even if I did have some on me, they'd probably be expired. But I don't have any at all, not even expired ones."

"Oh, um ..." Hope looked up at him. He was frowning. Even frowns looked so good on him. "Well, your friend Summer thought of everything when she packed that bag for me. She included, um, condoms."

Luke's eyes widened and his face lit up. "Yeah?"

"Yep."

"Can you get them?"

"Yep. You'll have to let go of me, though."

He opened his hands and Hope went to the wheelie. The box was at the bottom and in a second she was holding it. It was brightly colored and there were *flavors*. She was pondering that when Luke snatched it out of her hands, picked her up and placed her on the bed. Actually he threw her. She bounced a little. His hands were shaking. So were hers.

"Oh, man." Luke stood by the side of the bed and looked down at her, like you'd look at a present someone had given you. "Bless you, Summer. A whole box."

Hope wanted to smile but somehow she'd lost control of her muscles. Heat was rippling under her skin, glowing, melting her. It was a miracle she could breathe.

Luke bent forward, backlit and burnished gold, like some ancient god. He reached out and a shiver went through her. He unbuttoned her jeans, the back of his fingers whispering across her belly. Even greater heat was concentrating there. He knelt on the bed, making her roll gently toward him. He unzipped her jeans and his hands tugged gently, sliding them down her legs and then sliding his hands back up to her hips. Summer's underwear was sexier than what Hope usually wore, which was white cotton athletic underwear. This was lingerie — a scrap of mint green stretchy lace with matching bra.

Luke hooked his fingers in the elastic waistband of the panties and pulled them down. Slowly, slowly.

Hope couldn't see anything but Luke's eyes, blazing with heat. He pulled those pretty panties off her feet and threw them to the floor.

"Open your legs," he whispered.

"Okay." Her voice came out on a soft breath. They were back to whispering.

It was so quiet in the room she could hear the rustle of her heels moving across the bedspread. Naked below her waist she was completely open to him.

Luke blew out a powerful breath. "I can either take off your sweater and bra or undress myself. I can't do both. Sorry. This should be long and drawn out but that train left the station a while ago. Can you do the rest yourself?"

Could she? Hope moved her fingers. They were working. "Yeah."

Lifting herself up slightly, she pulled the sweater off and threw it somewhere, hoping Summer wouldn't mind the way her clothes were being treated.

Luke had already pulled off his tee, unbuttoned his jeans and was shucking them. "Bra," he reminded her, as if she'd somehow forgotten.

She hadn't forgotten. Her fingers felt numb. The bra had a front clasp which was fortunate, because she didn't know if she'd have the coordination to reach around behind her back. It came off at the exact moment Luke pulled down his briefs and ... *oh*.

He was huge, so hard his penis was almost flat against his stomach. Deep red and shiny at the top.

Completely and totally unlike any penis she'd ever seen in real life.

Everything about him was just so fine, like a Greek god, only blond. And aroused. Long, hard muscles, broad shoulders, not an ounce of fat, just pure male. Both of them were naked. Luke had one big warm hand on her ankle. She was spread-eagled on the bed, completely open to him. It didn't even occur to her to be embarrassed though he was probably seeing more of her than any of her fumbling lovers ever had. And he clearly liked what he was seeing because when she moved her legs even further apart, his penis, impossibly, rose a little.

And her vagina clenched. And was getting wet. All of this was her body reacting without any input from her mind at all. She didn't have to psych herself into arousal like she usually did. Her body was enthusiastically arousing itself. Just looking at Luke did the trick.

And then he mounted her and it was almost overstimulation. The feel of him against the whole front of her body was amazing. Like warm steel, with that warm steel rod at the front. He bent his head and licked her neck and ohmygod yes. The neck was an erogenous zone. She'd read about it but had never experienced it. He licked behind her ear, nipped her skin slightly and she jolted, the electric thrill almost too much to bear.

Somehow he'd found the time to put that condom on and was positioned right there, at her opening. Strong hairy thighs opened her legs up even more as he kissed her ear. It sent shivers over her entire body.

"Okay?"

What was he asking? Whatever it was, she was fine with it. More than fine. In fact, whatever he wanted should be happening *right now*.

But she couldn't answer because he was kissing her. There were other ways to answer, though, in another language. She lifted her hips and clutched his buttocks and that was a language he understood. He made a sound deep in his chest and thrust forward hard.

It hurt, just a little. She wriggled, trying to accommodate him.

"Sorry," he gasped.

His face was against her neck and she could feel the puff of air as he spoke. He dropped kisses against her jawline, up the side of her face, back down. His mouth settled over hers and he gave her sweet little first-prom date kisses. Such a contrast from his penis inside her, like two entirely different men were making love to her.

He wasn't moving. She was wet now and wanted him to move. Now.

Hope shifted her head and bit him on the jaw.

"Luke. Rangers lead the way."

"Oh yeah." He kissed her deeply then and moved.

MIDNIGHT KISS

Lorne Resnick pulled into what once had been a driveway, though now it was barely visible through the weeds. He drove under a big faded sign, HAPPY TRAILS TRAILER PARK, onto a rutted path and killed the engine when the path basically dried up.

So, this is where Court Redfield had sent him. He scouted the terrain before opening the door. He was good with situational awareness. He was good with all of it, though the Army hadn't appreciated his gifts at all. He waited for that little spurt of bile, for the sudden flush of anger, but it only lasted a second. Because, lucky him. Since the military had treated him like shit he'd ended up in a covert position in the CIA's secret army, when special activities at the CIA was being run by Court Redfield. Court took them private, outside the power structure of the government. A tight little unit answerable to no one except Redfield himself. Almost ten times the pay and the only rule was *get the job done*.

Resnick was good at getting the job done once you untied his hands.

So he became the general of Court Redfield's own private army and then damned if Redfield didn't declare his candidacy for the Big One. He'd win, too. Redfield knew a lot of secrets and he didn't play nice. Resnick was going to be the right-hand man of the goddamned President of the United States.

Maybe even his surrogate son, since Redfield's own son seemed to be a fuckhead who didn't want anything to do with his old man.

Resnick understood that, down to the bone, only his old man had been nothing like Court Redfield. His old man had been a nasty drunk who couldn't hold down a job and made the people around him pay for his failings. Why Bard Redfield hated his father so much was a mystery, but it did create a sort of a job opening.

Resnick was exactly the kind of guy a father would be proud of. At least a father who wasn't like his own asshole father.

Resnick was going to do Redfield's bidding and make himself indispensable and move up in the world. Right up to the right-hand side of the most powerful man in the world.

He sat for a moment in the California sunshine, hands dangling over the steering wheel, and let the images run through his head. Money and power, his for the asking. Women too. Women followed money and power like pigs to the trough. They were programmed for it. Resnick was on a trajectory that led right to the top.

Since he'd joined Redfield's private army his domestic bank account had swelled, but it was a shadow of what he had stashed abroad. He owned his own condo in DC but he also owned a working ranch in Argentina, a beachfront property in Aruba and a hotel in Tirana. All in the name of a holding company no one could trace back to him. Redfield himself had showed him how.

There was more, much more, ahead of him. He just had to not fuck up. He'd fucked up — once! — in the military and had barely avoided a court martial but it had been the best thing to happen to him. Court Redfield had recognized talent and had scooped him up.

And Court Redfield would soon be the most powerful man in the world, so that worked out just fine.

Resnick shook himself. He was here for a purpose, not to daydream about marvelous futures. Though it was hard not to, hard not to look around this hardscrabble trailer park and reflect on how far he'd come. Because this was exactly the kind of place he'd come from. Where dreams had been ground into the dust so long ago they were barely memories.

He got out of the SUV and stuck his Colt 1911 in his waistband, smoothing his jacket over it. He wore extra-thin leather shooting gloves. The Colt was scrubbed of all identifying marks and he'd loaded it using latex gloves. If anything happened, nothing could connect him to the gun and the gun itself would disappear in pieces thrown out the window over a radius of miles.

There were plenty more guns where that came from. His boss could choose from a whole arsenal of untraceables.

There was plenty of everything, actually. Weapons, IDs, hardware, money, transport. He had access to it all, and it was all the best. The only thing Resnick had to do was not fuck up.

Be a weapon. Point and shoot.

Resnick did a careful scan, 360°. There were no security cameras and hadn't been since he turned off onto the country road. There had been three on the road from the city but none here.

No cameras and no people.

The place looked deserted, but it wasn't. There were ancient rusted cars up on blocks but there were also a few working vehicles in sight. They were old and battered, but in use.

All the trailer homes were locked up tight but there were signs of life. A trash-can barbecue with an irregular pile of chopped wood to one side. Dingy stained sheets flapping in the wind, hung from a line of plastic cord running from a trailer to a nearby tree. A supermarket pot of daisies on a rickety porch. There could well be people inside but they were probably sleeping off a bender or high.

Resnick knew these people. They were his people. He knew what the trailer homes were like inside. He knew what they smelled like. He knew that many trailers would have a plastic tarp taped over the window frames instead of glass. He knew the residents all had substance abuse problems, impulse control problems, mental problems. Problems with the law and with what was in their heads. They'd been his people once, but not any more. He'd grown up in a trailer park marginally better than this one, but just as hopeless and ugly. Ten years ago, walking around this place would have given him the creeps, as if he'd been pulled back into the hell he'd grown up in. Now, he felt nothing. This place had no power over him. He was someone else, someone with no connections to this kind of place, where hope died an ugly death.

He was a warrior. A top-level security contractor who would soon be the right-hand man of the president of the United States. Nothing at all to do with the hungry, thin boy, son of Jimbo Resnick, alcoholic mechanic who couldn't keep a job and who was a sadist. Whose son was terrified of him. That boy was gone.

He straightened his shoulders and started walking the trailer park in a grid. North to south. East to west. Nobody came out of the trailer homes to challenge him. He didn't even hear human voices, just a dog barking in the distance.

When he finished, he stopped in the middle of the intersection of a couple of dusty paths. One led to what maybe had been a small canteen or grocery shop. One led to what had once been a swimming pool but was now cracked cement with putrid green scum on the bottom.

This was his one lead and it went nowhere. Resnick didn't know where to go after this, so he needed to squeeze this intel until something popped out. He was not going to disappoint Senator Redfield.

He took another 360° scan of the area. Deserted and silent and run down. What would anyone do with this place? It was dead. Well, maybe not quite dead. There were a few signs of life and if people lived here, then there had to be a manager, of sorts. Someone to pay the monthly rent to, someone to intervene if there were fights.

Where he'd grown up, the manager had been a big bruiser, more like a bouncer than a manager. If the water wasn't running, he wasn't your guy. If you didn't pay, though, he got right in your face. This place had to have a guy like that. Even legally, someone had to be in charge.

He set out to find that guy and finally, down a path that could barely be seen, he came across a cabin that was badly maintained and needed a coat of paint. It was isolated, fairly far from most of the trailers. You'd have to want to come here, you wouldn't stumble across it. There was nothing around it anyone would want to see.

Which was fine, in Resnick's book.

A board was nailed to the wooden siding. There was writing on it, in faded paint. Manager, Happy Trails Trailer Park. If it was Resnick's call, he wouldn't advertise that he was the manager of this shithole. It wasn't anything to be proud of.

He walked slowly up to the porch, hands out and loose. Nobody could see the 1911 in his waistband, or the ankle holster, or the Todd knife in its Kydex sheath clipped to the inside of his front right pocket, which he kept sharp as a scalpel.

The door opened with a creak. A man stood just inside the doorway, his face in shadow. It was hard to make out his features and Resnick was sure that was deliberate.

They stood staring at each other. Resnick took his measure. Tall, old, very skinny. He looked malnourished, like someone who didn't take care of himself. Resnick needed intel this guy probably had. He could beat it out of him, trick it out of him or buy it from him.

"Whaddya want?" The man asked. Not even a stab at *Can I help you?* "We're full up."

Sure, Resnick thought. *Bustling little business you've got here. Don't know how you can manage it all.*

"Don't need a slot," he said. Slowly, keeping both hands in view, he pulled a photo out of his shirt pocket. The reason he was here. The first time he'd seen the photo, it hadn't clicked. It was just one woman, like a million others. Maybe prettier than most but the world was full of pretty women. What did the Senator want with her? Maybe she'd seen something or maybe she'd heard something? Maybe they'd fucked and she wanted money. For whatever reason, the Senator wanted her dead, so Resnick was going to kill her.

But then he'd looked again and realized exactly what was going on.

She looked exactly like the Senator's son, Bard.

Who'd clearly had an accident with a condom twenty-five or thirty years ago.

Resnick held the photo out in the palm of his hand. His left hand. His right was down by his side, fist open. Ready to reach for his weapon at any moment. He hoped it wouldn't come to that. Yet.

The old man frowned. "What's that?" he asked, pointing to Resnick's hand. Resnick walked forward a few steps and held his palm up shoulder high. The photograph was clear at that distance.

The old man was shaking his head but Resnick had seen the slight step back, the widening of rheumy blue eyes. The wrinkles around his mouth had tightened.

"You ever see this woman around here?" he asked.

"Nope. Never seen her before in my life." The old man was already backing away, about ready to slam the door in Resnick's face. Not that that would stop him. The old door was essentially cracked plywood. A strong wind could bring it down.

The old man was shuffling as he moved back into the cabin, trying to shut the cabin door, but Resnick was fast and he was strong. The old man didn't — *couldn't* — put up anything Resnick recognized as resistance. In a moment, the old man was sitting in a kitchen chair, tied down with duct tape that had been on a kitchen counter. If it hadn't been there, Resnick would have used the filthy kitchen towels draped over the sink, or an electrical cord ripped off a lamp.

Anything would have done. Resnick had been trained and trained well and knew how to improvise. This was nothing. The old man was weak and terrified. Resnick could have kept him in the chair through intimidation alone.

But that would have taken longer and Resnick didn't want to waste any more time here than he had to. The place depressed the hell out of him.

The old man was panting. He'd put up a little resistance and it had tired him out. His face was covered in sweat and his chest was heaving. Shit, he had to get intel before the old man's heart blew.

Man, Resnick was going to eat a bullet before he got like that.

Casually, he placed the muzzle of his 1911 right on the old guy's knee and watched as his face froze. Yep, he had the geezer's attention. He knew what a bullet to the knee meant.

Resnick pressed down on the gun to give his words a little added meaning.

"Okay, this is what I want. The woman in that picture is Hope Ellis. She was here. I could see you recognized her. I want to know exactly when she was here and what she said and you'd better give it to me straight because otherwise ..." He smiled down into those weeping eyes, listening to the man's terrified wheezing. "You know the rest. Now talk."

A quarter of an hour later, he walked back out the door.

So — Hope Ellis had been here yesterday. The

old man chased her off quickly. She'd been accompanied by a man the geezer described as 'tall and strong'. Which could mean anything. A boyfriend? But the background info the Senator had provided on Hope Ellis didn't include a boyfriend, tall and strong or otherwise. So that was an unknown quantity. The boyfriend wasn't armed or surely he would have pulled it.

The thing was, the geezer recognized her. He didn't know her as Hope Ellis but as Cathy Benson, a little girl who'd lived with her single mother here in the trailer park maybe twenty-five years ago but had died, together with her mother, in a car accident. The geezer wasn't absolutely sure when. Wasn't sure about anything but the fact that she'd died. Still, the little girl had been very pretty and had had dark hair, green eyes and a narrow face just like Hope Ellis. And the photograph was of the woman he'd seen yesterday. He was sure of that.

The geezer had been crying by the time he told it all to Resnick, who'd interrogated hundreds of prisoners. Terror and weeping did not make a man a good source of intel. Sometimes they lied, just to give something up.

If so, tough luck.

When Resnick was absolutely certain the man had given him everything he knew, he pulled the Todd knife and carefully slid it right in between the third and fourth rib, straight into the heart, and watched as the geezer died. It was a quick death, for which the old man should have been grateful. Quick and clean. No bleeding, all the blood stayed inside the chest cavity.

On entering the cabin, Resnick had noticed a nice collection of cheap rotgut whiskey bottles that were mostly empty. One was still three-quarters full, and doubtless would have been just another empty by nightfall. Resnick carefully carried the body to the messy, smelly cot and laid the man down. He poured the contents of the bottle on some dirty blankets he placed over the dead body and lit them up.

He stayed long enough to make sure the fire caught and would burn the hut down completely.

When the fire brigade came, they'd find what was probably a common scene in these difficult times. An old man, living in poverty, who drank too much, setting himself on fire with the cheap cigar Resnick had found and placed on the bed, leaving the box of matches on the floor next to the bed.

The police would come and stay maybe half an hour. Maybe.

Sacramento, like most cities these days, was strapped for cash. Police departments were understaffed and underpaid. They'd take in what had happened in a glance — sad old man getting drunk and smoking in bed. Nothing to see here, folks. Move on.

Autopsies cost around five grand and Medicare didn't cover it. Resnick was betting the old man had no family to demand and pay for an autopsy. The authorities would find a charred cadaver no one cared about and no one was going to probe around the burned skin for puncture wounds. Burned corpses were disgusting. Resnick had seen a lot of them while operational. They were grotesque and stank. Only the most hardened coroner would want anything to do with a burned body.

Resnick had extracted what he could from the geezer and was good to go.

He'd already muddied his license plates, front and back. He was riding a Suburban, black, like a billion other Suburbans out there. True, a Suburban in a place like this was unusual, but he had an app for that, literally. He pulled up a surveyor's map of the area and sent up a mini drone, overlapping the drone's footage with the map on his tablet.

There was another way out that intersected with the highway ten miles up. But it was entirely possible that video cameras along the main highway had caught him driving into the trailer park. But if so, they'd also have caught Hope Ellis and whoever was with her.

He sat in his truck and quickly worked the problem. He had the exact GPS coordinates of three of the closest videocams. They were connected to the Traffic Department of the Municipality of Sacramento. Sacramento had not spent much on cybersecurity, that was for sure. It took him a quarter of an hour working from his phone, and he was in the entire system.

Hope Ellis and the man had been here the day

before, so he ran footage from 9 am onward. The closest videocam on the highway didn't cover the actual turnoff. He had to deduce it by the turning on of the indicator light. Resnick himself switched on the indicator light at the very last minute, out of habit. He'd trained himself to always consider himself followed and rarely gave much advance notice as to what he was going to do. Some people were like him. Others turned on the lights five minutes before turning.

There were two hundred twenty cars in the time frame between 9 am and 5 pm. This was going to require a bigger and better monitor than his phone and was going to take time.

On his way back to the motel room that hadn't bothered with ID and whose surveillance cameras were switched off, he stopped by a drive-through hamburger place, making sure his cap's bill hid his face. He drove to the motel, ate his cheeseburger and went to work.

Four hours later, he had seven cars that were possible. Three had a single passenger. He grabbed the license plates of the four that were left. Three were registered in Sacramento to private citizens and the fourth was a corporate car he couldn't see into.

He sat back, thinking. A corporate car. Sounded right. Owned by a company registered in Aruba. Which was owned by two other companies. From experience, Resnick knew that this was a rabbit hole. He wasn't going to find out anything by chasing down who owned the car on paper. That was irrelevant. He was going to get somewhere by chasing down the car itself.

It was going to take time. He was going to have to monitor all the traffic cams in Sacramento. Luckily, he had a program that could speed it up but it would still take a long time.

After five hours, he ordered a steak and fries from a nearby diner and then got back down to work, knowing it would probably take all night.

Sooner or later he'd find Hope Ellis and the guy. And smoke them. Court Redfield had been very clear on that.

This was important to Redfield. Resnick knew he'd move way up that greasy pole if he accomplished this mission. Just the thought of being the power behind the throne to the President of the United States gave him goosebumps. The Presidency was such a long long way from the trailer park he'd grown up in.

Oh yeah, he'd accomplish this mission. Hope Ellis was a dead woman walking.

Thirteen

How was she expected to reason her way through this with Luke ... right there? Right in her face? So very handsome, even with that grim expression. How could he be so good looking yet so very serious? All the good looking men Hope had ever seen had expressions ranging from smiling to sulky but not serious. And they'd been on screens or in glossy magazines, never in meatspace. And certainly never so close to her.

Really close. She'd spent all night with her nose right up against his skin, with his body close up against her. And a lot of time with him *inside* her. She knew how he smelled. Some intoxicating blend of soap and testosterone that should be classified as a Schedule 1 drug, certainly addictive for anyone possessing two X chromosomes. Should absolutely be against the law.

If every male on earth smelled like that, felt like that, no work would get done. Ever. Women would just sit around, smelling and touching their males.

Not that Luke was *her* male. He was ... she had no idea what he was to her. He hadn't run screaming after they'd made love, there was that. Any of the times. She hadn't had men run screaming from her bed, but most of them were more interested in her algorithms than in her. And she hadn't been all that impressed with her four — no, three lovers. One of them hadn't really been a lover, not in the technical sense of the term. He'd tried, but his systems had malfunctioned.

None of them had been even remotely like Luke.

The others had eventually left, but Luke hadn't. But then again, at the moment, he was professionally attached at the hip to her. Was he with her just because she was his job?

"You okay?"

Hope was jolted out of her thoughts by his low voice, thankful that her face was buried against his shoulder, so he couldn't see her blush. She was more than okay. It felt like she finally understood sex. Like she'd been eating wax fruit all these years and finally someone had handed her an apple. A real one, juicy and sweet.

Mmmm.

She ran his words around her head, trying to focus. Was she okay?

Why yes, yes she was. She was more than okay.

"I'm fine," she said, smiling. There wasn't much to smile about. A good friend had been murdered because he knew something about her past. Geraldo had died because of something in her past. That past was murky, unknown, and was reaching out with clawed fingers to catch her and drag her down.

And yet.

And yet here she was in the arms of the most attractive man she'd ever seen, who'd loved her all night and who was still holding her tightly. She'd come to know his body almost as well as her own. To know the smell of his skin, the way he'd tighten his arms each time she moved. His taste when he kissed her. The way the light caught on the dark blond hairs on his chest and the light hairs along his forearms.

He was incredibly strong. The muscles she was touching were hard as wood, though warm. She felt like a fairy-tale princess behind magic walls, protected from the dragons outside.

Luke pulled away and tucked his chin down to look her in the eyes. She met his gaze calmly.

"You sure?"

"Yeah." She said the words on a sigh and rested her cheek against his shoulder.

It was true. Hope was a planner. To do her job, she needed to keep a lot of data in her head and it all had to be structured. Time was one of the elements she kept in her head and it was omnipresent in all her processing. Her life was one eternal timeline. But right now, it felt like she had stepped outside of time. There was no past and no future, just an eternal now, wrapped in a strong man's arms.

Not to mention the fact that those strong arms seemed to have swept away all the thoughts in her head. Though right now she didn't need thoughts so much as the man himself.

Wow. That was primitive thinking. One night of really good sex regressed her about ten thousand years, punching her right back into the Stone Age.

But — how on earth could she have known? Have realized what it meant to be *held?* Her parents had never hugged her, not that she could recall. Her best friends, Felicity, Riley and Emma, hugged her but she hadn't seen any of them for two years now. What few boyfriends she'd had weren't big touchers. One had been so awkward he never touched her until he'd lunged at her suddenly, having worked up the courage to do so entirely inside his own head. He'd essentially humped her through their clothes like a German shepherd humping the couch pillow.

Not huggers, any of them.

Oh man, it was so great being held. She didn't have to do anything. She was draped over Luke bonelessly, touching as much of him with as much of her as possible. They smelled of sex and each other. She could hear his heartbeat against her ear and feel it against her skin. He had one long strong arm around her back, stroking her buttocks and one big hand against the back of her head.

Hope realized that for the very first time in her life she felt *safe*. There was someone else between her and the world, this world that was sometimes cruel and always cold and indifferent and had lately been trying to take big bites out of her.

Luke wasn't cruel and he wasn't cold and indifferent. For now, at least. And what else was there but the now?

"I'm glad you're okay." Luke pressed a kiss to the top of her head and let his own head fall back to the pillow. "I, um, I haven't had a lot of practice lately. That first time, I didn't know if I'd remember how to do it right."

A laugh exploded out of her.

"That's funny?" he asked, voice lazy, ruffling her hair.

"Yeah, that's really funny. I think I've had a lot less practice than you and with, um, guys whose main relationship is and always will be more with their computers than with real life women."

His hand stopped. "That's so weird."

She frowned. "What's weird?"

He lifted his head again. "You're so beautiful and so smart. I can't imagine any man not wanting to take you to bed."

She traced the line of his pecs with a finger. Man, this was a *chest*. He had this intriguing valley between his pecs, a little scrum of blond hairs softening the skin and arrowing down to … um … oh yeah. "That's really nice of you to say that, but you don't need to flatter me."

"Whoa." He blinked, surprised. "I'm not flattering you, Hope. I'm assuming you sometimes look into a mirror. You're gorgeous. Just ... perfect. The only women I've seen who are as good looking as you are, are the wives and girlfriends of my teammates at ASI. They all seem to have lucked out in the female department."

"Felicity's very pretty," Hope agreed.

"You're prettier." She looked up at him in surprise. Luke's mouth was set, as if stating a law. What he was saying was ridiculous but Hope didn't want to argue it. And anyway what he was saying was flattering. Untrue, but flattering. No one had ever flattered her looks before. Her mind, yes. Absolutely. Her gaming skills, sure. But looks? Nope.

But somehow Luke, this amazingly handsome man, seemed taken with her looks. Who was she to look a gift horse in the mouth?

In the earthquake that was her life, she was taking it moment by moment. Pretty soon they'd have to get out of bed and start working on the mystery of her past, on the puzzle of her parentage. And there wasn't going to be a happy ending, guaranteed. Sometime in the past, people had abandoned her as a little girl. Just left her. Hope would find out how and maybe who, but not why. There was no why. There was no way that was justifiable.

So there was pain and sadness in her immediate future. But not right now. Nope. Right now, there was warmth and strength and, judging from the growing column of flesh hardening against her thigh, sex.

Their eyes met and again, there was this momentous electric connection. She could almost feel her molecules melding with his, it was that profound. He'd been looking at her with a soft gaze but all of a sudden his gaze sharpened, features tightening. Two days ago she wouldn't have recognized that look. She'd have put it down to him suddenly solving a complex math problem or the soldierly equivalent. Now she was familiar with it.

It was very specific and it meant that mind-blowing sex was on its way. Coming soon.

Luke shifted a little and rolled over so that she was under him. Oh yeah. The missionary position. She was all for it, even though apparently some people found it boring. Hope couldn't even imagine being bored with the missionary position. It was, if anything, even too exciting. Her arms were around his neck, holding him close. She'd tried to put her arms around his shoulders but they were too broad. She ended up holding onto his shoulder in the storm of sex, simply to keep herself grounded. He was very heavy for someone so lean, all this delicious weight bearing down on her, his broad shoulders blocking out the world.

Her legs opened automatically and he settled between them, so naturally. As if it were his rightful place in the world. And he slid right in, certain of his welcome.

His face was right above hers now, smiling down into her eyes, a devilish cast to his features All that grimness gone, replaced by heat and desire.

Oh God, yes.

She lifted herself slightly and his mouth covered hers. Their mouths met with almost a physical click, perfect. Their mouths were made for this, for this exact kiss.

Both of them sighed at the same time, then laughed, their bellies meeting.

And then it all went to hell.

"I think —" Luke began and his cell rang. The refrain of *Wild Thing*. At that moment, Hope hated Jimi Hendrix, who'd died twenty years before she'd been born. If she could have, she'd have exhumed him, resuscitated him and then strangled him.

They looked at each other for a second, two, as the refrain started up again. Luke's head hung down between his shoulders in defeat.

"I have to get that," he said apologetically. "It's the ring tone for ASI. Maybe they have news."

"Yeah." Hope looked to the side so he wouldn't see the disappointment in her eyes. They were on borrowed time. Maybe there wouldn't ever be a chance to make love again.

Her entire body protested when he slid out of her. When Luke lifted himself away, she felt cold, as if a blanket of ice had descended. She unfurled her hands, a moment ago full of warm hard male, now clutching the covers instead of Luke.

She reached down and pulled on the sweater and jeans next to the bed, plucking them from the floor where they fell the night before.

He rolled over and grabbed the cell on the night stand, right next to his gun. She'd noticed that he'd never been far from that gun. Like she was never far from her laptop.

He pulled on his tee and jeans, really fast.

Luke glanced at the screen and his face tightened, that grim look back.

"Felicity, talk to me."

Hope startled, sat up to look over his shoulder. Felicity's pretty face filled the screen. She was in an office.

"I didn't dare call Hope's cell so I called you. Can you pass me to her?"

"Sure." Luke turned and passed her his cell. "Put it on speakerphone."

She did, keeping it so they could both watch the monitor. She kept the video function off, though probably up in Portland it would be clear that they were really close to each other. It was still fairly early in the morning. They weren't dummies at ASI.

Felicity didn't make any suggestive comments at all. She looked pale and worried. "Honey? Our system is under attack."

Hope frowned, turned the video function on. "Another DoS?" Troubling but not devastating.

Felicity shook her head. "Multi-vector volumetric DDoS."

A Distributed Denial of Service. Now, *that* was serious. "Against ASI? Your company? Why?"

Felicity's mouth turned down. "We — I — suspect it has to do with you."

Hope met Luke's grim gaze. Turned back to the screen. "Me?"

"Yeah. Under the DDoS, someone is probing our activities over the past three days. And —" She hesitated which was totally unlike Felicity.

"Yeah?"

"There was a search for your name. Specifically. It's an attack aimed at crashing our system while finding out information about you in stealth mode. It was hard to catch."

"How —" Hope's mouth was dry. "How could they possibly know?"

She felt a tremor begin deep in her body, coming from the very core of her, her insides freezing. All that warmth from last night dissipating like a spaceship leaking heat in deep space. Inside her was a dark and airless space and she recognized it as something she'd lived with all her life. The past two days were an exception.

Felicity shook her head. "Somehow they — whoever they are — found out about our friendship. Emma and Riley have been hacked, too. Or attempts have been made. Emma's bank and Riley's company are undergoing a DDoS, too."

"Jesus," Hope breathed. This was — this was almost worse than Kyle being killed. She'd been fond of Kyle. But she loved Felicity and Emma and Riley. If anything happened to them because of her …

She jumped as something warm and heavy fell across her shoulders. Luke's arm.

She glanced up at him, at that grim unsmiling mouth. He looked pissed.

"Goddamn," he said, a muscle twitching in his cheek. "Is there any way to find out the origin?"

"No." Felicity's voice was sad. "It's coming from various sources —"

Hope straightened. "Actually," she said, "there might be a way. I developed a program that searches for underlying constants in data streams. A DDoS usually ramps up. When did it start?"

"Two hours ago. We were all asleep. I was in bed. I set up an alert system to ping me and it did at 7:07 this morning."

"I'm so sorry, Felicity. Just when you need your rest. This is all my fault."

Felicity waved her hand. "It's not," she said fiercely. "It's not your fault."

"Damn right," Luke growled. "It's this fucker's fault, not yours."

Hope drew in a deep breath, held it, let it out in a long slow stream, just like she'd been taught in the yoga course she took many years ago while working at the NSA. The course hadn't lasted. Yoga had proved a flimsy defense against the massive stress of her job.

"Okay. Felicity, can you send me your records of the first five minutes of the attack? Was it recorded?"

"Of course. Good thinking. The first five minutes

would be before the botnet was fully formed."

"Yeah. I have a program that does a data dive for constants. The bots will be shifting but there will be constants in the command and control structure. I designed it as a tool to find stuff in massive streams of data, with a low signal-to-noise ratio. But it will work here, too. Let's see if we can also trace it back to its origin. I'm sending it to you now."

"Right now they're masking," Felicity warned. "Bouncing around the world."

"Of course they are. But I think if we let the program work, give it some time, it can trace the origins, too."

"So this is another of your programs, Ms. Ellis?" A new voice. Basso profundo, almost too deep for her speakers. A man appeared. Very ugly, with a crooked welt of a scar on his jaw. Hope knew who he was. Felicity had given her a run down of the bosses of ASI. Douglas Kowalski. Some called him 'the Senior' because of his former rank in the Navy. Hope had no idea how 'senior' could be a rank, but still. Ugly and ferocious-looking, he was one of the good guys.

"Hope, please."

Douglas Kowalski had a voice like God. God wouldn't address her as Ms. Ellis.

The man dipped his head slightly. It was as if he were in the room, looking her right in the eyes. She was glad she was on his good side because he looked fierce enough to eat her for breakfast if she were his enemy.

"Hope. Judging by the noises Felicity here is making —" he nodded his head at Felicity. She could see a slice of Felicity's intent face, staring at her computer. "That program is something else. Can we buy it off you? Or at least pay you for the use? I understand it protects against —" He side-eyed Felicity.

"DDoS." Her voice was preoccupied. She didn't look away from the screen.

The Senior nodded. "What she said."

"God no!" Hope held her hands up. "We've gone over this before. You and your company are helping me figure out what's going on, probably saving my life. You're under attack now because of *me*. You're welcome to anything I've developed. Now and ever will develop. To the end of time."

He hung his head for a moment, jaws working. As if he were chewing on a problem. He lifted his head suddenly and seemingly looked her straight in the eyes. "Well, how about this? Can we offer you a job?"

Hope's jaw fell open. "A *what?*"

"A job," he replied. "You know. You work for us and we pay you. Felicity here says that you are super smart and a hard worker. Coming from her, that's incredible praise. And she said that already the two programs you've sent are worth a lot of money. From what I understand, you didn't like the job you had. Felicity will tell you what working with us is like." Suddenly a slender hand appeared on the screen next to his cheek, with a thumb up. Something like a smile appeared on his face. "Our conditions are good and Felicity needs a hand. Not only now but after her twins are born. She's got too big a work load as it is. We'd love to have you."

A sudden elbow in her ribs nearly knocked her to the floor. Luke, turning to her with a fierce expression, bright blue eyes nearly glowing. "Say yes!" he urged. "You'll love it at ASI. Say yes!"

She couldn't tear her gaze away from him.

"Yes," he prompted, nudging her with his shoulder.

"Ahm ... yes?" she answered.

Luke fist-pumped and the Senior's mouth twitched, which Hope interpreted as a smile. She had long experience interpreting nerd body language. Soldier body language was different but sort of the same. She suspected they had issues expressing their emotions as much as nerds did.

"Excellent," the Senior said. "Felicity's carrying too heavy a load right now so I'm glad that she has someone as good as she is to help carry it."

"*Almost* as good as she is," Hope corrected with a smile.

"I heard that! No way!" Felicity's voice floated in the background. "As good as or better."

Hope rolled her eyes and shook her head.

"Either way we're looking forward to welcoming you to ASI, Hope," the Senior said. "You already had our attention and the full resources of the company at your disposal, so that doesn't change. I understand that as soon as your present troubles are over, you'll need to relocate and that will take time, but consider yourself on our payroll as of right now."

Hope's eyes rounded. "Wait! That's not …"

But he'd disappeared and all she saw was Felicity's pretty face. She was pale but had an ironic smile on her face. "That's the Senior. He and Midnight are the closest things to God on this earth. Welcome aboard the Good Ship ASI. It's great here."

Her voice was light, but looking closer Hope could see the lines of fatigue on her face. She was too pale and though she was halfway through a difficult pregnancy, she looked like she'd lost weight, not put any on. Luke had said that though she felt sick, she insisted on working just as hard as she could. If she couldn't come in to work, she worked from home. She'd clearly gone in to work early this morning.

Hope imagined she'd welcome a hand and was very happy to give it. Happy to take some of the load off. Felicity had always been a good friend to her and now it was time to pay that back.

Plus — a new job. With new challenges. And, um, working with Luke.

Yeah, that.

Luke encouraged her to take it but who knew what he was thinking?

But … working with Luke.

Felicity was staring into the camera, head slightly cocked. There was only one thing Hope could say.

"Glad to be on board, honey. As soon as we —" She drew in a deep breath, searching for the right words. "As soon as we sort all of this out, we'll be up there and I'll pick up the slack."

Felicity blew out a breath. Her face relaxed and she almost looked like her old self. "The company keeps a studio apartment for new hires until they can find something they want. So you'll have a place to stay."

Hope blinked. She'd changed jobs and cities twice and no new employer had showed even the slightest interest in where she lived or if she had trouble finding an apartment.

"Wow. That's ah —"

"Yeah." Felicity gave her a blinding smile and there was some real relief in there. She was happy Hope was coming but clearly she was also happy that there was someone she could offload some of the work to. "It's a great place to work. You'll love it." She suddenly turned sheet white. "Whoa. Sorry. Gotta run."

Hope didn't have a chance to say goodbye, the screen simply blackened.

"She went to barf," Luke said sadly. "She's been doing a lot of that. Metal just hates it but he's helpless to stop it."

Poor poor Felicity. Hope herself had always been really healthy and had thrown up exactly twice in her life. The experience had been worse than horrible. Vomiting several times a day? For *months?* No, thanks.

Luke bent and gave her a quick kiss. Lifted his mouth and frowned. Bent and gave her a longer kiss and everything just melted away. All her troubles, the mysteries surrounding the past, the DNA — all of it gone. Up in smoke. It was impossible to remember fear and anxiety while in his arms. The only thing she could perceive was his soft lips surrounded by wiry stubble that gave her that tingle of contrasting textures. His tongue was soft, the hands holding her were hard.

He was hard all over. Holding him never got old. Her mind simply disappeared as she turned into a creature of skin and blood and hormones. Heat and desire.

He was infinitely dangerous. A bomb could have gone off in the room and she wouldn't have noticed.

Luke lifted his head and frowned down at her. "You're dangerous, woman."

Hope laughed and pushed at his shoulders. "I was just thinking the same thing about you. That you're dangerous."

"Yeah?" That had him smiling. "I definitely am. I'm a really good shot."

"Not dangerous that way. My whole life is upended. I am maybe related to a criminal. Someone who wants me dead, anyway. I'm definitely not who I thought I was. I seem to have just accepted a job across the country from my home on the basis of maybe a two-minute interview. And all I could think about was you."

He was holding her upper arms, which was probably a good thing because her instinct was to just lean forward and rest her head on those luscious pecs. Just let it all go. Relinquish any attempt at control. Let him take care of everything. Which was the most un-Hope-like thought she'd ever had. She was used to taking care of herself, had been doing it for as long as she could remember. She never put her troubles in anyone's hands.

Except, apparently, now.

He was looking down at her and managed to both smile and scowl at the same time.

"What?"

He bent to kiss the tip of her nose. Which no one had ever done. Hope wasn't used to being cuddled.

"So I guess we'll be colleagues now."

"Mm."

"And fraternization and flirting on the job are frowned on."

Her eyes widened. This was the very first time she'd ever been faced with the idea of a romantic work relationship. Or was it a romantic relationship at work? Work romance? Whatever the hell they were called.

Man. She'd just found Luke and was now expected to treat him like some remote relative? That was going to hurt.

"Okay."

"Unless ..." he said.

Unless ... Hope was running alternatives through her processor and wasn't finding any. "Unless?"

"Unless we go in as a couple. Already established, that way no one could say anything. Like Felicity and Metal. They just started like that and no one questioned it."

Her mind whirred emptily. Was he saying what she thought he was saying? He couldn't be, could he?

Luke reached out a long finger and gently closed her jaw, which had dropped. "For a smart lady, you're looking really clueless."

She nodded. Yep. Anything she said could be completely wrong if she was reading this the wrong way.

"I am suggesting that we become a couple. Like — a real one. That people know about." He frowned. "Fuck. That sounded really awkward. But I think you know what I mean."

She nodded. Continued to stare up at him.

"So, ahm, how about it?"

She just looked at him, without even blinking.

"Hope?" He waved a hand in front of her face. "Are you in there?"

She was, she was. She was just frozen. He was proposing — what? She couldn't even picture it. Hope hadn't ever been part of a couple, not for anything more than a week, if that. And to be a couple inside a group of people who were friends, well ...

For a moment, a strange feeling shot through her, zipping along her nerves, so intense she felt it skimming over her skin, thrumming through her entire body.

Happiness. Pure, radiant joy. She never thought much about the future but in that instant she had a vision of herself working with Felicity, a good friend, with Luke, her whatever-he-was-to-her. With the rest of the gang that Felicity said was really great. A whole building of *friends*. Plus Luke.

Maybe going out in the evenings, together. Or seeing them on the weekend.

Plus Luke.

To *belong*. To him, to that life.

It was a vision of her own future better than any she'd ever had before and it was almost scary how much she wanted it. Terrifying, because once she'd seen her future — or at least *that* future — nothing else would do. Anything else seemed cold and barren and lifeless.

She'd gone ahead and projected her desires on a blank canvas, something she never did. She made a point of not wanting things so she wouldn't be disappointed. It always worked, but somehow that mechanism suddenly broke. Shattered into a million pieces.

She wanted this. She wanted it fiercely.

This was so freaking scary.

"Hey." Luke pulled her to him and it was exactly what she needed, that sense of sinking into him, fitting in beneath his skin. Reassured by the feel of his heart beating beneath her ear, strong and steady. A beat a second. "Is this about us being a couple? I'm pretty easy to get on with, promise. Are you scared?"

"No." Whether it worked or not, she suddenly realized she wanted a shot at coupledom. With Luke and no one else.

"Good," he grunted and held her more tightly. They stood there until her own heartbeat slowed, matched his.

He kissed her hair. "About the job. It'll be fine. Promise. You'll be treated like a princess."

She smiled against his shirt. "They already treat Felicity like a queen."

He bent his head until his chin rested on the top of hers. "They do. Rightly. Whatever perks you had in your previous job, they'll top them. The Senior and Midnight have been looking for someone to help Felicity for a while. And now that they've found her — you — they'll make sure you want to stay. And trust me when I say no one will harass you. Ever."

Her jobs had all been high powered and interesting but the human element had always been missing. This sounded like the job of her dreams. Nobody could chase her away.

But he thought she needed convincing and tightened his arms around her. "And like I said, they pay well. Really well."

She sighed, her chest lifting and falling. "I don't care."

It was true. They could pay her a dollar a year and she'd still take the job. There were a lot of things to worry about, including someone trying to kill her, but money wasn't one of them.

He sighed and she followed the movements of that magnificent chest. He should sigh more often while she was holding him. Just sigh all the time, his chest expanding under her arms. "You might not care now but money is useful. As a matter of fact—" He pulled away and looked down at her. "This might be a good moment to confess that I don't have any."

Oh god, he was just so handsome, like a fierce Viking that could turn unexpectedly tender.

"What? Any what?"

"Money." He smiled at her. Her mind completely disengaged and for a moment she forgot what money was even for. He gave a crooked smile. "I don't have any. The lawyers ate everything I had and all my dad's savings. All I have is a little trust fund my grandmother left me and that my dad refused to touch and refused to allow me to touch. But it's ok. Like I said, ASI pays really well and I'll be back on my feet by the end of the year. Don't worry about it."

She blinked. "Money? I'm not worried about it. As a matter of fact —" she stopped, embarrassed.

He heard the change in tone and pulled his head back. "As a matter of fact …?"

This was just one more tile in the mosaic of befuddlement that formed part of her life. Before she told him, she held on to his forearms. Maybe in an attempt to read him, feel his reaction. Under her fingers the muscles were clear and defined, like an anatomy text.

Maybe she could read his emotions, too.

Tilting her head back, she watched his face carefully. "As a matter of fact, I'm —" her throat tightened and she coughed to loosen it up. "I'm rich."

If she was expecting some big reaction, she was disappointed. His eyebrows rose. That was it. "You're rich? Good for you."

"Unexpectedly rich. I've been living off my earnings for years, since my first job. When my — my parents died, I received a notice in the mail that there were two bank accounts in my name at a bank based in Luxembourg that had a branch office in Boston."

Now he was scowling. "That's weird."

"Thank you. It is, isn't it? What was even more weird was the amounts. Ten million dollars in one account and about half a million in the other. And the names. The accounts had names. The ten million dollar account was in my name, only it was Hope Catherine Ellis."

"I don't think that's so weird. You have to assign an identifying name to accounts, so I guess your parents just put your name on the account."

"Well, that's the thing. That's not my name."

He frowned. "Hope Ellis isn't your name?"

"Yes, it is. But my name isn't Hope Catherine Ellis. I'm like Jack Reacher with no middle name. Hope No Middle Name Ellis. I don't know where the Catherine comes in. But it's not my name."

"Does that make a difference? I mean, you could

call an account Numbnuts and it wouldn't matter. If it's yours, it's yours. Right?"

She nodded.

"What's the other one called?"

"Something *really* weird." Hope pulled away from him, a little unsettled. Talking about this just reminded her of all the question marks in her life that looked like they would never be answered. She hated it that these bank accounts, popping up out of nowhere, messed so much with her head. She didn't need the money, she didn't *want* the money. Her needs were fairly modest and her skills were such that she'd always earn more than she needed. In the past couple of years alone, she'd socked away over 200K. She didn't like having too many clothes because it just made her decision tree longer and harder every morning. She totally got Zuckerberg with his hundred identical gray tees. A bigger apartment just meant more to clean. The things she loved — dinners with her few friends, movies and books and brand new tech — she could easily afford and she didn't want things she couldn't afford.

She could tell Luke was the same way. Not once had he mentioned money in connection to himself. He'd been wiped out financially, but the man clearly had serious skills and was confident he'd be okay by the end of the year. Because that was what he was, what they both were — survivors. He didn't have expensive clothes, was comfortable in his skin. She was sure he was exactly the same whether he had ten dollars or ten million dollars in the bank.

That was massively attractive. The few non-nerds she'd dated had been climbers, fascinated by money. A couple of lawyers and three men in banking. One of the men in banking had been an analyst and they'd met on the job, both fascinated by numbers. Only to her, the flow of data itself had been what she was interested in, not particularly what the data represented. He was fascinated by the money. All of them ate money, slept money, breathed money. And it was essentially all they could talk about.

It had stopped her from sleeping with any of them. In most cases, it stopped her from accepting a second date.

In Hope's humble opinion, money was just about the most boring thing on the face of the earth, besides sports. You could only eat so much, only wear one set of clothes at a time.

Which was why she was more puzzled than delighted when she found out her parents — who at this point weren't her parents at all — had left her millions. She didn't need that much money. What she needed were answers.

Luke nudged her shoulder. He didn't seem to be put out when she disappeared inside her own head, which was an enormous mark in his favor. "Weird?"

"Huh?"

He smiled down at her. "You said the other bank account's name was weird. Or weirder than having it called by a name that is your name, only not."

"Yeah." Hope grabbed her laptop and moved to the living room. Luke followed. She opened up her home banking account. She didn't bother trying to hide the password. Luke was watching her, anyway, instead of what she was typing in. "So, first of all, it's strange having two bank accounts. Why two? They are both mine. Why split it into two accounts, one large and one smaller? One with my name plus an extra middle name and the other —"

She sat back to allow Luke to see the screen properly. He squinted. There were two accounts listed with their numbers and a name. One Hope Catherine Ellis and the other ...

"Immortals?"

Hope sighed. "Yep. Immortals. I googled it. Immortals is a movie about Greek gods, a fantasy sports league, another movie, this time about vampires. A series of fantasy books. The members of the French Academy are called The Immortals. But I can't see what any of that has to do with me."

"Wait." Luke scrunched his brow. "The Immortals. Huh. The Emperor of Persia's guards were called the Immortals."

She sat up. "Yeah? When was this?"

Luke put his hand on her shoulder. "About two thousand five hundred years ago. The Achemenid Empire. When I was a kid I was crazy about military history. The Immortals were an elite unit, ten thousand strong. They were ferocious. Think '300'."

"The movie or the graphic novel?"

"Both. They had really cool gear and they always numbered ten thousand. If someone died, or was seriously wounded or sick, another Immortal immediately took his place."

"Huh. That's interesting but I don't see —" Something lit up in her head. "Say that again."

"About the Immortals?"

She nodded. "About them being always ten thousand strong."

"Okay. They were essentially both the Imperial Guard and the standing army of the Persians. There were ten thousand of them. Always. Forever. Never less and never more than that. Any member of the elite force that died or was wounded or sick was immediately replaced from a separate force created as a pool to keep the main force at exactly ten thousand. It was why they were called the Immortals, as if no one ever died, because their ranks were never depleted."

"Oh my gosh." Hope scrolled through the financial history of the second, smaller account, Immortals. "These accounts were set up in 2013. Originally the larger account was ten million dollars, exactly. But you know keeping accounts costs money, they make you pay to keep your money for you. And they pay close to zero percent interest so the amounts go down slowly."

Luke nodded.

She pointed to the two amounts. "So the original ten million, deposited seven years ago, is now

$9,897,445. But the Immortals account has remained exactly the same, unchanging. Do you see?"

"Yeah. Someone went to a lot of trouble to keep that sum unchanged. So?"

"So, it's not a question of the money, per se. If it were, there'd only be one account. Splitting the money into two accounts makes no sense if it's about the money. But it makes a lot of sense if the Immortals account is about the number, not the money."

Something deep inside her started thrumming. The same something that happened when she solved a tricky software issue or saw a pattern in the data. Only more this time. Stronger. She could feel her heart beating in her chest but it also seemed like she could hear the earth breathing, some cosmic rhythm that reached out to the stars. This was what truth felt like.

She went to Tor and started digging deeper until she got to bedrock, then typed in the exact number of the Immortals account, including commas and the period.

A green link popped up on the dark screen. It glowed and seemed to throb. It looked dangerous.

"Wait." Luke squeezed her shoulder gently and bent forward, until his face was next to hers. She could feel the heat of him. Glancing sideways she could see the blond fuzz that would soon be pale scruff over his tanned skin. The temptation to kiss him was so strong she had to mentally bolt herself to the chair.

He went into the bedroom and brought back his own laptop. Hope was an electronics snob and had to refrain from sniffing when she saw it.

"I heard that." Luke was smiling as he set his laptop up next to hers. Hers looked like a different species.

"I didn't say anything," she protested.

"You didn't have to. It's clear what you think of it."

The blood rushed to her cheeks. "I — um —"

He laughed. "It's OK. I don't have to perform magic on my computer like you do. And ASI is assigning me a new one, it's ready at the office and Felicity has already given it her kiss of approval. This is my old one and I guess she'll just have it taken out back and shot."

Out of mercy. Hope thought it, but didn't say it.

"You take us to the point on this computer where all I have to do is click," he said. "I don't think I can be trusted to do more than press a key. If it's a destructive virus it will have killed an ancient broken-down steed instead of a thoroughbred. I know your laptop is surrounded by magic incantations and spells but why risk it?"

Hope switched to his laptop, entered Tor, drilled down down down again until all that was left was a dark screen and a small white field in the middle. She entered the number exactly without taking her eyes from the screen.

"Wow." Out of the corner of her eye she could

see Luke's surprise. "You didn't need to check. Huh."

"It was only 9 digits, two commas and a period. When I was a kid I won a prize because I could recite pi to the two hundredth digit. I have a good head for numbers."

"You surely do." He nudged her a little out of the way and sat down in front of his laptop. "I'll do the honors."

He looked as intrigued as she did. She was going to feel foolish if the number led nowhere. But somehow she thought something would happen, though she had no idea what.

"Hit it," she commanded, and his finger hovered. "Wait."

The screen dissolved and a man appeared. He was leaning on a cane and took a few halting steps forward.

Hope gasped. "I know who that is! That's Frank Glass! He died over five years ago. This looks like it was late in his illness." The man on the screen looked very ill, emaciated and bald. His expensive clothes hung on him.

Luke narrowed his eyes. "*The* Frank Glass?" He leaned forward a little. "Yeah, it is. Man, he looks awful."

"He wouldn't allow himself to be photographed the last six months of his life. You can see why. He died of a glioblastoma, a very aggressive brain tumor."

Frank Glass was a living legend, the man who almost single-handedly made AI and quantum computing possible and possibly commercial. From nothing, he'd made over a hundred billion dollars, but more than that, he'd revolutionized computers, the way we understood intelligence. He'd expanded humanity's boundaries. She'd cried the day she read his obituary in the newspapers, and had gone to a nearby church and lit a candle for him.

The image was super clear even on Luke's super crap screen. Glass looked exhausted and at least sixty years old, though she knew he'd only been 46 when he died.

Glass sighed deeply and for a moment his hand trembled on the handle of his cane. His head dipped down, looking at the ground. Then he looked up and smiled sadly.

"Hello, Hope," he said. "Congratulations on solving the puzzle. You're seeing this after I'm dead. I'm Frank Glass. I'm your uncle."

Fourteen

Washington, DC

Court Redfield thought long and hard about joining Resnick in Sacramento, where it all started. To make sure it was done right this time. It would be like travelling back in time, but not in a good way. He'd always hated the place. It smelled of dust and neglect and regret. Washington had always smelled like power to him. The perfume of the big time — a place where powerful men lived powerful lives. The center, not the provinces.

Court read history and he loved Roman history above all. He hadn't enjoyed his period as a Senator — too much kowtowing to morons — but he'd loved the idea of it. He identified with the biographies of the Romans he'd read. He knew that though life in the provinces might have been sweet, a real man of power needed to be in Rome. Just as he needed to be in Washington. Because one day he'd end up Imperator.

Sacramento was the dusty outlying provinces and he'd hoped never to go back. California was lost to his party anyway, so he'd planned on sending his vice presidential candidate to campaign there.

In the end, he'd decided to stay in Washington, and use a very secure videoconference app. Resnick was in a parade rest position. Good old Resnick. Loyal as ever. Goddammit, why the fuck couldn't his *son* behave like his employee? Court was aiming at the highest office in the land, a position of almost unimaginable power. He should have his son by his side, not a member of his Pretorian Guard.

As soon as the connection was established, Resnick spoke.

"Morning sir," he said. "I think I have their location pinpointed. A man and a woman. The woman has been confirmed as being Hope Ellis, formerly Catherine Benson. I've sent a drone to their location. As soon as I have confirmation, I'll wait until nightfall to strike."

A smile crossed Court's face for the first time that day. "Excellent."

"Sir." Resnick's head bowed. It was a gesture of fealty.

"End this," Court said. "Everyone involved. And don't be seen."

Resnick's head bowed once more. Court knew how Resnick viewed him and what he was thinking.

Thy will be done.

Sacramento

Luke was a former Ranger. He got a lot of shit from the squids at ASI about SEALs being so badass, but Ranger training was one of the toughest in the world. Ranger School was sixty-two days of hell. Every single thread in the Ranger cloth tab was soaked in blood and every single molecule of the metal tab was paid for in blood, sweat and tears.

To earn his tab, he'd trained twenty hours a day, averaging three and a half hours of sleep, carrying ninety pounds of gear, patrolling more than two hundred miles throughout the course. Every day he had live fire drills and there was the constant threat of ambushes by Red Team.

That was the training.

He'd seen brutal combat over three deployments, had been shot at constantly. He was unshockable. Or so he thought.

But right now, it was a good thing he was sitting down. Because it felt like he'd been gut punched.

Hope looked like someone had switched her off. Her face was bloodless. He'd only ever seen that color in dead men. She had that same look — waxy and lifeless.

"What?" she whispered.

Whatever was going on in that goddamned screen, Luke had to tend to Hope first. Shock could kill — he knew that. And though he was falling in love with her, right now he felt like she was his teammate and he had to protect her. He reached out and froze the monitor.

"Sit down." Hope turned her head to him, her eyes following slowly. She couldn't coordinate her movements. She didn't even know she

"Down, honey." Putting a hand on her shoulders, he pushed gently until she sat back down in the chair next to his. She resisted, then suddenly lost all resistance, and simply plopped down. Her hands were shaking.

In a moment, he had a tumbler with two fingers of whiskey and put it into her shaking hand. "Drink this." She looked at him, completely unfocused, uncomprehending. As if he'd spoken to her in a foreign language. He cupped the hand holding the tumbler and nudged it up toward her mouth. "Drink." Luke put command in his voice. He'd commanded men in battle. He knew how to make people obey.

She drank the whiskey in a couple of swallows and coughed. Some color slowly came back to her face.

"Good girl," he said and gently tightened his grip on her shoulder. Reminding her she wasn't alone in this. "So. We need to watch this. You ready?"

And his admiration for her, already strong, went up several notches. She sat up straight, nodded.

"Yes." And reached out herself to click the video back on.

Luke sat back down in the other chair, sliding it as close to hers as it could get, and took her hand. It was small and icy cold.

Frank Glass appeared again on the screen, emaciated, with only wisps of blond hair on his bald head, gray skin hanging off his jawline. Luke had seen many wounded men, but rarely any sick men. This man had death written all over him. You could see his skull beneath the skin.

He hadn't followed Glass's story at all. Luke wasn't in the computer world. Glass had been famous for being famous, as far as he was concerned. And he'd died when Luke had been on a mission and they hadn't had access to any news that didn't come from HQ.

But for someone in the world of computers, apparently, Glass was a very big deal. Their god.

And, apparently, Hope's uncle.

Hope was sitting on the edge of her seat, face forward, the monitor's light reflected off her pale face.

"Before I tell you your story, my darling niece, I'm going to need to sit down." He reached out with his cane and pulled a rolling office chair towards him. "Sorry. Not doing too well these days. But you'd know that. The tech press is speculating on when I'll die. The stock price of Glass Inc will change and some people will make a lot of money. And some will lose a lot of money."

He was in some kind of studio. There was no furniture at all besides the chair. Some kind of bland backdrop of an indeterminate gray-brown, featureless. Just the sick man, sitting down in a chair, telling his story.

The camera must have been on a tripod because it was rock steady. He was probably alone in that room.

He sighed, a small rattle sounding when he exhaled. This was one sick dude. A small smile played around his lips as he hooked the cane on the arm of the office chair and folded his veiny hands in his lap.

"So. Now that I have your attention, I'll assure you that you can verify what I say. I am your uncle. Your mother, Lucy Benson, was my sister. Half sister, which is why we don't — didn't — share a last name. But I left a vial of my blood with my lawyer, Morris Cannon, in Mountain View. You can google him. He has instructions to give it to you when you ask. The DNA analysis will prove that I am telling the truth, but in the meantime, I am just going to have to ask you to take my word for it."

Luke was interested in what the man was saying but he was more interested in how Hope was taking this. Glass stopped and wheezed for a moment and Luke watched her. That look of absolute shock was gone, but she was intensely focused.

Focused, but ok. She was holding up. Luke settled back and waited for the sick man to catch his breath to tell his story.

"The truth," Glass wheezed. "I've been waiting a long time to tell you the truth. Maybe I would have waited forever but I don't have much time left. It started in my head —" he stopped for a coughing fit that left him shaken. "Sorry. It's spread to the lungs. This isn't how I imagined telling you. I imagined telling you in person, then hugging you. Tight."

Glass cut away and on the monitor appeared the photograph of a young woman. California-cute, very blonde, blue-eyed, with big hair. Luke had never seen her before but neither had Hope. She frowned, but otherwise didn't react.

The screen cut back to Glass. "That was your mother, Hope."

Luke turned to Hope as she gasped. Her hand reached out for his and he folded her hand in his fist. Her skin was icy cold.

He hit pause.

"You okay?" he asked quietly.

Luke couldn't imagine anything more stressful than this. Discovering you weren't who you thought you were. You were someone else entirely. And now discovering who she really was. Everything about her face was sharper, as if she'd lost weight she didn't have to lose in the past few minutes.

"I — I don't know." She spoke as if having to catch her breath. As if someone had punched her in the stomach. "None of this makes any kind of sense."

Luke believed firmly in the ripping-off-the-bandage-fast theory of bad things. Get it all over with quickly. "Let's hear it all," he said firmly. She nodded and he pressed Play.

"Or rather Cathy. That's the name on your birth certificate. Catherine Frances Benson. Frances was the name of our maternal grandmother, Frances Caldwell. Our mother married twice. First husband was Thomas Glass and she had me, and second husband was Bob Benson. Both marriages ended in divorce. Mom and Lucy ended up living in a trailer park in Sacramento. Happy Trails Trailer Park. It was temporary and only because Bob Benson cleaned out our mom's bank account before disappearing. Lucy was 16 and I was 24, trying to put myself through Stanford on a scholarship and working three jobs when Benson lit out. I helped as much as I could but I couldn't do much. Lucy worked after school and on weekends. She was a really hard worker."

He smiled and suddenly Luke could see the man he'd been. He remembered now reading articles. In the first flush of success of his new generation of computers and smart objects, he'd been a young god. Tall, blond, good-looking in a nerdy sort of way. Nothing like the stooped, bald sack of bones on the monitor.

"Lucy was really smart and funny. Got straight As in school. The year Lucy graduated from high school, our mom died. She was never the same after Benson left and she just smoked and drank herself to death.

Lucy helped as much as she could but mom just wanted to die ... and she did. But anyone who was around Lucy for any amount of time knew she was going places. I was going places, too. We were going to make it. She graduated class valedictorian and enrolled in a local junior college, business major. Was doing really well. She was destined for the big time."

Luke hit pause again, glanced at Hope. "How you doing? Is this all too much for you?"

Hope took a big breath, let it out slowly in a controlled stream. Luke recognized a stress reliever. "It's a lot to take in. I don't — I don't even know if it's true. That woman, the one who is supposed to be my mother, doesn't look anything like me. None of this is making any sense to me."

"Do you want to stop, pick this up later?"

"God, no." Hope sat up straighter. "No. Whatever Frank Glass has to tell me, I have to know. None of this feels real, but it is real. Real enough to get someone killed. Data is life."

Luke nodded and pressed play again.

Data is life. Hope was right. Only he called it intel. And intel saved lives, he knew that from painful personal experience. Someone was after Hope. Or Cathy, or whatever the fuck she was called. He didn't care what her real name was. All he cared about was that she be kept safe. And to keep

her safe he needed intel this crazy dead genius, Frank Glass, was providing.

Glass's head had been bowed. He lifted it slowly,

in jerks, as if it hurt to move. "My dearest Cathy — I can't think of you as Hope — I've been waiting so long to tell you the truth. And now I can't wait any longer because I'm out of time. My doctors say I'll be lucky to last another three months, but no guarantees. I must do this now or you will never know the truth. It all goes back to the summer Lucy, your mother, was 22. She'd just gotten her bachelor's degree and was applying to graduate schools. We saw each other maybe once a month, once every two months. One day she took the bus to Mountain View to spend the weekend with me and she had stars in her eyes. Almost literally. She ... shone. I knew she was too pretty and too bright not to have boyfriends but she never let them slow her down, or knock her off her course. But this guy ... she met a young soldier who was between deployments and he just knocked her sideways. I met him. He was knocked sideways too. Seemed nice enough, though really grim, for someone as sunny-natured as Lucy. He'd just qualified as a Navy SEAL. At the time I didn't really know what that was, but I'm good at research. Everyone nowadays knows about SEALs, the tip of the spear and all that, but I didn't then. He scared me. Lucy was head over heels in love with a man who ran into danger for a living. With a gun. And something else scared me. He was Bard Redfield, Court Redfield's only child. Court Redfield was a state representative at the time, a man on the rise and burning with ambition. He went on to become California's governor, Deputy Director of the CIA, currently a Senator. They say that eventually he wants to run for President. And he is a cold-hearted ruthless son of a bitch."

This time Hope pressed pause. She kept her finger on the button, frozen.

She was still for so long Luke started worrying. "Hope? Honey?"

She didn't answer. Just drew in a deep breath and pressed the pause button again.

On screen, Frank Glass unfroze.

"Court Redfield had no intention of letting his only child marry 'trailer park trash'." Glass's hands rose, trembling, as he made air quotes. The video glitched. It had been edited. He reappeared, sitting down as before, but with a sweater on.

"Sorry," he wheezed. "Had to stop to catch my breath. It's getting harder and harder. Okay. To pick up where I left off, in April of 1990, Bard disappeared on a mission and Lucy heard nothing from him. Then his father showed up." His face tightened, grooves running down his cheeks. "Lucy said he scared her. Showed up in this huge black SUV, with two bodyguards, armed and standing at attention outside. He came in, didn't sit down, told her Bard had been killed in action. He never wanted to see Lucy again. Told her never to contact him." He sighed, bowed his head. "Two days later she found out she was pregnant."

Luke looked sharply at Hope. She was still, barely

breathing. There it was. The reason for everything that had happened to her. And he saw, with a sudden uncomfortable flash, that it was going to end in heartbreak.

The monitor showed a different image. Hope drew in a shocked breath.

"There he is. Hubbard Redfield. Known as Bard," came Glass's voice offscreen.

Up on the screen was a photograph of a young man in dress whites. Luke could read his uniform like a book. He was a SEAL, which meant he had discipline and smarts. Among the many medals decorating his chest was a Navy Cross and a Silver Star. The man was brave and had seen combat. He had that young/old look of men who'd been in combat while young. Their bodies were still supple and able and they were at their physical peak but something inside them would never be young again.

He was compelling — grimly handsome with a narrow face, dark hair, green eyes.

He looked exactly like Hope, down to the slightly uptilted eyes, narrow nose, well-defined mouth. There could be no doubt at all they were related.

Hope was staring, hand over mouth, frozen. Luke reached out and pulled her gently toward him. She was stiff, unyielding, more like a life-sized doll than a person. Shock had hollowed her out. It was awkward holding on to her like that but he didn't yield. She needed to feel human contact. He held her less like a woman he cared for and more like a wounded comrade. She'd been hit, was bleeding, even if it didn't show.

He held the back of her head, giving her the comfort of his body heat. One hand shielding her head, one hand against her back, protecting the head and the torso. She lay her forehead against his shoulder and shuddered out a breath.

Fuck it. Luke opened his arms, picked her up out of the chair and settled her onto his lap.

He held her tightly, tucking her head in under his chin. Making her warm, making her feel safe.

Shock — even psychological trauma — could be deadly. Her blood would have rushed to the core vital organs, leaving her dazed and confused. He gently held her hand, which was icy, and surreptitiously took her pulse. Fifty beats per second.

Acute stress disorder it was called, and it wasn't fun.

"I look just like him," she whispered, her breath puffing against the skin of his neck. "I've never looked like anyone."

"Ah, honey." Luke's heart broke, just a little. She'd been so alone all her life, essentially without any kind of family. Luke resembled his father, but he was the spitting image of his paternal grandfather. It had been a family joke. He also looked like his cousin Brian, except Brian had dark hair. Everywhere Luke looked in his family, he could see bits of himself. Cousin Roger, who'd joined the Marines and was almost as good a shot as he was, had the same build.

Cousin Mary, who had the same color hair he had, was as tone deaf as he was. At big family gatherings, Aunt Emily, who played the piano really badly, would accompany him and Mary as they sang classic rock. It sounded like a tortured cats convention and everyone loved it.

Hope was shaking.

A slow burn was taking place inside him. A terrible wrong had been done to this beautiful young woman who didn't have any meanness in her. Someone had played with her life, tossing her around like some doll to be manipulated to satisfy someone's agenda. Careless people had wounded her grievously. *Maybe her own blood.*

This was exactly the opposite of Luke's experience, where the people closest to him loved him and cared for him. The ones who meant him harm had nothing to do with him. He tried his best to shoot their faces off.

A low whimpering sound came from her and it broke his heart just a little more. It was the sound of extreme pain, from someone who was used to hiding pain because there was no one to care.

Well, he cared. He fucking cared. A lot.

"Hey," he said, voice low. He held her more tightly against him, trying to quell the trembling, trying to warm her up. Her narrow torso was tight, unmoving. "Breathe," he whispered against her ear. "In and out." Air exploded out of her and she drew in a great shuddering breath. "That's my girl. Breathe deeply. You're in shock. Do you want me to turn the video off? We could have something to eat, you can let some of this settle. It's a lot to take in."

"No." Hope placed her hands on his chest as she sat up, shook her dark hair out of her eyes. Her eyes were bright but she hadn't shed tears. "No, I need to listen to it all. Data —"

"Is life," he finished for her and smiled as he laid his hand against her face. She looked so delicate and yet was so strong. Her world had just been upended, everything she knew about herself was a lie. Yet she wasn't losing it.

Luke remembered Ross Stuart, his team's corpsman, who got word while on a training mission that his wife had left him. He went on a four day bender and his teammates had to cover for him. And take his guns away.

"Let's finish this."

She moved to get off his lap but Luke tightened his hold. It made him feel better when she was in his arms. "Stay."

She nodded, shifted until she was watching the screen. He reached out to click play but she stopped his hand and clicked it herself.

At that moment, Luke knew she'd be okay. More was in store, probably all of it bad, but she was strong enough to bear it. One thing was for sure. She wasn't alone any more. She had him.

The face of Frank Glass filled the screen again, looking even worse than before, if that was possible.

"I have to be honest with you, my dear. I urged your mother to terminate the pregnancy. Lucy was trying so hard but she already had so many counts against her and was just starting courses to get her MBA. Becoming a single mother so young was ... unfortunate."

His head rose and his exhausted eyes stared right into the camera. It was like he was looking right at them.

"But Cathy — Hope — if you're listening to this, know that your mother loved you from the instant she found out she was expecting you. She loved you wholly and fiercely. She wouldn't hear of terminating the pregnancy and for the short time she was able to mother you, she was a fabulous mother. She loved you with all her heart."

Luke angled his head sideways to look Hope in the face. Those words had cracked her open. Silent tears were tracking down her cheeks. She looked over her shoulder at him then back at the screen. He had to work not to react to the sadness in her eyes.

He didn't try to comfort her or console her. Those tears and that sadness were real and were justified. Nothing he could say would make it all untrue. Her entire life had been a lie and she had somehow understood that without understanding why.

The why was still a mystery but the rest wasn't.

Frank Glass continued. "It wasn't easy, being a single mother and trying to get a degree. I helped as much as I could, though I was struggling too. You were a charming child, my dear. Sunny and easy-going and very, very bright. It was — it was working. Lucy got her MBA. You're in tech, so you know my story. By the time you were nearly five, I'd had my IPO and was going to move you two out of the trailer park. But then Lucy saw a newspaper article about Court Redfield. Pictured with his son, who'd been wounded in war.

"It electrified Lucy. She realized Bard was alive. She wrote to him, c/o an FPO address. She wrote letter after letter after letter. She wrote to the Navy. She sent endless photos of you. When she received no answers, I tried to get her to stop writing and sending snapshots because it was breaking her heart. And mine. But she was absolutely sure that if he knew about you, he'd come back to her and to you. And then —" His voice cracked.

He drew in a deep wheezing breath, covered his face with a trembling hand.

"And then you and your mother were run off the road by a truck."

Luke tightened his arms around Hope at the shocking words. Her hands were so cold he curled her fists into his. Looked like the next part of the story was going to be even worse than the beginning.

"The state trooper who found the car called me in. We went to high school together. He said it was vehicular manslaughter, the car was T-boned. The truck that ran into you was parked on a side street and accelerated into Lucy's car. It was a devastating impact and Lucy was killed immediately. But then my friend told me you were still breathing. I begged him with everything in me to hide you until I arrived. To this day I am grateful to him, and have put his two kids through college. Because if he hadn't —" Glass stared hard into the camera lens. "If he hadn't, you'd be dead."

Luke reached out his hand again. "Do you want to stop? Digest what you've heard?" How could she not want to stop? Right now, it looked like her father had killed her mother and had tried to kill her. Of all the terrible things Luke had seen in combat, this was the worst thing he could think of. The man tasked with loving you trying cold-heartedly to kill you. Every cell in his body was repulsed by the idea.

"No." Hope's voice was quiet. "No, I need to hear the rest."

Luke's hand hovered over the keyboard. "You sure?"

"Absolutely."

Luke clicked and Glass lived and breathed again on the screen, though he was in the ground these past five years.

"I knew if you were to live, I had to do something and do it fast. My state trooper friend took you to a hospital two hundred miles away. He took a big risk because you were badly concussed. You could have died on the way. But someone wanted you dead, and would have gotten to you if they knew you'd survived. I bribed the coroner and the mortuary company and anyone else that was necessary to say that there were two deaths. At the funeral there were two coffins, one a tiny white one. If you go to the St. Ursula Cemetery in Sacramento you'll see two small marble tombstones in the ground. One for Lucy Benson and one for Catherine Benson. You were in a coma under another name in a hospital far away while the funeral was held. I paid cash for treatment. You were in a coma for a long time and in that time I was really busy. I made mistakes, but I was young and this was all brand new to me."

He broke away, coughing.

Luke put his head next to hers. "Do you remember any of this?" he asked quietly. He felt it against his skin when she shook her head. But he was also feeling her sorrow and pain. This story was devastating to him. He couldn't imagine the earthquake going on inside her.

Glass continued. "Your mother was friends with a brother and sister living at Happy Trails. They weren't too good at holding jobs but they weren't bad people either. I gave them a lot of money and promised them a very healthy income for life if they would take you far, far away, to the other side of the continent, and pretend to be your parents. You weren't ever to come to California. I procured some fake ID for all three. The fake ID improved over the years until the backstory for all three of you was perfect.

"Bob and Rachel Sanderson left Sacramento with

you on a private jet and set up in Boston as Neil and Sandra Ellis with their daughter, Hope." His mouth turned down. "I need to apologize to you, Cathy. I suspect Bob and Rachel didn't make good parents. I kept tabs on them and it was clear they weren't doing much parenting. I told them to put you in a good boarding school when you were ten. I think everyone was relieved and I know you thrived there. I got regular reports. You have no idea how hard it was for me to stay away from you. You are my only living relative. I never married. When I die, I'll leave you a very nice sum but not my whole fortune. I need to make sure my company survives my death, to safeguard my employees. I would have traded all my money to be with you as you grew up. But it was too dangerous. Whoever tried to kill you — whether Bard or his father Court — will still want you dead." He shrugged, clearly exhausted. "I hate them both because they deprived me of your mother and of watching you grow up. Of being your uncle, a part of your life. The best I could do for you was the Sandersons, secrecy and the money. But you've done just fine on your own. I can't tell you how proud I am of you. But I have to warn you — never let your guard down, ever. Keep this knowledge to yourself. Court Redfield is a Senator now and though I'm not political, I've heard that in a couple of years he wants to run for President. An illegitimate child in the family could ruin those chances. I don't know how Bard turned out. He was a hard man when I met him, and he's spent his entire life in combat. Court Redfield is coldly ambitious and his hero warrior son is part of his legend. Someone killed once and he'd kill again, certainly if your existence threatens a run for the presidency. I won't live to see whether he wins the presidency or not, but the danger you were in as a little girl is more acute now. Court Redfield is ruthless, honey. And Bard probably is too. You do not want them as enemies.

"I wish —" The video glitched then came back on. The backdrop was different and Frank Glass had on a gray sweater instead of a black one. There was no way to tell how much time had gone by. Glass looked a little worse. Maybe he'd waited 24 hours. Maybe he'd waited a week. There was no way to tell. "I wish I could stay alive to help you. But I can't. I have all the money in the world and I won't outlast the year. All I can do is point you in a useful direction. I have sources who told me that in his time at the CIA, Court Redfield set up what could be considered a private army, made up of ruthless former Special Operations soldiers. Those sources said that they were a kill team and eliminated some inconvenient people. Senator Deaver of Montana, Marcy Lamott, an investigative journalist. I heard that he had a brutal run in with Black Inc last year. Jacob Black hates Court Redfield's guts. If you are ever cornered, turn to Jacob Black. Tell him you are my niece. Tell him this story."

The video glitched again and when Glass came

back on the monitor he was wearing a green hoodie that hung off him. His eyes were deeply sunk in his head and he looked exhausted. Almost unable to keep his head up. He reached out to the camera lens.

"Sorry. Had some internal bleeding. Oh God, how I wish I could see you, hug you, my miracle of a niece. So beautiful and so smart. An evil man changed the course of our lives forever years ago. And now," he sighed, "I fear at some point you're going to have to go on the run again. Use the money I left you. Remember that I love you and your mother loved you. You don't deserve anything that has happened to you. You don't deserve any of this. But my one word to you, if Court Redfield or Bard Redfield find you, is —" his bruised-looking eyes burned into the camera. "*Run.*"

Fifteen

Hope wanted to stay forever just the way she was. Wrapped in Luke Reynolds' strong arms, feeling his heat and strength penetrate down to her bones. Chills were running through her body. Frank Glass's words left her feeling raw, like the words had flayed skin away from her body. Oh how she'd love to stay right here, burrowed against Luke's chest. She'd crawl right inside him if she could. Just crack his chest open and find refuge inside him.

But — that wasn't the way the world worked, was it? As a child she'd managed to deal with her parents' indifference by focusing on her studies and computers. Like finding a boulder in the road and walking around it. But however indifferent her parents had been, they hadn't been physically dangerous to her.

It looked like the Redfield family *was* dangerous. Not dangerous in the rabid dog sense but in the snake sense. Lying in wait for her.

She wasn't going to let them do that.

Luke kissed the top of her head, though she barely felt it. She heard his words more as a rumbling in his chest than as a voice. "Wow. That's a lot to take in. I think we should find a safer place for you than here and — where are you going?"

Hope had slid off his lap and was making for her phone.

"Hope, honey." Luke stood up and she marveled all over again at how tall he was. How strong. And yet all his strength wasn't going to save her from the snakes. Only cunning would. And that's where she came in. She didn't have much physical strength but she did have smarts. He cocked his head as she pulled out her cell and made it even more impregnable and untraceable. Before it would have been really hard to trace her phone. Now it was impossible. All communications would be routed through three satellites and there would be a slight time lag but it was worth it. "What are you doing?" he asked.

She started her search.

"We have a name now. My — my uncle told me to contact Jacob Black and that's exactly what I'm going to do. I'm looking up his number right now."

Luke's hand enveloped hers, stopping her from her online research. He looked her in the eyes, seemingly walking around inside her head. Right now though what was dominant wasn't what was in her head, it was what was in her heart.

Rage.

If you'd asked her, Hope would have sworn she didn't have any anger in her. She was always even-tempered, forgiving, understanding. Never angry. A wuss, really. Luckily, she'd never been bullied because she probably would have caved in. Even with the Boss from Hell, she'd opted to quit and look for work elsewhere rather than to confront him. All she wanted was the quiet life. To be left alone to work without distractions. Certainly not the distractions of violent emotions.

Or so she thought. All of that was *wrong*. She was *burning* with rage. Her rage could blow up the entire city of Sacramento. All her life she'd felt something was wrong, that she didn't fit the space life had carved out for her. She could barely articulate her feelings but once, over a lot of wine, she'd confessed those feelings to Felicity, who had completely understood.

Felicity's past was an enigma, much of it to her, too. She'd been born under another name and had spent her childhood in Witness Protection, where no one could know the truth of her family. They'd changed names and identities twice. She too had felt completely unrooted, living her life at a distance.

Hope's entire life was a lie. Someone — either Court Redfield or his son Bard or both — had had her mother killed. Either her father or her grandfather had wiped Lucy Benson — whose only fault apparently had been to love Bard Redfield — out of existence and had tried to kill *her*, too. For — for what? An issue of reputation? Her uncle hadn't mentioned Lucy seeking financial aid from the Redfields.

No, she'd tried to bring Hope up as best she could, and had been guilty only of trying to contact the man she'd loved, who was the father of her child, and who she'd thought was dead.

Men like that — who'd swat away innocent lives simply because they were inconvenient — were the scum of the earth. Men like that had cast a shadow over her that she'd subconsciously felt all her life.

She switched to her laptop and sent the entire file recorded by her uncle to Felicity, who was surrounded by security guys, with instructions to disseminate it as widely as she could in the company and to forward it to Don Temple at the FBI. She'd worked briefly with Don while she was at the NSA, tracking down a cyberterrorist. Whoever it was who wanted her dead, who had killed her mother, tried to kill her and had murdered poor Kyle and Geraldo would be outed. She knew Don. Don wasn't going to be swayed by a Redfield.

She could feel the blood in her face, the heat in her veins. That chill plaguing her was gone. The anger had swept absolutely everything away in a wave of red-hot rage.

"Look at you," Luke murmured. "Woman on a mission."

"Damn right." She was typing furiously. "Someone's been playing with my life since I was a child. That someone killed my mother and killed Kyle and my doorman and whichever Redfield it is, he is going *down*."

"Yeah, he is. No question." Luke placed his large hand over hers, stilling them over her keyboard. "Don't bother looking for Black's number, I have it. Tomorrow we're going back to Portland and we'll start focusing on which of the Redfields killed your mother and tried to kill you." His eyes narrowed as he looked at her intently, features tight and grim. "Four murderers went free under my watch. That will never happen again. Whoever it is will go down, I promise you."

He looked deadly serious and she knew he meant every word. After a lifetime of being on her own, it looked like she had ... an ally.

A lover, too.

Totally and inappropriately, she was aroused. That hot rage had also, um, turned her on. Instead of being meek and mild Hope Ellis, who never took the initiative, who felt a mild tingle — akin to the joy of reaching the next level of Doom — when she liked a guy, this brand new Hope Ellis, who was another person entirely, felt sexual desire bubble up in her and swirl like a whirlwind.

"Luke," she said. It was an entirely new voice. Deep and smoky and so unlike her own she barely recognized it.

But Luke recognized it. He looked at her sharply and understood immediately.

She'd just heard a story of death. Her mother — dead. Her uncle — dead. But she wasn't dead. She was alive. *Alive.*

Every cell in her body pulsed with life and desire.

And Luke felt that desire, too. Oh yeah. Eyes narrowed until only a shard of light blue was showing, features drawn, cheekbones dark with color. Luke Reynolds desired *her* and everything about him showed it.

They came together like magnets, with an almost audible click, their bodies fitting together naturally, as if they'd done this thousands of times before. When she lifted herself just this much and he bent his head this specific amount, their mouths met and clung. She knew the taste of him now, and the smell of him and the feel of him. He was both familiar and brand new and exciting beyond words.

He lifted her one-armed and walked backward. "Not going to make it to the bedroom," he said, his voice thick.

She could barely hear him above what felt like a hot wind whistling in her head. The bedroom? God, no. That was *miles* away.

"Right now." She sucked on his lower lip. "Right *now*."

Her entire body was on fire, glowing with heat. There was such coldness in the world but there was heat right here, between them. Hope was ready to simply drop to the floor and have sex. Luke didn't drop to the floor but took two steps to the table. In those two steps, he managed to get all her clothes off. Hope didn't know how he managed it, all she knew was that their mouths were separated for a moment and she felt cool air on her chest. Her pants — she had no idea what happened to them. By some miracle, Luke was naked too.

His hand travelled down her body, thumb brushing over a nipple that was so sensitive it was almost painful, over her belly and down. He cupped her, where she was wet for him. Hope covered his hand with hers and pressed down.

He pushed out a breath, lifted her onto the table and stepped between her legs. Oh God, she was on fire.

Something crackled and she realized he'd had the presence of mind to put on a condom. The time it took him to put it on, leaning away from her, was intolerable. She needed to touch all of him she could because Luke was life itself. Was heat and light and life. A part of her had been dead all her life and was now fully alive.

Luke entered her and she arched her back in pleasure. They were both so excited that it didn't last long, but then it didn't have to. They held each other tightly as she convulsed. One hard stroke, then another and he followed her.

Luke's sweaty face fell onto her shoulder as he panted, "I'll get it right

next time. But we'll need to be in the bed."

She held his head, smiling at the ceiling, happy.

"Okay," she whispered. "Let's go to bed."

Luke lay in bed, one hand behind his head, one arm around his woman. She wasn't asleep but she wasn't quite awake, either. If she felt anything like him, she was boneless with pleasure.

Luke felt — well, he felt *great*. Better than he had in years. If he weren't feeling so very relaxed, like someone had massaged him nearly to death, he'd have jumped out of bed and gone for a fifty-mile run. Or done a hundred pushups. He felt perfectly capable of doing them except he was really comfortable where he was and anyway, he didn't want to disturb Hope. He tried to think of her as Cathy but it didn't fit. Hope was Hope and that was exactly what he felt right now. Hope.

Frank Glass's video was now at ASI and they were taking care to show it to a select group of responsible journalists that Summer, Jack Delvaux's wife, had chosen. Summer had run one of the country's best political blogs, Area8, until she started writing books. But the fiery investigative journalist was still there and she had the grenade in her hands, finger in the pin, ready to pull.

Her hands were steady.

They were safe.

Hope's secrets were now out in the light of day and sunlight disinfected. It also set free. She was going to be fiercely protected until the story came out and the Redfields couldn't hurt her. She had nothing to be afraid of now and soon could get on with her life. Which Luke was determined would include him. No question. He was not letting her go.

No other woman intrigued him like she did, with her superpower intelligence and that delicate fairy-like beauty. She was pure magic and she was the opposite of heavy maintenance. The few women he'd dated these past years had been like *work*. A job, and not a pleasant one at that. He'd spent his time slaloming around the poles of their obsessions and dislikes and feelings. They'd constantly sought reassurance about their looks, taking offense when he had no idea he'd said something wrong. Crumbling at the first sign of difficulty.

Luke had almost convinced himself there was something deeply wrong with him. That he was too old-fashioned, too cold, too hot, too stiff, too loose, too much or not enough. Something. Relationships were so fucking hard and he just didn't seem to have the knack.

And then, Hope. Who was as low maintenance as they come. If anything he found himself all but doing cartwheels in front of her to get her attention when she was immersed in her computer, conjuring up God knows what dark arts. It was a little exciting that she was smarter than he was. Well, a lot exciting. He didn't care, his ego wasn't bruised. He was a better shot than she was. We all have our talents.

In a terrible situation, with her life on the line and on the run, Luke had never heard her complain, not once. She rolled with the punches and took what came at her. That was his understanding of the world. That's the way his parents rolled, facing difficulties head on, without complaint. And as a Ranger, he and his teammates had bitched in funny filthy language all the time about the sand, the food, the showers, but never complained about the real hardships of going on patrol, going into danger day after fucking day. No one complained about that. They'd all been naturally brave and stoic.

Hope was like that.

She resonated with him. She'd struck a match that just lit him up, opened him up.

Including his stomach. Yeah, strange but true. Luke hadn't felt hunger since, well since the Sigma Phi Five. Food held no appeal and he had to force himself to eat. With Hope, he was hungry. Ravenous, in fact. Hungry for food, for sex, for her company. For life. For her.

And for the first time in a very long time he thought about the future. His, specifically. And in a positive way. During combat operations, you don't think about the future and you don't think about the past, you are fully focused on surviving the present moment. Survival took up his entire hard disk. Trying his damndest to keep his men alive and himself, too, while he was at it.

The future was this massive unknowable dark

mountain far away in the distance that he couldn't climb because there was the mountain of survival right in front of him. Even back at the FOBs, no one thought of the future. The most you could think of was planning the next mission, the next patrol.

Right now, the future stretched out before him like an upland meadow in spring. Full of unicorns and flowers and butterflies.

He smiled to himself at the turn his own brain was taking. Well, not unicorns and flowers and butterflies, no. But he could think about a future where Hope was in his life. Maybe — if he played his cards right — living with him. Maybe even … *married* to him. That would be great, but a stretch. He wasn't that big a catch. He was an ex-soldier, ex-cop who would forever be linked to a huge scandal. Someday in the future people would only remember his name, a murder and vicious kids, but it wouldn't be clear who did what and what role he played. He was the good guy but that was sometimes lost. The parents of the killers had spent a lot of money to muddy the waters and make him out to be an incompetent cop. That kind of mud stuck.

He had no money.

True, he was about to join ASI, a really good, solid company full of friends. But it would take a while for him to get back on a solid financial footing.

Luckily, it appeared Hope didn't care about that. About any of it. She had what the Reynolds family had always had, an ability to see to the heart of things and not be distracted by appearances.

So ... there seemed to be a real possibility that she would be in his life, maybe living with him. Working with him in the Pearl, at ASI. Yeah.

Oh, man.

His stomach rumbled. But first food.

"I heard that," she said dreamily, eyes closed. Luke looked down at her, at the delicate profile, the fine features, the creamy skin. A view that could be his for the rest of his life. Would be his if he had anything to say about it.

He laughed. Another new thing in his life. Laughter. "Yeah? You up for some food?"

She drew in a deep breath and then her stomach rumbled, too. A cute little girly growl. "I guess I am."

Her eyes popped open and their gazes locked. A smile spread across his face. It took a moment for him to recognize what his face was doing, it felt so alien. He'd been doing a lot of that lately, straining some muscles in his face.

"There's pancake mix and real maple syrup. I can make pancakes if there's a mix involved."

She frowned, a little line appearing between her dark eyebrows. "I have no idea what time it is but I think it's late. I think it might be ... dinner time and not breakfast time?"

"Hmm." The reliable clock in Luke's head said 8.15 pm. 20.15 in military time. "You've never eaten breakfast food for dinner?"

Hope smiled. "All the time. Especially if I'm on a

work jag. Cornflakes and milk are my go-tos, no matter the time of day."

Well, cornflakes for dinner for her was over. It was going to be Luke's mission to make sure she ate well at regular intervals.

It was good to have a mission again.

He threw back the covers and headed to the bathroom for a quick shower, picking up a change of clothes along the way. There was a weird sound behind him and he looked over his shoulder at her.

Hope was sitting up in bed, blankets around her waist. She was staring at him. At his ass, really. Looking like she liked what she saw. He liked what he saw too. Her beautiful face, mouth slightly open as she stared at him. The elegant slender lines of her torso, the delicate collar bones, the perfect small breasts. With aroused nipples.

His dick rose straight up when he saw that. Totally uncontrolled and uncontrollable. From zero to hero in a second. He couldn't have stopped himself if he'd tried. He was half turned toward her and she couldn't help but see.

Another one of those flushes rose from her small breasts to her face. She huffed out a breath, as if letting off steam rising inside her and he could feel his dick swell. She turned a brighter shade of pink, a small smile playing around her mouth. A heart beat was visible in her left breast.

Their bodies were talking to each other. No need for words. But he used them anyway.

"Don't really need breakfast/dinner. Or a shower," he offered. It was hard to keep the hope out of his voice. Because right now the thought of anything that wasn't rushing over to her, climbing right on top of her and sliding right in, where he belonged, seemed insane.

She breathed hard, in and out, delectable mouth slightly open. He remembered that mouth. Above all his dick remembered that mouth and he was now officially as hard as a rock.

She wasn't talking, just sort of vibrating there on the bed. Was that an invitation? If it was, the answer was yes. He turned completely, his dick flat against his stomach and was about to stride over when she raised a shaking hand, palm up.

Stop.

He sighed.

"You are temptation itself, but I think we need to eat something and check in with Felicity. See how she's doing. I haven't heard from her and I'm a little worried."

He tried one more time. "We could shower at the same time," he said sneakily. "Save time, conserve water. A twofer."

She smiled at him and he felt like a light had switched on inside him. She didn't smile enough. Come to think of it, he didn't smile enough, either. They were going to deal with her situation and then they were going to get on with their lives, which would involve smiling, a lot.

Hope pulled up the covers and leaned over to get something off the floor. He couldn't see what it was, but whatever it was, it was going to cover her up and that wasn't good.

"Nice try, slick, but no. Fun and games are for later." The smile took the punch from her words.

He gave a heartfelt sigh that could be heard across the room and headed for the bathroom, slumped over in defeat, making sure to drag his feet.

He heard a giggle at his back and smiled secretly as he walked into the bathroom.

Yeah. He wanted more of that.

Luke was pure sinful temptation. Hope had to dig her fingernails into her palms to refrain from springing out of bed and hurling herself across the room at him. Why not? Just looking at him made her eyeballs boil. He was just so ... fine. Those long lean lines, those broad shoulders and that lean waist, all muscle with not a molecule of fat on him ... he was like a Platonic ideal of man. A couple of times in despair at her lack of fitness, Hope had joined a gym and there had been plenty of muscular men but their muscles had looked fake compared to Luke's. Stuccoed on or glued on. Some were so muscle-bound they waddled.

Not Luke. Man, he moved like a panther —

gracefully and without a wasted motion. And those muscles were *real*. He was real, too. A man with a heart and emotions he wasn't afraid to express, unlike the nerds she knew, who had such abysmal social skills. Luke was a man, in the real sense of the term. Deep, mature, secure in himself.

But — they had things to do and they had to eat something because she knew first-hand what happened to your mind when you forgot to eat. Plus, she really did want to check in with Felicity.

And they'd be going to bed later anyway. Together. To have sex. Again. What an amazingly delicious thought. Mainly, her sexual encounters had been of the one-and-done variety. Both parties reluctant to repeat the experience. Not here. With Luke, it looked like sex was on the agenda for a long time to come. Sort of on tap. Like beer, only better.

She shivered with delight. She was uncovering such darkness, even evil, in her past. A pall cast over her life by either her father or her grandfather or both. A curse. It would take time to clear everything up and she would do her damndest to bring whoever had killed her mother and tried to kill her to justice. To shatter the shackles that had been holding her down all her life and to set herself free.

She was absolutely set on bringing the second half of her life into the open air and the sunshine and freeing herself. Because the future was going to be different. A new city, a new job, a new life and above all a new man, awaited her.

She'd been shocked by the video recording and yet she hadn't been. Some part of her, maybe even at the cellular level, knew that something in her life was askew. Her earliest memory was of a shiny red bike in Boston for Christmas. She knew she'd been sick but she had no memory of it. She was better and had begged for a bike and there it was — under the small Christmas tree the Ellises — the Sandersons really — had erected. She'd been five and she had no memories at all before that moment.

Like lightning illuminating a landscape until then cloaked in darkness, Frank Glass's video shed shocking light over the bleak past. But at least now she knew. Something sad and mysterious had always kept her back, kept her separate from other people. Her only friends had been Felicity, Emma and Riley, and they'd had strange upbringings too.

But the dark, sad past felt now like a heavy carapace she was shedding, pieces falling to the floor, leaving her light and free. The past couldn't be changed, but the future could.

And there it was, her future, right there, opening the bathroom door and walking out. Rumpled, not elegant, exactly her type. She distrusted men who cared too much about how they looked.

His clothes were clean but not pressed. A slightly wrinkled long-sleeved black tee, black jeans, black boots, hair up in damp spikes. Clean shaven, without the blond scruff softening the angular planes of his face. She preferred the scruff and made a note to herself to tell him.

Heartbreakingly beautiful. And, cherry on top, a good guy. A really good guy. The kind who ran into burning buildings to save people.

Life had fucked her up and then, in a bid to gain her forgiveness, had thrown Luke and a new life her way.

Okay. Yeah, she'd take it.

Luke walked up to her, eyes fixed on hers the entire way, tilted her face up to his with a finger under her chin, and kissed her gently. Warmth coursed through her, under her skin, like honey. She closed her eyes and savored it. One of many many kisses to come.

She opened her eyes to see him looking down at her.

"My turn in the shower. And after —" She smiled. "I heard talk of pancakes. Were you serious or were you just blowing smoke?"

Oh God, when he smiled widely there was a dimple in his cheek that had been hidden by his beard! A dimple! Wild overkill! He didn't need a dimple to be insanely attractive, but there it was.

"Yes, ma'am. Pancakes are definitely in your future. Would I lie to you?"

"No," she whispered, looking him directly in the eyes. Suddenly serious.

He sobered, face drawn. "No. Damn right. I won't ever lie to you. You've had enough lies in your life. And enough injustice." He held out his cell to her. There was a message from Felicity. **Got the vid. Forwarded to your FBI friend. Also forwarded to Bud. He'll raise hell.**

"Bud? Who's Bud?"

"Remember I told you about my boss? How he was willing to go to the wall for me before I called him off? He never forgave me for that because he believes in justice the way other men believe in God. His name is Bud Morrison and by sending that video we are sure he will know exactly who to forward it to. Probably the FBI and certainly the state police. The Redfields are powerful in California but Court Redfield is in campaign mode and vulnerable. Bud will send it to someone he trusts and whoever is responsible for your mother's death, trying to murder you and the death of your friend is going down."

"I already had Felicity send it to a special agent I know at the FBI," she said. "You can text Commissioner Gordon — er — Commissioner Morrison his name."

Luke flashed her a blinding smile.

She showered fast, dressed in a turquoise sweat suit Summer had provided and walked into the kitchen. She watched Luke stir the pancake mix, pour it into a hot skillet and make a stack of dollar pancakes. Perfectly round, all the same size. The one time she'd tried pancakes they'd looked like the spines on Godzilla's back. Plus they were totally inedible.

These tasted fantastic. Crisp on the outside, soft on the inside. A little like the guy who'd made them

— hard on the outside and soft on the inside.

Something occurred to her. "Your friend Bud won't have any jurisdiction in California. He might be police Commissioner in Portland but that won't help in California. And the crime was a long time ago. Can someone still be brought to justice?"

Luke's face turned sharp and hard. "There's no statute of limitations on murder. It could be a hundred years ago and it wouldn't make any difference. And no, Bud won't have jurisdiction but he has pull. He is highly respected in the law enforcement community. The only reason he backed down in my case is because I forced him to. I saw he was going to go down with me and I didn't want that. But it still burns and he's not going to allow that a second time."

"Luke." Hope put a hand on his. Felt the strength and the tension. "Court Redfield is a very powerful man. And he is backed by powerful people. I don't pay much attention to politics, but even I know he stands a good chance to get the nomination and win the election. That is power, more than a Commissioner can ever wield."

"Well, Bud wouldn't be on the front lines, but he is in a position to contact the people who will be on the front lines. And Summer is busy writing a book but she'll know the right people in the media to contact."

Hope smiled. "You know when I said I didn't pay much attention to politics? Because politics never made sense to me."

Luke nodded.

"The little I know about politics I got from reading Summer's blog. Area8. She made it all make sense. So — she works for ASI too? In what capacity? From what I understand she's a journalist. Not an expert on security."

Luke's hand turned until he could clasp hers. "Not working for ASI, no. But her husband does. Jack Delvaux. His family was wiped out by a man high up in politics and this kind of thing is what he was born to fight. He is focused like a laser beam on politicians ruining people's lives. Once he gets wind of this he'll be like Bud — unable to let it go. And everyone else at ASI is like that, starting from the top. The other Big Boss, John Huntington, and the Senior will make sure the Redfields are brought to justice. It's a formidable place, ASI. They'd protect you even if you didn't work there, because of Felicity and now me. And when you join, you'll be part of the family."

Part of the family. Hope did her very best not to get emotional at those words, but it was impossible. Here, in this very comfortable, anonymous house in Sacramento, she'd found her true family. Luke and the men and women he worked with. It was really all she'd ever wanted in life, without knowing she wanted it.

Wanted was the wrong word. She craved it. Never to be alone again … it was almost too good to be true.

But there was something she had to know.

Hope pushed away the plate where the pancakes were a distant memory and brought up her cell. She squeezed Luke's hand and let it go. "I need you to do something for me."

"Anything," he said.

That distracted her for a moment. "Really? What if I asked you to run up Mount Hood or ... or give me a million dollars?"

"You say those things like they are impossible. I'm a runner. I'd run up Mount Hood for you, absolutely. It would probably take me about eight hours but I'd definitely do it. And I don't have a million dollars, I told you I'm almost wiped out financially. But if you want a million dollars, I'll just pay it to you over ten or twenty years. No problem. Whoa. Where's this from?"

Hope didn't know what he was talking about until she felt coolness on her cheeks and touched them. Her fingers came away wet. She was leaking water from her eyes. Or rather, she was crying. She'd cried earlier, too. Man, this was so not her.

"I never cry," she said, taken aback. "Never. Not even at Les Mis."

"Uh huh." Luke wiped her cheeks with his thumbs. "Not crying. Gotcha."

Felicity, Emma and Riley would do anything for her, but this — this was a declaration of something approaching love. Hope tried to think of a man who'd do something for her, something hard and that required sacrifice, and came up blank.

"Thank you," she whispered.

He bent and kissed her, briefly. "I have no idea what you're thanking me for but I guess I'll take it." He waggled his eyebrows. "A grateful woman is always a wonderful thing."

She knew what he was doing. She'd had a moment in which she felt raw and vulnerable. It had probably been pretty visible and Luke, notwithstanding his tough guy appearance, was really observant.

In that moment, Hope felt like she'd been flayed alive. Someone had just come along and taken away her skin and all her defenses. In that moment, a wrong word, a wrong move, and she'd have been devastated. Like the rebel base when all the shields suddenly went down and there was the Death Star, ready to kill.

Her defenses had been so high and deep all her life, all the life she could remember at any rate, that she thought they were part of her. But they weren't. Her defenses were artificial. Her disconnection from life had been created.

She was the way she was because a greedy and cruel man, or men, had killed her mother and robbed her of her future.

Well, that was stopping, right now.

"You said you'd get me Jacob Black's number. So can you?"

Luke blinked, frowned. "What?"

"Frank Glass told me to talk to Jacob Black. That he knows the man who is possibly my father. The man who possibly killed my mother. I want to talk to him, find out what Bard Redfield is like."

"Whoa. When you said that before, I thought you were kidding." Luke took an involuntary step back. "Is that — is that wise? Don't you think we should wait until —"

"No." Hope was as sure of this as she was of 2 + 2 = 4. She'd waited long enough. Her entire life, in fact. She wanted to set wheels in motion right now, and follow through with them up in Portland, with her team at her back. The thought of having that team shot warmth through her entire body. But whatever was going to happen, whatever her new life was, it had to start *right now*. Impatience bubbled under her skin. The past was dead. She was shedding her past like a snake shedding its skin and something new, previously unsuspected, was unfolding within her. That dead carapace was lying shattered at her feet and the new Hope was taking her first breaths. Whatever was going to happen next in her life, it was going to be completely different from what was before. "I don't want to wait another moment more. If Jacob Black knows the man who is my father, and maybe tried to have me and my mother killed, I want to talk to him. There's this huge black hole in my head where my life should be. I need to start filling in the blanks."

Luke stood looking at her, mouth a thin line.

Clearly, he didn't agree. Hope waited for him to make counterarguments. Whatever he said, it wouldn't sway her, but he deserved her listening to him. He swallowed and she prepared to *try* to listen to him over the drumbeat of impatience filling her chest, but in the end, he simply nodded as he bent over his cell. "Okay. If that's what you want."

Tears sprang in her eyes that she impatiently dashed away. God, a lifetime of never crying and here she was, springing leaks everywhere. *Thank you, Luke,* she said in her head, but not aloud. He didn't agree with her, but it was what she wanted, so he was going to help her do it. If he'd fought her on this, she wouldn't have known what to do. But he hadn't.

"Wait, wait!"

He was scrolling through his contacts list and she stopped him, alarmed. Holding out her hand, she said, "May I?"

"Sure." Without hesitation, he handed her his phone. It was a nice one but not as nice as hers which was the beta of a new type of phone. She added a stronger layer of encryption, turned off the location setting with a secret app that worked when the phone was off. And switched it from being a cell to a satphone, which a year ago would have been impossible.

"There you go." She handed it back to him. "I added 256-bit AES encryption, plus a WPA2. Your location setting is temporarily switched off and you now hold a satphone and not a cellphone, so you're not operating off the local cell tower. As of this moment, your phone cannot be tracked."

He cocked his head. "So let me get this straight. You essentially cast a magic spell over my phone that makes it invisible and you turned it into a powerful wizard."

"That's right." Luke was handling his phone gingerly, as if it might wake up and bite him. "By the way, as soon as we get back to Portland, you're changing phones. This one is primitive."

He made a choking sound. "Yeah, uh … it's the latest model."

"Primitive." She clucked her tongue. Latest model if you were a caveman. "Can you call Jacob Black? I didn't disable the ID function so he'll see who is calling if you're in his system."

Luke scrolled and tapped, on speakerphone. On the second ring, it was picked up, and a man appeared on the cell's monitor.

Jacob Black.

Hope didn't pay that much attention to corporate gossip but Jacob Black was a living legend. Founder and owner of what was by all accounts one of the largest and most powerful security companies in the world. Also a billionaire several times over. That didn't faze her. In tech, she'd dealt with billionaires before. Most of them were like children, only with money. Tech smart and life stupid.

Jacob Black didn't look even remotely like a child. He had a hard, narrow face burnt dark brown by the sun and reflective sunglasses that gave him a robotic look. In the background was a harsh blue sky with a bright pitiless sun that gave an intense glare. Everything else was a dun color — the street, the walls of the buildings, the men dressed for battle in desert camo. There was a lot of mechanical noise in the background.

Luke had caught Black in the middle of something, but neither his voice nor his expression betrayed impatience. "Hang on, Luke, let me get out of the street." The monitor's images bounced up and down as Black entered a building and shut a heavy door behind him. The image again stabilized, focused on Black's dark, hard face. "So, what can I do for you?" he asked.

Which was a remarkable statement for a multi-billionaire warrior to make. Hope had known some tech giants who answered their phones with a barked, "What?"

What can I do for you was a strange thing for such a powerful man to say. And yet his expression hadn't changed. He wasn't irritated or angry. Just waiting to hear what Luke had to say.

Luke didn't mince words. "Sir, you know Bard Redfield, correct?"

If he was puzzled at the question, Black didn't show it. "I do. He was my first commanding officer."

"And your opinion of him?"

"Excellent." Black's expression changed slightly. His brows drew together and his lips thinned. "He was my XO in the darkest days of Iraq. He's a fine man, the best. *And my friend.*"

The emphasis on those last words was clear. Bard Redfield was Black's friend and Black wasn't going to like it if someone spoke ill of him.

Hope was a little intimidated. Granted, Black was a billion miles away. In Afghanistan, would be her guess, though that background could have been any combat zone in a desert area. There were a lot of those. There was nothing he could do to her on the other side of the world. Still, she shrank back a little. Thick black eyebrows were drawn down over his blade of a nose in a scowl. He'd taken his sunglasses off and she could see that his eyes were almost black. And cold.

Luke wasn't intimidated at all. "Okay. This is the situation. I am here with a young woman who is Bard Redfield's biological child. By a woman Bard apparently loved, who lived in Sacramento. They —"

Black interrupted. "She is *Lucy Benson's* daughter?"

Luke glanced at her then turned back to the screen. "Yes. This is confirmed by DNA."

Black didn't seem to be listening. "Let me see her," he demanded. "Right now."

Luke glanced again at Hope and when she nodded, turned the cell to her, framing her face.

"Jesus fucking Christ," Black breathed. "I don't know your name, but you are the spitting image of Bard. He has no idea you exist, none at all. Lucy was the love of his life and he never had a serious affair after her. She just blew him off after he was wounded. He never got over her and he thinks of her to this day. If it's money you want, Bard will give you the shirt off his back."

Hope's voice turned cold and crisp. "I don't want money, Mr. Black. Not a dime. I'm fine. But I do want to know if my father tried to have me killed."

Jacob Black seemed like the very epitome of an unflappable man but his features went slack for a moment. "Have you *killed?* Bard?"

He was surprised? The idea of a warrior, a man who'd been a soldier all his life and had served in war zones, being an actual killer wasn't an impossible stretch, she thought. In essence a soldier was a professional killer. But Hope had two soldiers right before her — Luke and Jacob Black. Luke technically wasn't a soldier any more but he was about to become a security expert for a company made up of former soldiers like himself. Jacob Black too wasn't a government soldier but was the head of a highly successful company made up of former warriors. Telling both of them that Bard Redfield was already a killer anyway wasn't a smart move.

"Unlike you, Mr. Black, I don't know him. I only know that I had a DNA analysis done and it pinged on the Redfields. The next thing I know, the friend who did the DNA analysis is dead. I have remote access to my surveillance system, and masked, armed men broke into my apartment that same day. Luckily I was able to escape. I don't like to think of what they'd have done to me if I'd been there. Someone doesn't want me around. And for the record, I have been told that Lucy Benson, my — my mother, thought Bard Redfield had died. Court Redfield went to see her to tell her Bard had been killed and that she should never contact any of the Redfields again. She was pregnant with me but didn't know it yet. Five years later, she read an article and discovered that Bard was alive. She tried to contact him with photos of me and a few days later she was dead and I was in a coma."

Black frowned. "You remember all of this?"

As if. "No. I remember nothing and this was as much of a surprise to me as it is to you. Luke and I watched a video recorded by my uncle, Frank Glass, who told me the story."

Black's face changed. "Frank … Lucy's brother was Frank Glass?"

"Half brother, apparently, but yes. Did you know him?"

"Bard told me about his affair with Lucy once when he was very drunk. He said she had a half brother named Frank, a real nerdy guy. I had no idea we were talking about Frank Glass."

"I don't think he was *the* Frank Glass at the time. I think he was just a bright kid with good ideas." Hope wanted to bring the conversation around to what she needed. "So — twenty-five years ago someone had my mother killed, tried to kill me and would have if my uncle hadn't acted quickly. He had me taken to a hospital far away from the scene of the accident, had me declared dead and relocated me under another name. When I tried to find a match of my DNA and it was found by a good friend of mine, someone killed him and sent what looked like a team of hitmen to my apartment. They also killed the doorman. That someone might be my father. That's why I called. You know him and know what he is capable of. Is he capable of this?"

Black's face tightened. "Never. Never in a million years would Bard have been capable of hurting Lucy in any way. And hurting his own daughter? There's just no way. But I'll bet you anything his father would be capable."

Luke shot her a quick glance. "Court Redfield?"

"Yeah. God, Bard hated his father's guts, still does. The old man is a psychopath."

"That psychopath is gearing up for a run for the Presidency," Hope said dryly. "And he just might win. If he's the one responsible for all of this, he does not want anyone to know about me and he's shown that he is willing to kill. But I refuse to lie low, in hiding, because of him."

Suddenly her shoulders were taken in a strong grip. Luke's arm around her. He was a warm wall of strength by her side. She leaned into him.

Black nodded sharply. "Understood. I'm going to call Bard. Right now. He's Stateside, the last I heard. He's going to be absolutely stoked at your existence and enraged at his father."

Luke glanced at her and she gave a small shake of her head.

"Absolutely not." Luke's face hardened. "Not going to happen. Hope will decide when and how she contacts her father. Not anyone else."

Jacob Black was immensely powerful and rich. His company essentially had the resources of a small country and Black was its king. Luke had no money and no power. And yet there was no question who would win this. Luke was like a force of nature.

Black held up huge, calloused hands. "Okay, okay. But tell him soon. That guy has missed Lucy almost all his adult life. He needs to know about his daughter. About — what's your name?"

"Hope. Hope Ellis. That guy — or his father — had my mother killed," Hope said sharply. "I'm not going to expose myself to him until I'm certain who is responsible for my mother's death and my friend's death."

"Well, it wasn't Bard. You need to talk to him soon." The force of Black's will seemed to come through the screen. Hope could almost see magnetic lines of power emanating from him. Man, this was one powerful dude.

"Fuck that." And then Luke stepped forward and it was like the battle of Jedi warriors because she could see *his* lines of male power meeting Black's halfway and there was almost a shimmer in the Force. "Hope will talk to him when she feels safe doing so. And not a second before. I'm not going to risk her safety because you think Bard Redfield is a good guy. A lot of good guys go bad. You know that as well as I do."

There was a male staring contest, like an elk battle only without antlers, and Black stood down. "Bard would be incapable of hurting Hope, and I know for a fact that he'd welcome her with open arms. But I respect that you can't take my word for that. Not when her safety is at risk."

Luke nodded and his taut body language relaxed. "I have your word you won't say anything to him?" Luke asked.

Black bent his head slightly. "You have my word. But I'd like to give you two his private cell. It's a number he will always answer and only he will answer it."

"Yes." Hope surprised herself by how much she wanted that number. A portal maybe, to another world. Or the engine of her death. But a number that would at least end this feeling of being a molecule lost in space that had accompanied her for her entire lifetime. "Please. I'd very much like his number."

"I'm texting it to you," Black said. "And consider me at your disposal. If you want to arrange a meeting, I can be there as a sort of guarantor. Say the word and I'll be there as fast as I can get there. I owe it to him."

Considering he was in the field, and was a very busy man, it was quite an offer.

Hope glanced at Luke and ran a quick finger

across her throat.

"Okay then." Luke brought the screen back to his own face. "Thanks for your time, sir. We really appreciate it and we'll be in touch. Thanks for sending Redfield's cell number."

"Call him," Black urged.

"We will. We just don't know when." Luke broke the connection.

Silence. Hope was trying to assimilate all this information. Jacob Black was known as a powerful man but she had never heard a word against his character, unlike some of the contractor types she'd worked with at the NSA. He'd never cheated or corrupted, that she was aware of, in a business rife with corruption. It seemed like every month a contractor went to jail for trying to game the system. Which made sense, because the PMC business was huge.

No one ever so much as breathed a word against Jacob Black, which meant he was either clean or so ruthless no one dared open their mouths.

But Luke was easy with him and that counted for a lot with her.

She must have looked like a dork, standing there, lost in her thoughts because Luke took her gently by the arm. "Come on. I think this calls for alcohol. We'll talk it over and do what you think is best."

What was best? Her thoughts were such a jumble.

She made a living, and a good one at that, by thinking clearly. Her thinking was usually linear, rational, logical and she was capable of keeping a lot of data in her head while making decisions. But now there were all these elements and she didn't know what relationship they bore to each other. Her mother wasn't the mother she'd known but a woman she didn't remember, Lucy. Her father was a warrior and the son of a man who was immensely powerful and might become the most powerful man in the world. He also might have killed her mother and tried to have her killed. Or maybe it was his father. Her uncle was Frank Glass.

And then there was Luke.

There was nowhere to put these thoughts in order. No way to draw conclusions and no way to understand what to do next.

Luke walked her over to a cabinet with some high-end liquor bottles and cut glass tumblers turned upside down to avoid gathering dust.

How do you keep a safe house where no one lived clean? Did regular cleaners come in, say, twice a month? Or just after it had been used as a safe house, to clear out the pizza boxes?

It was an organizational issue, she thought as he poured out a glass with a finger of amber liquid. But surely a safe house was used on an irregular basis so there'd have to be a data base that —

It happened all at once, in slow motion. The pretty cut-crystal glass on the sideboard blew up in a cascade of red. She turned to Luke but he — he wasn't there. He was diving to the floor and taking her with him. She landed on her back, the breath driven right out of her by his heavy weight on top of her. He looked so lean yet he was really heavy. It was hard to breathe and she tried to push him off but her hands kept slipping in something red ...

And time, which had slowed down, suddenly rushed back in like a tide held back. Someone had shot at them! And she'd been hit! She looked at her red hands but couldn't figure out where she'd been hit.

She hadn't been hit. But Luke had.

"Luke!" Hope tried to get him to lift up a bit to see him better but he pushed her down, arms over her head, protecting her. "You've been shot! Let me see!" she cried. Pushing hard, she couldn't budge him. Her hands were bright red and sticky with blood. "You need medical care!"

He wasn't listening, focused on his cellphone. Of all the times ... but then she saw what he was looking at. It was a view of the surrounding area around the house, in windows on the cell screen. It looked similar to the app she had for security for her apartment.

She frantically searched his screen but it was empty of people. The images were a greenish ghostly tint which she recognized as night vision. "Who shot at us? I don't see him."

"Neither do I, damn it. And I don't understand how he could aim and hit me, we were away from the windows and the curtains are drawn anyway."

She was studying the static images carefully.

"Thermal?"

"Fuck," he said. "Yeah. We don't dare stand up. We're relatively safe on the floor but we can't stay here forever. Listen, stay here for a second while I go get thermal blankets, that will hide our thermal signature. You're okay here behind the couch. The shot came from the front."

Her throat tightened. She didn't want Luke to leave her, there was safety while she was touching his strong lean body. But there was someone out there and they were sitting ducks as they were.

Luke planted both hands on the ground in front of her and lifted himself off. His left arm was shaking and as he rose behind the couch, she gasped. His entire left side was soaked in blood. He'd been shot in the back and the exit wound from his left shoulder was a bloody hole in his flesh. It hadn't hit an artery and it didn't look like it had gone through bone, but it looked dangerous and immensely painful.

There was no expression on Luke's face, but his skin was grey and clammy.

"Let me go! Tell me where the blankets are and I'll get them."

"No." His face tightened even further. "Stay right here, don't move."

Before she could answer he was up in a deep crouch, hiding behind furniture. Across the room was a closet and he headed right for it, crawling along the ground, leaving a horrible trail of blood.

In a second, he was wrapped in the foil blanket

which would mask his thermal signature and he was armed, holding a sleek black pistol in his hand, and dragging a small duffel behind him. He crawled back, wrapped her in the other foil blanket and sat up with his back to the couch.

"Even if they have the house surrounded, there are two rooms between us and the outside walls in this direction. Fuck! How did they get past the guard?"

"I'm sure there are security cams at the guard station." Hope picked up his cell, ignoring the streaks of red, scrolling through until she found what she was looking for. "Nope. They are all offline. Though, I think — here. This must be the security cam from under the eaves of the roof of the guardhouse. But there's no one there."

Luke was breathing heavily. "Impossible. It's guarded 24/7. That's the point of having a guard." He studied the image of a brightly lit, empty cubicle. "Fuck. Look at that." He pointed to the bottom of the small window. Hope squinted but could only make out two small dark blobs.

"What?"

"Shoes." Luke's voice was grim. Yeah. If they'd killed the guard to get in there'd be a body, and she was looking at it.

Blood from Luke's shoulder wound was dripping onto the tile floor.

"We need to call 911 and an ambulance!" Hope tried and failed to keep the fear and anxiety out of her voice. Luke himself seemed the picture of thoughtful calm, though he'd been shot. With a bullet. Out of a gun.

God.

That wound needed packing. It would need surgery and IV antibiotics but right now, the most important thing was to stop the bleeding. Presumably there were tea towels in the kitchen she could use or she could rip up a sheet, but the kitchen and the sheets might as well have been in Siberia or on the moon. The Mylar foil blanket around her shoulders was completely unrippable. Mylar was used as cladding for space capsules reentering the atmosphere.

Wait ...

The jacket of her sweat suit! She shucked it off quickly and rolled it into a ball, leaving the sleeves free. Luke watched her out of the corner of his eye but said nothing. She rose on her knees, facing him.

"This is going to hurt," she warned.

He nodded. Set his jaw. His face was grayer than before.

Hope gently tried to lift his long-sleeved tee but he gave an involuntary moan and beads of sweat broke out on his forehead. "I'll need to cut this off you," she whispered. The thought of sprinting across to the kitchen to get scissors was daunting. Impossible.

Luke bent a little, jaws clenched and lips white, to slide a knife out from his boots. Hope's eyes widened. She'd had no idea it was there. He handed it to her. It was a stiletto, the edges honed like a razor blade. Exactly what she needed.

"Hold still." He became a rock, even though his nerve endings must be screaming with pain. She did her best to slit the heavy cotton as quickly as she could without jostling him. When she sliced through the collar, the tee fell open. No point in trying to get it off him, all she needed was access to ...she saw his shoulder for the first time and swallowed heavily ... the wound. God.

The wound was awful. The worst thing she'd ever seen. Worse than the time her neighbor's German shepherd had been run over by a truck and reduced to a sack of blood and broken bones.

The wound was open, the size of her fist, butchered flesh flayed away from the terrible exit hole. Blood was seeping out fast. It had to stop. She didn't know much first aid but this she knew. The bleeding had to stop and it had to stop right now. There was nothing to stitch him up with, even if she knew how, which she didn't. No idea how to put a tourniquet around a shoulder.

No, the only possible thing was to put pressure on the wound and bind it until he could receive medical care.

And that would hurt like crazy.

Hope was holding the sweat suit top. She met Luke's eyes. "I'm going to have to do this. Pack your wound. And it's going to hurt."

He held her gaze. If possible, his face was even

grayer than before. "Now might be a good time to say that I think I love you. No, scratch that. I know I love you."

Hope nearly lost her hold on the soft material. Her mind turned entirely blank with shock. "What? I —"

But he looked so awful, in such pain, that she couldn't continue. First priority here was to staunch his bleeding so that this wonderful brave man who'd just crazily said he was in love with her would not die on her. After declaring his love. That would really suck.

"Hold on," she said shakily as she mapped out in her head what to do. Place the folded up material directly over the wound — thank God the jacket was clean — and wrap one arm of the jacket over his left shoulder and the other around his chest and tie the two arms together across his back. Good thing the material was super stretchy otherwise the two arms would never have met across that broad back. "Ready? You'll have to hold still."

He nodded and she pressed the wad of material over the terrible wound. Luke held rock steady but a hissing moan escaped him and he turned a color she'd never seen on living flesh.

Hope took his hand, pressed it over the material and grabbed the two arms. She shuffled until she was behind him, stretching the two arms until she could tie a tight knot over his back. Every muscle in his body was taut and quivering. She pressed a kiss he probably couldn't feel over the shoulder blade and shuffled back around to look him in the face.

"What's next?" she asked.

"Calling it in." He held up his phone. "That spell you cast will still hold, right?"

He was joking. Surely he wouldn't — couldn't — joke if he were dying, right? She nodded shakily.

His left hand had no grasping power. He simply placed his cell in the palm that was lying on his lap, limp and still, and went to his contact list and pushed an icon.

"Speakerphone," she said. "On low."

He nodded and slid the volume control way down.

He called it in to 911, identifying himself as a former police officer with the Portland PD and giving the address. "We're pinned down and I am wounded. Be prepared for an armed response. Don't know how many hostiles." He closed the connection. "They'll be here in ten minutes."

Hope watched Luke's face carefully. "Do we have ten minutes?"

"I hope so. We —"

A fusillade of gunfire interrupted him and he threw himself over her reflexively, grunting with pain. He shouldn't be moving with a wound like that. The gunfire raked the house, left to right and right to left. The windows were bulletproof and simply starred but the bullets went through the walls. It was a sustained fusillade, violent and terrifying, smashing furniture and ceramics. Bits of wood and glass floated in the air.

And not a sound of the shots, just of the damage.

"They don't know where we are," he murmured into her ear. She could feel his heartbeat against her back, steady and regular. Her own heart was hammering so hard she was afraid it would beat itself right out of her chest. "So they're just pumping in bullets. And damn, they're all silenced."

"Can you check the security cams?"

His head bowed as he looked at his cell, scrolling through, jaws clenched. "Nothing. It's got to be a fucking —"

"Drone." They said the word at the same time. Hope had no idea what that meant, if it was good or bad. Bad probably. It also meant that they — whoever they were — came ready for business. A drone with a silenced machine gun.

Great. Just great. They were being hunted by a Borg.

She turned her head up and studied Luke's face, trying to take her cues from him. But his face expressed nothing but extreme stress. White and sweaty and taut. It was horrible because this situation — she had no idea what to do with it. And she wanted to live through it.

Oh man, yes, she wanted to live through it. She wanted to live. The desire to live rose up in her with raging ferocity, surprising her. If you'd asked her before to list her characteristics, strong will for survival would have been dead last. Not even there, really.

But not now. She had so much to live for. The promise of a new love, a new life, even that new job with Felicity's company. Moving to a new city. A new dream life, a life where she *fit*. Where there was a place for her. Where she was welcome. Someone was trying to take that away from her. Someone felt she was inconvenient. And while they were at it, they were more than willing to kill a good man in the process.

Rage simmered.

Luke grabbed her hands, holding them tightly. His hands were scarily cold. Under that pressure bandage, she knew, he was still bleeding, though she hoped with all her heart not as profusely as before.

Luke squeezed her hands so hard she was startled. "Listen to me," he said urgently. "I just sent out the bat-signal. The closest ASI and Black Inc people are coming as fast as they can make it but it won't be fast enough. I think that drone is going to make its way around the perimeter of the house. The sensors can't pick it up so we don't know its location. That puts us at a huge disadvantage. It will just keep —"

He threw himself over her as another strafing commenced. It went from the furthest wall to about ten feet from them. If it was strafing strategically, it was very possible that the next round would be their section of the house. Luke was sprawled over her. He'd take the bullet, she wouldn't.

Again, the fusillade was eerily silent, the destruction it caused the only sound, fragments of wood, metal and textiles fogging the air. When it stopped, Luke lifted himself up and off her with a grunt. She felt wetness and checked her back. He'd bled through the improvised pressure bandage.

God.

Luke rolled over until they were both flat on the ground, face to face.

He clutched her shoulder with his good hand. "Listen." Voice low and urgent. "Next time that drone comes our way we might not be so lucky."

Yeah. Being shot in the shoulder was plenty lucky.

He shucked the foil blanket. "This is what we're going to do. I'm going to run over there —" he pointed toward the bedrooms, "without the blanket. It'll be programmed to target moving sources of heat. I'll run fast and hit the ground in the corridor, covering myself up again. The drone will shoot but I should be ok. While I'm running, I want you to keep your blanket on and head for the door next to the kitchen. It's the gun locker and it's as protected as a safe room. Bullets won't penetrate and you'll be safe. There's a keypad to open the door under the hunting print to the right. Use your knuckle covered by the foil blanket. That way you won't leave fingerprints and they won't be able to see the heat signature on the keys you've touched if they enter. The code is 84765. Can you remember that?"

If they penetrated the house in time for the keypad keys to keep a lingering heat from her fingers, she and Luke would be in terrible trouble. She would be, rather. Luke would be dead.

She could remember the numbers. Numbers were her friends. "Sure. 84765. But there's no way I'm leaving you, and there's no way you're going to try to draw them away. That's insane."

He smiled, face waxy now, nostrils and lips dead white. His eyes were exhausted and sad. "It's the only way honey. That drone is here to soften us up. They're hoping the drone killed us, but no matter what, whoever is out there will be coming in soon to check on the damage. If I — if I die, you'll be left alone to face them and they will take you out in an instant. I can't let that happen. If you're in the gun locker, you'll be safe until our guys can make it. The gun locker will withstand anything, including grenades and maybe even an RPG. If they are conscious of sound discipline they won't use grenades or an RPG though. I can plan to keep the drone shooting in the wrong direction until you're inside the locker.

This was not ok, but Luke looked absolutely determined. His determined look was different from that of the men she was used to dealing with. Their looks were stubborn. His was the look of a man who simply could not be swayed and that terrified her. She'd just found him and she couldn't lose him, simply couldn't.

He wasn't going to be swayed by the mention of danger or the fact that he'd probably die, something that would be a major deterrent for most of the men she knew.

That wasn't going to work here.

So in the short time she had before he gathered his strength for what might well be a last sprint, she had to convince him to do the thing that would save his life.

She clutched his hand. "Listen, if that drone has thermal imaging a bloom of heat and light will burn its receptors, for a moment at least, until the subset of instructions closes the lens. So we need to create a controlled fire. But not one that will kill us in the locker if it spreads. Which leaves that fancy fireplace. Can you turn on the gas fire remotely?"

His eyes widened for a moment then he nodded. "It might just work," he murmured.

"Of course it will." She was exasperated.

That earned her a small smile.

"When I turn it on, we could make a small Molotov cocktail and toss it onto the fire to make it flare. That will really blind the drone." He spoke with effort, through clenched teeth.

"Um. We'd have to toss it exactly into the fire. That's hard."

It was his turn to look exasperated. "I am a very good baseball player and I have excellent aim."

He also had a bullet wound in his shoulder but maybe now was not the time to mention that. Luke got to his knees, with a difficulty he tried to disguise, thermal blanket over him. He started to shuffle toward the drinks cabinet but she stopped him.

"Let me." Before he could protest, she duck-walked under the thermal blanket, grabbed a bottle and a lighter near the little forest of candles and made it back in record time. "Here."

Luke was staring at the bottle.

"What?" she asked impatiently.

He had a peculiar expression on his face. "This is a 40-year-old single malt. It probably costs three hundred dollars."

Hope heroically refrained from rolling her eyes. "Then take a big slug or three before you toss it. Probably act as a pain killer. You don't need to aim. Reducing your pain would probably be worth being slightly soused."

Luke's eyes narrowed. "I don't get soused on a few slugs."

"*Luke.*" God, now was not the time for him to get all macho on her, when he'd been so good up until now. "Light the fire and throw the damned bottle. And then we run."

He gave a sharp nod, thumbed an app on his cell while taking a couple of healthy slugs of the amber liquor. The instant they heard the whoosh of the fireplace lighting, he capped the bottle and threw it. He didn't peek around the corner and he didn't even turn around. He threw it backhand over the couch.

As they moved as fast as they could while crouched, she chanced a look over her shoulder and damned if he hadn't thrown it perfectly. The entire fireplace area was in flames. The intensity of the light and heat must have thrown the drone into disarray because another fusillade of bullets came immediately, killing a couch, a cabinet and two expensive-looking vases.

By the time the bullets stopped, Luke was pulling the door of the gun locker closed. It closed with the soft whump of an expensive car door. The instant it was closed, Luke put his back to the wall and slumped down. He looked terrifyingly white. He looked — no, she wasn't going there.

"Whoa, that was one perfect pitch, slick. I don't think I've ever seen anyone throw like that before. I'm glad you got a taste of that super expensive whisky, otherwise such a shame for it to go to waste. Though it wasn't really a waste, was it? It will probably save our lives."

She was babbling through chattering teeth as she tried in vain to find something else to use as a pressure bandage because her sweat suit jacket was sodden with blood. She had on a soft tee, the only soft thing inside this gun locker which had enough weaponry neatly aligned along the walls on special hooks and foam cutouts to start a war. Against the far wall was even an array of knives, the blades a dull black but which looked wicked sharp. Guns, machine guns, other guns that looked like they belonged to Men in Black, ropes with hooks, neatly stacked boxes of what she could only presume was ammunition other things she had no name for …

Everything except something that could work as a pressure bandage. She whipped off the tee, folded it and untied the sleeves of the jacket behind Luke's back. He was barely conscious and she had to gently bend him forward to get at the sleeves.

Peeling off the jacket, she winced at the wound, at the broken flesh. God he needed medical care! Placing the folded material over the wound and pressing, she retied the jacket over it. He grunted when she pressed against the wound and opened his eyes. He tried to smile when he saw her in only a sports bra.

"Pretty," he slurred, and closed his eyes again.

In the movies you weren't supposed to sleep. That might be only for concussions — but maybe it applied to bullet wounds, too.

"Hey, hey Luke!" she shook his unwounded shoulder, just enough to keep him awake. His eyes popped open. "There's a really weird smell in here."

"Hoppes," he said, closing his eyes, and smiled again.

"Hops? Like what you make beer with?"

"No," he said. He was slurring his words a little. "Hoppes, gun solvent."

Who the hell cared? It could be Chanel N° 5 for all she cared. She just wanted to keep Luke talking.

"Let me have your cell." He held it out without opening his eyes. "Luke, look at me. Hand me your cell." His eyes were slitted, he was having problems keeping them open. To her horror, blood was seeping out again from under the makeshift bandage. She couldn't remember how much blood the human body held but he had lost a good chunk of it.

The cell was open. The security app was easy to figure out but showed nothing. Security cams existed only at the front and back doors and they were free. However, the front door security cam showed an unusually bright light. The augmented fire in the fireplace. *God, please don't set the entire house on fire!* Was the gun locker fireproofed? If not they had the pleasant option of being suffocated or burnt to death. After which, the bullets would start cooking off and riddle their burnt-to-a-crisp bodies with bullet holes.

They were a coroner's nightmare in waiting.

Muffled sounds of gunfire damage. The drone was hitting another part of the house. Presumably soon someone would report something to the police.

"Call the good guys, find out where they are." She held the cell flat in her hand so Luke could touch the screen with a trembling finger.

"Hey Luke, five mikes out," a deep voice announced.

"Five minutes," Luke slurred.

That was good news, though a lot could happen in five minutes.

A faint tinkling sound. The drone had targeted the area where the gun locker was. It was bulletproof though maybe not fireproof. Like a video game where you were under attack by the dragon, the wizard and the evil king's minions.

And your sword was broken.

Her personal sword was slumped against the wall, breathing heavily.

Not too many cards left to play.

"Hey Luke. Luke!" She shook him again, gently. He struggled to sit up straighter. "Is this gun locker fireproof?"

That shocked him into awareness. "It won't catch fire, but it probably doesn't have a separate air system."

Which meant they could be smoked out if the house caught fire.

"Has the fire spread?" The words were slurred but still comprehensible.

"Dunno." She held up his phone with the security apps program running. "No security cams in the house, just at the front and back entrances. But one of the security cams is picking up a big source of light. I could write a little algo comparing the lumens to known sources of heat and extrapolate but it would be pointless. What?"

He'd made a snorting sound. "Nothing."

"Do you want me to call our guys again? Because they'd feel pretty bad if they rushed to get here and all they found was our charred remains."

He shook his head. "They're — they're coming as fast as they can. And they'll see the fire. The vans have extinguishers."

"So ... now it's a battle between the speed of the fire, if flammable objects catch on, and the speed of the good guy vans? And we don't dare go out because there's a fire-breathing drone out there and presumably bad guys not too far away."

That faint smile was still there as he nodded.

Was that her imagination or did she smell smoke? As a way to die, a bullet felt better than being burned alive.

She bent to her cell. "Then there's one last thing left to try. Call the dogs off."

He blinked. "Wha —?"

She punched in the number Jacob Black had given her. "Calling my father. If he's behind this, nothing lost, we're where we were. If he's not, then I'll appeal to his fatherly instincts. If he has any."

Didn't want to think about her own father trying to have her killed, because it was too monstrous.

Her finger hovered over the cell screen. She might be making a mistake. She might be saving their lives.

The lady or the tiger?

She touched the call button. It rang and was picked up almost immediately. Black had said it was his private cell. Hope kept the video function off.

"Redfield," a deep voice said. "Who is this?"

"Mr. Redfield …" How weird to call the man who was her father mister. On the other hand, she never called the man she thought was her father Dad, either. He'd always been Neil to her. She checked on Luke. He was even grayer than before but he'd dipped into reserves and was watching her attentively, one hand curled around his gun. He was down but apparently not out. Not yet.

She took a deep breath. This was for Luke, too. "Mr. Redfield, Jacob Black gave me your number. My name is Hope Ellis. But I was born Catherine Benson. I have recently found out that my mother's name was Lucy Benson. Mr. Redfield, I have reason to believe I am your daughter."

She switched on the video function and heard a gasp. He switched on his video function and she gasped.

She'd seen the photograph but in real life it was just amazing. She looked just like him. Same narrow face, same deep green eyes, same high cheekbones. And beyond the features, something more. A deep family resemblance.

Genes at work.

No one could doubt they were related, and closely.

The man looked shocked. She was shocked too, though she'd had a while to chew on the situation, get used to it.

There'd been a part of her that hadn't really believed any of this. Though she'd been trained to think in binary terms — something either was or wasn't — and there'd been ample evidence showing that what Frank Glass had told her about her past was true, some part of her still found the whole thing outlandish.

That part was gone.

She was Bard Redfield's daughter. The proof was

in her face.

Redfield spoke. "You're — you're Lucy's daughter?"

"And yours. Apparently."

He didn't even deny it. It would be like denying that the earth rotated around the sun.

"Where is she?" He'd moved his face closer to the screen, there was an urgency there. And she realized that he thought her mother was still alive. "Did she send you to me?"

Hope felt stupid, like shock had wiped away half her IQ. "No, no she didn't. She —" she swallowed. "My mother is dead. She was killed. Someone ran her car off the road. I was in the car too but I survived. I don't remember anything about her." All of a sudden her eyes filled with tears and for the first time she mourned the mother she couldn't remember. "Mr. Redfield, I think your father had her killed."

His face closed up like a fist, hard and angular. She would have been afraid of this man if she'd been in the same room with him. For an instant the temptation was huge to just hang up. Her phone was untraceable. He'd never know where she was.

But a tiny wisp of smoke, so faint it was almost invisible, ghosted into the locker. She and Luke could die in here.

This man might help. He might not. If not, if he had sent killers after her, she and Luke were in trouble. Maybe lost.

Her own face closed up. "I have DNA analyses

that prove what I am saying. They are with a lawyer," she lied. "My lawyer has instructions to send the results to all the major press outlets and online press. It would be a scandal your father doesn't need at the start of his campaign."

"Fuck my father and fuck his campaign," he said sharply. "You say my father had Lucy *killed?*"

"In 1995, or so my uncle told me. And he's trying to kill me. I am with an operative of ASI in a Black Inc safe house in Sacramento. An armed drone is attempting to kill us. My friend is hit. He's bleeding badly. We are in the safe house's gun locker but to get here we had to start a fire, which I think is now out of control. We can't leave the locker because the drone is outside, together with the man or men operating it. But if we don't leave very soon, we'll burn in here."

She panned the room so he could see, lingering on Luke, on his gray sweaty face, on the blood-soaked improvised bandage on his shoulder.

She brought the phone back to her, talking fast, the words tripping over themselves. "We're in real trouble here. If it's not you coming after us, then I think it's your father who sent these people. Black Inc is coming but I don't know if they'll get here in time. Can you call our attackers off?"

The man's face was even tighter. "Goddamn right I can. Can you stay on the line?"

She nodded. "Hurry," she whispered. The smell of smoke was unmistakable. Luke coughed. Oh god, had the bullet gone through his lungs? How could you tell? "Hurry," she said again.

"Be right back. I'm switching to another phone."

Hope let the phone clatter to the ground and fell to her knees next to Luke. Closer to the floor there was an acrid smell that made her cough. Worse, it made Luke cough, leaving him weak. He leaned his head against the locker wall and closed his eyes.

"No!" Hope yelled, taking him by his good shoulder and pulling him forward. It was horrible to feel how lax he was, this super strong former soldier. He felt like a rag doll, barely able to sit upright. His entire side was red, the blood glistening, fresh. He coughed again, weakly.

The tendrils of smoke were visible, a gray pall in the small room. She lifted Luke's phone and saw the shadows of flames dancing on the walls through the entrance security cameras. There was no way to know how far the fire had spread but if smoke was already penetrating the gun locker, they were in trouble.

One thing was for sure — Hope would rather take her chances with the Borg than wait in a small room to be roasted alive. The very thought of being trapped there while a fire raged made her skin prickle. Even something that gave them a small chance of survival was better than simply waiting here to burn.

She mapped out the house in her head. Assuming the flames were concentrated for the moment in the living room area and kitchen, maybe she could help

Luke up and they could make their way to the garage. He couldn't crouch, he'd fall over. But she'd make sure that they were covered with the thermal blanket and anyway at least as far as the corridor the flames would mask their presence.

The plan was a little vague after that. Dragging Luke to the car and driving like a bat out of hell was the only thing to do. With no idea where the attackers were, she could be driving herself and Luke straight into their path. The drone could certainly follow them and maybe shoot straight into the roof of the vehicle. She wasn't much of a driver and was perfectly capable of driving them into a tree if someone was shooting at them.

In the movies it looked easy but she knew herself. The chances of her driving them away to safety were very close to nil.

The chances of them burning alive in here were 100%.

No question what she had to do though she was scared to death. Maybe she couldn't even bear Luke's weight and they'd slump to the ground outside and be burned to a crisp almost immediately.

One thing for sure. She wasn't leaving Luke. No way. He was wounded because of her. All he'd done was work to protect her. He wouldn't leave her and she wouldn't leave him.

She loved him.

It came in a blinding flash of utter clarity, maybe the last intuition of her life. Love had always seemed so far from anything she could ever experience, something not ever meant for her. But here it was. She admired him, cared for him. Loved him. Wanted to be with him for the rest of her life.

She'd cheated death twenty-five years ago but death had only been lying in wait. It was coming to claim her, maybe angry that she'd escaped it all those years ago. Maybe that was her destiny but it wasn't Luke's. It was wrong for Luke to die. Luke — so brave and so noble. A truly good man. He didn't deserve to die. She'd do everything in her power to keep him alive.

The smoke was thick enough now to be visible. It burned the eyes and throat and she was sure the air was hotter than a few minutes ago. Maybe the fire wasn't far off in the living room but was right outside that door.

They had to go, now.

"Up you go," she said, tugging at Luke's good arm. He coughed hard, without opening his eyes. "Up, Luke," she said again. His combat boots scrabbled on the floor until they found some purchase and he rose shakily to his feet. "Lean on me."

He did, heavily. Hope nearly staggered under his weight. What had seemed like a small shot at survival while he was on the floor now seemed almost impossible. They'd have to move fast but he was barely able to stay on his feet. God, she couldn't carry him, didn't think she could drag him if he fell.

Despair washed over her. Either they'd have to

walk through fire or be exposed to gunfire. Probably both. Even if they managed to make it to the garage, getting Luke into the vehicle was going to be hard.

The only way to deal with it was like dealing with an IT problem. Step by step. Solve problem one, go on to problem two.

Problem one — keeping Luke upright. She angled herself under his right shoulder, put his right arm around her, and snaked her left arm around his waist. Holding him up, barely.

Now to get going. The smell of smoke was intense and her eyes stung. God help them if the fire was right outside the gun locker. Guns ... she eyed the walls, filled with guns. Guns everywhere. Guns would help if she knew how to shoot, which she didn't. Luke already had his own gun. It hadn't left his hand in all this time. He wasn't letting it go, and it rested on her shoulder, clutched in his hand.

She didn't know if he had the strength to lift it, to shoot it. Even if he did, he certainly couldn't handle more than one.

When she opened the door, they'd be met by a wall of smoke, so she took in a deep breath and startled when a face appeared on her cell.

Bard Redfield.

"Shooter's gone." His face was drawn, his voice urgent. "Men from Black Inc are arriving right now. Get out of there as fast as you can."

"There's a shooting drone right outside!" It was hard to keep the panic from her voice.

"No. The drone has been taken down, man operating it is ... neutralized. Get out!"

Hope tried to study that face with such oddly familiar features, tried to see the truth in pixels on a small screen. Was this a ruse? Were the men outside, trying to kill them, *his* men? Was he simply trying to make things easier for his killers?

Was she going to lead Luke to his death? Wipe out that infinitesimal chance they had of surviving this?

That dark, weather-beaten face came closer, filled the screen. "Listen to me, Hope. I loved your mother with all my heart. I thought she'd left me when I was wounded. I had no idea —" His deep voice cracked. "No idea she'd been killed, no idea you existed. I would never ever harm you. You need to get out of that house and get to Black's men outside. You trust Jacob Black, right?"

She nodded, throat too tight to talk.

"Then trust them until I get a chance to earn your trust. But do this for me — *live*. Get out alive. I am coming for you as fast as I can."

"Luke needs medical attention, now."

"They all have medic training. Now go!"

Hope settled her shoulder more solidly under Luke's arm and reached out to open the gun locker door.

Behind the door was hell itself. Black smoke billowed in her face, acrid and oily, coating her throat. She and Luke immediately started coughing. Beyond the smoke were dark yellow flames reaching out with greedy fingers to the curtains. Her vision grew cloudy, it was hard to think. Lack of oxygen.

You were supposed to go low in a fire, below the rising smoke, but Hope couldn't get Luke to crouch. He'd fall over and she'd never get him back up again. They had to run. Now.

Luke was swaying. The only way for him to move was basically pulling him. "Luke!" she yelled. "We have to get out!"

He blinked, visibly groggy, then bent over coughing. Her arm was around him and she tried to push him forward. He looked at her, frowning and coughing. "Hope? Are you ok?"

She had a flash of genius. "No, I'm hurt Luke! We have to get out! Black's men are waiting for us outside!"

"Hurt? You're hurt? Where?"

Where was she hurt? Somewhere he couldn't see. "My back. I'm bleeding. We have to *get out now!*"

Luke's face hardened, the tendons in his neck stuck out with effort. "Hold on to me, honey."

She nodded. She was holding on to him to keep him standing. But if he thought he was leading her to safety that might make a difference, allow him to stay on his feet long enough to make it out.

A snazzy modern corrugated-paper floor lamp went up with a whoosh, the flames crackling so hard they couldn't hear each other any more.

In the distance were sirens. The fire brigade.

Come to save them, only it was too late. They had to save themselves.

She pushed forward with her arm across his back, using the strength of her entire body. He came with her, stumbling and unsteady. His labored breathing rose above the noise of the fire and he was leaning heavily on her.

Hope's lungs were on fire and it was hard to think, hard to see. Everything hurt — her lungs, her throat, her eyes. Straight ahead should be the door to the garage but she couldn't see it for the smoke. They were slowing down when they should be speeding up. A lone spark flew in the air and caught on her bare skin. Biting pain but she couldn't pay any attention. Then another spark and another, burning her skin.

Luke stumbled over a rug and almost fell. His entire weight rested on her for a moment and she nearly crumpled. She stopped and pushed against him until he stood upright again. Her knees and legs were trembling with the strain. She couldn't see, couldn't breathe, could barely move …

They bumped straight into a wall, Hope's head bouncing off it. They were trapped! Nowhere to go! Her hand reached out wildly and she felt hinges, the door. The handle was brass and hot but she pushed down, opened and there was blessed air! Sweet and smokeless and life-giving.

She bent a moment and wheezed in and out but she'd been propping Luke up and he fell. Hope caught him, struggling to keep him upright.

Hands reached for them and she recoiled in horror. "No!" she screamed. They'd found them and were going to kill them! She fought the hands wildly, kicking and screaming. Luke fell out of her grasp and slid to the concrete floor of the garage and she fell over him, shielding him. The idea of men wanting to hurt him when he was already so grievously injured burned in her chest. She'd die before she let that happen.

Hands reached for her again and she kicked out wildly, body splayed over Luke's.

His trembling hand came up with the gun. "Stay away from her, you fuckers!" he rasped, voice broken from the smoke.

They were surrounded by men, there was no hope. They all looked like insects, with hard carapaces, ski masks and goggles. One man took off the ski mask and the goggles and smiled.

The son of a bitch was *smiling!* In rage, Hope aimed a vicious kick that barely touched his shin which was covered by a sturdy boot anyway.

The man took her hand. "Ms. Ellis. Hope. We're here to save you and Luke, not hurt you. Jacob Black sent us. You're safe now. No one will hurt you."

She panted, searching his eyes. They were brown, cool and assessing. Then he smiled and they turned warm. "You're safe," he repeated.

His words finally penetrated. "Safe?" she whispered.

He nodded. "Yes you're safe, both of you. But we have to go now."

She glanced over. Luke was unconscious, face sweaty and sooty and completely colorless. She met the man's eyes. "Take care of him."

"We will." His voice was steady. "And we'll take care of you, too."

"I don't need it," she said, and passed out.

The next afternoon, a little dinged but feeling fine, Hope sat by Luke's hospital bed, holding his hand. He was sitting up and there was color back in his face. The surgeon said that his greatest risk had been blood loss, not the wound itself. He was stitched up, infused and taking the ribbing of two guys from ASI who'd flown down to see how he was doing and had orders to stay until he could be flown back to Portland.

Hope was starting work as soon as she could and Luke was under strictest doctor's orders to not even think of work for a month. He wasn't happy at the thought.

The two who were to accompany them back in the corporate jet, Raul Martinez and Pierce Jordan, were known as the 'twins', Luke said. They didn't look anything like each other but they'd been brothers-in-arms in the Navy as SEALs and they'd been through hell together. They'd been assigned a psychopath as a commanding officer in Afghanistan, a man who killed innocent civilians and reveled in it. Taking their career in their hands, they'd reported the commanding officer, who was then subjected to a court martial. The twins had paid a price, though. Their command had shunned them and they'd both quit and gone to work for ASI.

The twins were ribbing Luke for being rescued by a 'girl'. They winked at Hope as they said it. They were funny and annoying as hell. And they never shut up. Or rather Raul didn't. Pierce was less of a talker.

"I'm going to get so laid thanks to your story," Raul said, waggling his eyebrows like Groucho Marx. "The man known as Cool Hand Luke being rescued without getting off a shot."

"By a girl," Pierce said, for the billionth time.

It was a miracle Luke's eyes were still in his head, he was rolling them so much.

Her teeth set. "It wasn't like that." He didn't seem to be annoyed but Hope was. "Luke was very brave," she said stiffly and the twins laughed. It was really annoying that Luke laughed too.

Hope's teeth ground. Luke seemed incredibly relaxed for someone who'd been shot at and nearly burned to death. On the other hand, her nerves were shot. She still had the shakes.

Which was why she jumped at the soft knock at

the door.

A tall, gray-haired man stuck his head in the opening. "May I?"

Raul and Pierce stood at attention. Luke sat up straighter in his bed. The man who walked in had such a commanding presence Hope felt like saluting herself.

He walked in slowly, never taking his eyes from Hope and her heart started pounding and her hands shook.

Raul stuck a thumb out. "Gotta go see a guy about a thing," he said. Pierce nodded and they disappeared. Hope barely noticed. Her gaze was fixed on the man's face. A face that looked just like hers.

"Hope," he said softly.

She nodded, a huge lump in her throat rendering her incapable of speech. She felt so many emotions, all of them huge and unsettling, that she couldn't open her mouth for fear that she'd scream.

"I didn't know. I swear I didn't know. I thought your mother — Lucy — had left me. I'd been wounded and she didn't answer any of my letters. She seemed to disappear off the face of the earth. It was all my father. He didn't think she was worthy of a Redfield. Even though he wasn't worth her little finger. Your mother was so bright and so alive." He swallowed heavily. "She was pure magic and I loved her with all my heart. I've never loved another woman."

Hope swiped at the wetness on her cheeks. "I

don't remember her."

"You wouldn't. You were so small. And you were in a coma for months. I checked. There was a very young girl in a coma in a hospital in Modesto. A Jane Doe."

"Who was it? Was it your father who did this?" She finally found her voice but it was raw, as if the words were being torn out of her.

He nodded.

Her heart was still pounding. "Is he — is he dangerous to me? To us?" She glanced at Luke, who was watching her with a sad expression on his face. His grip on her hand was warm and strong and grounded her.

Something — a predatory shadow — passed across the man's face and she could see the warrior he was.

"No," he said firmly. "You'll read about it in the papers tomorrow. My father committed suicide. I confronted him and told him that I'd see him stand trial for conspiracy to murder Lucy and your friend Kyle and the doorman of your building. And for the attempted murder of his own granddaughter. And that we had Frank Glass's video. He has good spin doctors but there's no way to spin this. I'd make sure of it. I told him his life was over and left a gun on his desk. He then did the only honorable thing he has ever done in his life and used it. You're free."

A choking sob welled up inside her and she covered her mouth with her free hand.

Bard Redfield nodded. "You're free and you have a father. I want to be a part of your life as much as you'll allow. We have a lot to catch up on."

Underneath her hand, her mouth tilted up in a smile. He echoed it and turned to Luke. "I understand I have this young Ranger to thank for keeping you alive. You have my undying gratitude. She's very precious to me."

Luke grinned. "She did a pretty good job of saving herself, to tell the truth, sir. And she's precious to me, too."

Her heart overflowing, Hope remembered her manners. "I guess you two haven't been properly introduced. Luke, this is Colonel Bard Redfield, my — my father."

And wasn't that a kick to say?

"Colonel Redfield, this is …"

"I'd love it if you'd call me Dad," he said softly.

Her throat vibrated with emotion. "Dad," she said shakily. "Meet Luke Reynolds, my —"

"Fiancé," Luke said firmly. "I'm her fiancé. Pleased to meet you."

Hope brought a fist to her pounding heart.

She'd always wanted a family, a real one.

And here it was.

The End

You might also enjoy:

THE MIDNIGHT TRILOGY
1. Midnight Man
2. Midnight Run
3. Midnight Angel

The Midnight Trilogy Box Set

THE MEN OF MIDNIGHT
1. Midnight Vengeance
2. Midnight Promises
3. Midnight Secrets
4. Midnight Fire
5. Midnight Quest
6. Midnight Fever
7. Midnight Renegade

MIDNIGHT NOVELLA
Midnight Shadows

Don't Think Twice
Woman on the Run
Murphy's Law
A Fine Specimen
Port of Paradise

THE DANGEROUS TRILOGY
Dangerous Lover

Dangerous Secrets
Dangerous Passion

THE PROTECTORS TRILOGY
Into the Crossfire
Hotter than Wildfire
Nightfire

GHOST OPS TRILOGY
Heart of Danger
I Dream of Danger
Breaking Danger

HER BILLIONAIRE SERIES
CHARADE: Her Billionaire - Paris
MASQUERADE: Her Billionaire - Venice
ESCAPADE: Her Billionaire - London

NOVELLAS
Fatal Heat
Hot Secrets
Reckless Night
The Italian

About The Author

Lisa Marie Rice is eternally 30 years old and will never age. She is tall and willowy and beautiful. Men drop at her feet like ripe pears. She has won every major book prize in the world. She is a black belt with advanced degrees in archaeology, nuclear physics, and Tibetan literature. She is a concert pianist. Did I mention her Nobel Prize?

Of course, Lisa Marie Rice is a virtual woman and exists only at the keyboard when writing romance. She disappears when the monitor winks off.

Printed in Great Britain
by Amazon